UNFORGIVABLE
Sins

HARMONY A. HAUN

ISBN: 979-8-9868359-3-8 Paperback
ISBN: 979-8-9868359-2-1 e-book
ISBN: 979-8-9868359-4-5 Hardback

First edition

Author Contact: harmonyhaunauthor@gmail.com
IG: Harmonya.haun_author

Unforgivable Sins

Playlist on **Spotify**

Click Spotify link above

or scan QR Code

SCAN ME

Preface & Trigger Warnings

As an author, I am constantly aware and extremely nervous, about writing something that could potentially offend someone. Please know that it is NEVER my intent. That being said, I am human and I do make mistakes. I do not know everything, I am not the most educated person, and we all live lives that give us experiences no one else will understand or relate to. So, in the event that something I write EVER makes you feel uncomfortable or attacked in any way, please reach out to me. My Instagram DMs and/or email are always open and I genuinely care about my readers' experiences and feelings.

Now, please keep in mind this is a work of FICTION. I am trying to do my best to write authentically and to give real-life scenarios justice. I am writing a lot of this based on personal experience and some only from research, but again, this is a work of fiction.

POTENTIAL TRIGGERS: Adult language and content, trauma, abandonment, abuse (child and adult) both physically and emotionally, sexual assault, and suicide.

If you ever need to talk to someone, please seek help.
National Sexual Assault Line: 1-800-656-4673
Suicide & Crisis Line: 1-800-273-8255

DEDICATION

To all the women who grew up like Wendee, like me, and **refused** to follow the same path. To the women who were strong enough to break the cycle even though it's not always easy. Even though we're not always easy to love. You are amazing. You are beautiful. **You matter.** You are so worthy.

UNFORGIVABLE Sins

PROLOGUE

Dee

MASOCHIST BY SOPHIE ANN

I don't know why I constantly try to find my validation through the attention of toxic men. Scratch that, I *do* know why, but I continue to ignore my gut instinct. I ignore what brutal experience has taught me, which is, everyone lies. Everyone is selfish.

Everyone leaves.

Even knowing this, having it proven again and again, I choose to hold on to the hope that maybe, just *maybe*, the next one will be different.

The next one WILL be different.

I'm either stupidly optimistic or just a glutton for punishment. I'd like to agree with the saying that, *ignorance is bliss,* but that's a fucking lie. My ignorance only leads me down the same road of fucked up mistakes, scars, and infinitely more trauma at the hands of these toxic men.

And they don't make it easy, do they?

You see, the thing about toxic men is, they don't go around introducing themselves as manipulative pieces of shit. I mean, sure, some do, but not the majority. No, they camouflage themselves. They hunker down, and lie in wait, blending perfectly and innocuously into their beautiful façade, luring you in with their thick, dark hair and sexy eyes, that make you feel like you've never been seen until *they* see you. Their luscious lips and devious mouths, that do and say *all* the right things. Their strong, attentive hands, that make you *feel* all the right things.

And fuck, I so desperately want to FEEL something. A n y t h i n g. Am I even capable of feeling anything anymore? Have I ever truly felt the things a normal person should feel? Or have I been broken beyond repair? Perhaps I've been broken from the start.

Well, anyway, by the time you've figured out their schemes, seen through their smoke and mirrors, it's too late to try and break free. They're already clutching you in their claws, as they remove their camouflage to inflict their pain, knowing damn well you can't escape.

At least not without severe damage.

And I'm so damaged I wouldn't even know what to do with a decent man if I found one. I don't even *pretend* to aspire for a good man. Jesus, what would that be like? Do *good* men even exist? Or are they a fairytale made up for girls, by toxic men, to keep us looking? To keep us running straight into their destructive and cruel arms with hope, again and again.

All I know is I've never met one.

So, maybe I'm subconsciously staying on this fucked up merry-go-round so that I don't have to wander, blindly, searching for a new ride that may or may not even exist but one I sure as hell have no idea how to operate. I stay in the fucked-up world I've been thrown into, the world I've nurtured, so that I don't have to face my own self-camouflage and find my validation inside of myself, where deep down… I know I should.

Because where's the fun in that?

I'd rather focus on the finger that's pointing at someone else instead of the four pointing back at me. I would rather be a victim at the hands of some *asshole* than to admit that maybe I'm responsible too. Maybe I have some blame in how I turned out. How my *life* has turned out. Maybe I'm just as fucked up as these toxic men.

And so, here I am again, sitting across from a pair of deep, chocolate brown eyes, that seem to appraise me and worship me under their roaming, appreciative gaze, desperately hoping and praying that there's not
something camouflaged and lurking behind that teasing smile and those sexy dimples. No, this one WILL be different.

Little do I know…he's going to be the worst one yet.

Dee

I Can't Sleep by Autumn Kings

I jerk awake with a gasp, choking on a scream that's lodged in my throat. I push myself up off my stomach until I'm sitting on my knees. I reach a shaking hand up to my left cheek, gingerly touching it, before I pull my hand away and stare at it. I blink once, twice, three times, trying to pull myself back into reality. I expect to see blood. It felt so real.

It always feels so real.

Fuck this nightmare and its vivid intensity. Even though I can't remember everything, and all I get are glimpses, I still wish my mind would repress the memory like it has with so much of my childhood. I mean, I remember bits and pieces of growing up, but not nearly as much as I should. What I do remember is enough to confirm that what I refuse to remember must be beyond fucked up. My mind has taken pieces...no, chunks...of my life and locked them up inside Fort Knox.

So why not this memory too?

I sigh and drop my hand into my lap, rubbing at the ache in my wrists as I look around. I'm kneeling in the middle of my full-size bed in my tiny studio apartment. Light is filtering in through the open curtains of the one window in this shithole. I must have fallen asleep while I was attempting to get some work done. Sure enough, my laptop lies open and forgotten beside me.

I run my hands down my face in frustration. "Typical, Dee. Typical," I shake my head as I climb out of bed.

Hell, at least I managed to get some sleep, even though it came at the most inopportune time, when I desperately need to submit something. My blog had just started to really take off and I started seeing more income than just barely enough to pay my bills and eat ramen noodles every night when life decided to say, fuck you, Dee, as my life so often does. I haven't written anything worth a damn, much less *inspired*, in the past year and my readers are noticing.

I can't sleep.

I can't write.

I don't even want to leave my apartment to *get* inspired.

I can't seem to get my head on straight or do much of anything these days.

I walk over to the window, unlatch it, push it up and open, and step onto the fire escape landing. I inhale the hot, smoggy city air but instead of my shit reality, I imagine I'm on the porch of a remote cabin in the woods, cozy mug of coffee cupped in my hands, as I look out over a crystal-clear lake. I'd rather be anywhere else than here, but the honking of horns and people yelling obscenities at each other quickly dissolve any pretenses.

This is my sad and pitiful reality.

The sun is setting somewhere on the horizon, not that I can see it beyond the metal, mirrored skyscrapers surrounding me. Even on the fifth floor, I'm dwarfed by buildings as tall as mountains. Maybe I need to get out of the city. Maybe I should look into getting a cabin or house somewhere Upstate for a relaxing and renewing getaway.

Definitely a thought.

But for now, I just need to get out of this pathetic excuse of an apartment. I can start there. Baby steps. Get out into the world and be open to the stories, people, and places, that are out there waiting to be discovered. Waiting to be written. I can do this.

I take the time to care about my appearance for the first time in a year. I line my eyes with a thick layer of black eyeliner and a healthy coating of mascara that makes my green eyes pop in contrast, a light dusting of blush, and a bright, scarlet and sinful shade of red paints my lips. I style my dark brown hair in large, swirling curls, pinned down on the left side, behind my ear, the rest is free flowing down my back and over my right shoulder. A sleek black dress hugs my curves and ends just below my knees. There's a slight plunge in front, showing off my generous chest, but the selling point of this dress is the view from behind. The barely-there straps leave my back completely exposed from my shoulders all the way down to the base of my spine.

Sexy as hell and not at all slutty.

I smile at my reflection for the first time in a long time. Other than the dark circles under my eyes, that I can't completely hide with makeup, I look good. I feel good, too. It's a strange and new, yet familiar, feeling. I can do this.

The summer heat extends into the night and there's no need for a sweater or coat. I grip my clutch tightly as I walk down the bustling sidewalk. It doesn't really matter what time of day or night you decide to go out, it's always loud and busy. New York never sleeps and it sure as hell never notices you. All the people crammed into this city, these streets, these sidewalks, and no one fucking notices you. And why should they? There are a million others, just like you, walking these sidewalks. What makes you special? What makes you noticeable? The answer...abso-fucking-lutely nothing. You're no one here. Less than no one. That used to be a huge appeal to me. Now? It just makes me feel angry and sad.

And lonely.

How can I feel so alone when I'm literally surrounded by thousands of people?

I push those thoughts away as I enter the bar district. I slow my walk and finally lift my eyes up from the sidewalk, inspecting the illuminated signs, contemplating which one of these despicable places I'm going to step into. Marooner's on the Rocks, Mermaid's Saloon, Hangman's Hideaway? I shake my head and continue walking, nothing catching my eye. I'm about to close my eyes and randomly walk into one when a bright neon sign catches my eye.

Salvation Lights.

True to its name, the sign is glowing intensely, unmatched by any others. It stands out like a flashlight beam cutting across the darkness. I've never seen this place before, not that I'm surprised. I've been out of touch for a year and places come and go quickly here. Maybe it's the new type of atmosphere I need to bring back my inspiration. Just as I'm about to reach for the handle, a cold shiver runs down my spine, as if a finger just blazed a cold trail down my back. I spin around, my heart suddenly in my throat at the thought of some random stranger touching me so daringly and intimately.

But no one's here.

I let out a shaky, relieved breath, and then I see it. There, across the street, is another bar I've never seen before. It's shrouded in shadows, almost completely unnoticeable, but the neon sign is buzzing, flickering on and off.

Sinful Delights.

Before I even realize what I'm doing, my heels are clicking against the cobblestone, carrying me to this new, dark, and devious bar. Promises of danger and excitement whisper across my skin, calling to that familiar toxic, yet comfortable, feeling inside of me. This is what I know. This is what I'm good at. This is where I thrive.

Sinful Delights indeed.

Ready or not. Here I come.

I'm sitting alone at the bar, nursing my drink. I don't know what's wrong with me. I can't shake this unsettling feeling in my gut. This instinct that something isn't right, but what?

What's wrong with me?

I'd never consider myself to be a whore, by any means, but I am rather...*promiscuous*. I usually flourish in a place like this. I shine my brightest under the attention of men, with the help of a little liquid courage, a sexy outfit, and a lot of fucking confidence, which can go a long way. I know because I've done it before, time and time again. A little dancing, a little eye contact, a little touching, and a whole lot of flirting, and I could probably have any guy in this bar. So why am I sitting here, with my head down, trying my hardest *not* to be noticed?

I pick up my drink and take a big swig, the whiskey burning on its way down. They definitely aren't stingy with their alcohol here but that's about all I've noticed, not nearly insightful or inspiring enough for an article.

A sinfully hot new bar where you can get your money's worth of alcohol!

I mean, it's an attention-getter, sure, but what else is there about this place? Since I haven't taken my eyes off my drink, I can't tell you. I don't *actually* know if it's sinful *or* hot.

"What's a pretty thing like you doing sitting all alone?" A voice whispers, way too close to my ear, pulling me out of the internal conversation I was just having with myself.

I immediately smell the stench of cigarettes on his breath, and I have to swallow down the gag that's threatening to bring the alcohol I just downed back up my throat. An image of chocolate brown eyes flashes across my mind before I'm met with a different shade of brown eyes. A different pair of eyes that roam over me and assess me. Only these eyes aren't hiding a single thing. He's staring at me like I'm nothing more than prey. Nothing more than his next target.

His next victim.

It doesn't go unnoticed that he called me, *thing*. A pretty thing. Not a woman or even a girl, I'm just a *thing* to him. Looking at his weathered face, half hidden in black and grey stubble that looks like it's two weeks past due for a trim or shave, I can't help but be disgusted. He looks ragged as fuck and smells even worse.

Now, if I'm being honest, would it still piss me off to be called a *thing* if the person who said it was attractive? Probably not. We can lie to others, hell, we can lie to ourselves, try to appeal to a higher standard, but the truth of the matter is, looks matter. At least for initial interest. And this guy looks like Billy Bob in *Bad Santa*.

Gross.

"Not interested," I say blandly, returning my attention to my drink.

Good 'ole Billy Bob doesn't budge. Instead, he continues to stand too close to me as he reaches in his pocket and pulls out a pack of cigarettes. He sticks one between his thin lips, tosses the pack on the bar, and proceeds to light the cigarette with a Zippo. He slams the lid on the lighter closed then flicks it open only to slam it closed again, over and over while he continues to eye-fuck me.

He takes a thick drag of his cigarette and inhales deeply before he exhales the smoke and pulls it back in through his nose. I feel my top lip pull back in a disgusted sneer as he takes another drag.

"What's the matter with you?" He asks, voice tight, as he holds the smoke in his chest.

I turn my head to face him completely and give him cold, empty eyes. "Smoking is a filthy, disgusting habit and I'd appreciated it if you took your nasty habit somewhere else."

His hand is suddenly on me, gripping my jaw tightly, and then he blows his fucking cigarette smoke in my face. And just like that…

I'm terrified.

My heart is pounding in my chest, banging on my ribs to be let out, like a bird's wings fluttering violently against a steel-tight cage.

"You think you're better than me?" He sneers. "Because I hate to break it to you…*Princess*," he hisses the word in my face, "a pretty face and some amazing tits is all you are. Underneath, you're just as ugly as me or you wouldn't be here. But I don't give a fuck what's underneath unless we're talking about what's under that dress," he says, as he trails fingertips down my bare arm.

"Get your fucking hands off of me," I say through clenched teeth, fighting with everything I have against the fear that's threatening to make me freeze instead of fight.

He only squeezes my face harder. I dart a look around. Surely someone is going to see this and stop it, right? As if reading my mind, he leans in, his cigarette dangerously close to burning my skin, the sting from the smoke making my eyes water, and whispers,

"If you wanted someone to save you, you should have walked into Salvation instead." He removes the cigarette from his lips to grin at me, giving me a front row seat to his nasty, yellow stained teeth. "No one's going to save you here," he adds, his voice laced with poison and excitement. He licks his cracked lips before putting the cigarette back in his mouth, sucking in more disgusting smoke.

I can feel the bile creeping up my throat at the thought of him putting that awful mouth anywhere near me. I try to pull out of his grasp, but his fingers dig deeper into my skin. He's too strong. Why are men always too strong?

Suddenly, my face is jerked out of his grasp as the man is slammed into the bar by a very large and impressive body. His energy feels like a fucking force of nature. My eyes take in large biceps, bulging against a royal blue button-up shirt, and I get a whiff of leather, bourbon, and...*sin*. My eyes seem to travel up forever before I'm met with a steel-cut jaw, lips set in a hard, thin line, a straight nose, and a thick brow that's almost covered by a sweep of black hair, darker than a windowless pit of doom.

His hand is wrapped around Billy Bob's jaw, the same way Billy Bob's had just been on mine. I see his teeth clench and his nostrils flare as he continues to apply pressure. He slowly takes the cigarette that's getting ready to fall from Billy Bob's lips and turns it towards his face. He continues to squeeze until poor Bad Santa's lips are painfully pushed together from the sides.

My rescuer, I think, holds the burning end of the cigarette dangerously close to Billy Bob's eye and he finally seems to show some signs of intelligence. His eyes are wide with fear and he's whimpering, unable to fully use his voice, as his mouth is being forcefully squeezed shut. I swear I'll be able to hear the crack of his jaw soon and he knows it, too. He knows he's no longer the one in control, he's no longer the predator.

He's the prey.

I can hear my blood pounding too loudly in my ears, and then it dawns on me, it's much too quiet in the bar. The music is still playing, but the loud shouts, bursts of laughter, and general mayhem that was raging a few minutes ago has stopped. I glance around and, sure enough, everyone in our vicinity has stopped what they're doing to watch our little spectacle.

"Did you not hear her when she told you to let her go?" My rescuer's unusually calm, deep voice resonates inside of me.

It speaks to my body, to my soul, blossoming in my chest and setting a calm rhythm to my racing heart. He's like the steady foundation of drums, keeping the beat, and leading the music where it needs to go.

He's safe.

I shake my head at the insane thought. There's nothing safe about this man. He may have spoken just above a whisper but there's no denying his authoritative tone. His voice *demands* attention and obedience, and his words, although calm, are dripping with anger. In fact, his entire body seems to be dripping with it.

He's dangerous.

Billy Bob is still unable to talk, therefore, he can't answer the question, but his whimpers increase. My rescuer proceeds to put the cigarette out on his face, just below the corner of his eye. The poor creep tries to scream in pain, but it's muffled in his closed mouth, unable to fully escape as tears run down his cheeks, snot out of his nose, and the smell of burnt skin fills the air.

"The next time you so much as *look* at her," my rescuer's voice remains calm, steady, as if he's having a normal, everyday conversation and not threatening someone's life, "I will light a hundred cigarettes and put them out in each of your fucking eyes. Do you understand?"

The stranger manages to nod. My rescuer spins around, lifting the man up by his face, and throws him easily across the room. People scatter, letting the stranger fall to the floor and scramble to his feet. There's a crowd around us, everyone's eyes are on us. On *me*.

"Slightly, Cubby, get him the fuck out of here," my rescuer growls. "Better yet, take him to Hook, dock H2. It's time he meets The Crocodile."

"No!" Billy Bob yells. "Please, I'll never look at her again. I swear!"

Two men, one extremely tall and lanky and the other of average height but heavy around the middle, push through the crowd and take the stranger by the arms, escorting him out of the bar.

I watch as the two men drag my would-be attacker away. He's struggling and yelling as they pull him out of the bar.

"Please! Sinn, I'm not ready! Please!"

I watch until they pull him out of the doors, his voice fading, and then I feel *his* eyes on me. I feel his weighted gaze as if it's a physical thing on my face. On my face and not on my body. I slowly turn to face him and gasp once I see the entirety of his face.

His arctic blue eyes pierce right through my soul. Another image flashes in my mind. *His eyes.* I've seen these eyes before, there could never be any mistaking them, but I don't know how or where or when, I just know that I KNOW them. His eyes bore into mine with so much intensity that I start to squirm. I drop my gaze and take in the rest of his face. He's all hard, straight edges and perfection. Everything about him screams masculinity, except for his mouth that's just a tad bit too sensuous, too full.

Too sinful.

My mouth is watering. It's suddenly too wet and I'm forced to swallow down my own spit, practically choking on it, as he continues to stare at me with hard, cold eyes. His body is still taut with unleashed anger, and he clenches and unclenches his fists as he stares me down. Why is he angry with me? I didn't do anything.

Before I can gather my wits enough to ask him, or hell, even thank him for saving me, he storms off, disappearing into the crowd, leaving me stunned, speechless, and so fucking turned on I have to squeeze my thighs together for friction. When did that happen?

There's no denying the level of toxicity of this man is off the fucking charts and, if the wetness between my thighs is any indication, I'm all about it. And even though I know it's fucked up. Even though I know *I'm* fucked up for thinking it.

This is one trap I'm dying to fall into.

Sinn

ALL I FEEL IS YOU BY THE BROKEN VIEW

I feel her as soon as she walks through the damn doors. Her energy zaps across my skin with the force of a deadly fucking lightning bolt. It tingles and titillates my skin as if a torch made of hell fire is burning my nerve endings. Burning ME...*alive*. The intensity with which I feel her presence is excruciating, *maddening*, and exhilarating. Not to mentioned a fucking distracting nuisance as my cock twitches inside my pants at the mere sight of her exposed and bare back peeking through her long, silky hair. I wonder what all that flawless skin would look like with teeth marks marring it? *My* teeth marks.

I sit in my luxurious booth, raised up above the dance floor, and watch her like a hawk watches his prey. I watch her walk to the bar, oblivious to the heads turning, the eyes staring, the filthy fucking thoughts stirring... amongst other things. She climbs onto a bar stool, back straight and shoulders tense as she orders a drink. I can practically smell her fear from here. She radiates unease and uncertainty, which is not a good thing when you walk into a bar full of predators.

Men.

We can fucking smell an easy target a mile away and, she came alone, a weak and wounded fawn that strayed from the herd. Not a smart survival tactic.

Even though she chose to walk into this bar, the dark, mysterious, and daring choice, she's not like the regular patrons that stumble in here. The patrons who choose to walk into this bar are the kind that have completely given in to the devil on their shoulder and said to hell with the angel on the other one. But her... there's still a feel of... *innocence* about her. As if she hasn't quite given up yet, despite all the facts to the contrary, and the fact that she chose to walk into Sinful Delights instead of Salvation Lights.

Sure, they're just bar names, brands, but they're more than that, too. They're *symbolic*, obviously, giving you the option to choose between good and evil, light and dark. They call to an inner, subconscious desire that a person may not even be aware of. Despite what most people say, or how they try to live in the light of day, when night falls, and when they're alone, the majority of people feel the call of sinful desires.

But, in the end, when push comes to shove and they're standing between the two choices, those majority of people *do* choose to walk into Salvation Lights. They push their desires aside, in fear of eternal damnation, and make the safe choice. The *good* choice. The *right* choice.

Fucking cowards.

But who am I to judge? I call it like I see it, but I don't give a fuck either way. Their choices don't affect me one way or another. I own both bars and see the same benefits regardless of which one does better. I shouldn't give one more attention than the other, but I have to admit, lately I have a soft spot for Sinful Delights. I enjoy watching the depravity and it is infinitely more entertaining than Salvation Lights.

Which brings me back to the anomaly sitting at the bar.

Why is she here?

What possessed her to walk in here?

Before I can mull it over, a man walks up to her, pulling my focus back to the here and now. It took less than three minutes for her to be approached and I'm not at all surprised. What I am surprised by is the instantaneous jealousy lighting up my veins. The immense protectiveness I feel over her. Where the fuck is this coming from? Haven't I learned my lesson from the past? The one person I've ever tried to protect fucking DESTROYED me. She took the one thing I valued, the one thing that made me, *me*, and now I'm left as half the man I used to be. All because of *her* and yet I'm about to make the same goddamn mistake.

I watch as she tries to ignore him, and then he grabs her face and I snarl. His fucking filthy hands dare to touch her?! I clench my jaw as I feel the same rage I felt in the past rising up to greet me like an old, familiar lover.

"Sir? Sir, are you ok?"

I'm temporarily distracted by the piece of shit I was just having a meeting with. I move out of the booth and stand, never taking my eyes off of her and the fucking hand that's about to be amputated, as I address the guy sitting in my booth.

"Leave," I say, in a dangerously low warning.

"But, Sir, we haven't--"

I turn my head to face the idiot who dares talk back to me. He cowers under my stare, shrinking into the booth before he nods his head like a bobble-head doll and then jumps out of the booth, practically running away from me. He's lucky he's not my priority or I would have made him regret ever even *thinking* of talking back to me.

I stalk towards the bar. Her fear hangs heavy in the air now and I can hear her heart slamming inside of her chest. The sensory of it all pulls at the memory of that night.

The night I saved *her* and lost everything.

I should have walked away then, just like I should walk away now. So why the fuck don't I?

Before I can attempt to get my mind straight and talk myself out of it, I pull him off of her, slam his back into the bar, and take his disgusting face in my hand. Then, I squeeze his jaw the way he had been squeezing hers.

Hurting her.

Threatening her.

Terrifying her.

Well, he's about to feel that fear tenfold. I grab the cigarette that's dangling on his lips and turn the burning ember towards his face, threatening to put it out in his fucking eye. He doesn't deserve to even see her much less fucking touch her skin.

I can feel her eyes on me and it's fucking me up. It's distracting. I clench my jaw again, nostrils flaring, as the scent of her fills up my nose and muddles up my goddamn good sense. Who am I kidding? I've never had good sense. That's how I ended up here in the first place.

I blink, returning my focus to the man at my mercy, but I still feel her as if I don't have a fucking choice. I sense her fear dissipating and her heartbeat slowing. So much like the past and that memory stirs my rage even more.

"Did you not hear her when she told you to let her go?" My voice comes out calm, hiding the raging inferno inside of me.

Then again, I never have to raise my voice to threaten anyone. My actions do that for me. Case in point, I push the burning ember of the cigarette into his sensitive skin, right at the corner of his eye. I hear the hiss and smell of burning skin and it fucking delights me.

"The next time you so much as *look* at her, I will light a hundred cigarettes and put them out in each of your fucking eyes. Do you understand?"

The urge to crack his fucking jaw is thrumming through my veins with a vengeance. I have to rein in the rage. I lift him up by his face and throw him into the crowd. The crowd parts, letting him fall to the floor and then stumble to his feet, his legs shaky and unsteady underneath him.

"Slightly, Cubby, get him the fuck out of here," I growl. "Better yet, take him to Hook, dock H2. It's time he meets The Crocodile."

"No!" He yells. "Please, I'll never look at her again. I swear!"

I trust my Boys to do what I ask. They're the only ones that I trust. Well, them and Tink. They've been with me the longest and have never given me a reason to doubt them. They better not fucking start now.

"Please! Sinn, I'm not ready! Please!"

The man is yelling as he's pulled out of my bar, but I don't hear what he's begging for, my attention is on *her*. On her beautiful pale face, flushed with a mixture of alcohol, fear, and...*arousal*. I can smell it hanging in the air between us and it's like a damn aphrodisiac. I have to force my hands to remain at my sides instead of stroking my cock like I want to. Or even worse, touch *her*. She finally turns to look at me, her green eyes lock with mine, and I'm once again transported to the past. She gasps when she finally looks at me, *really* looks at me, and I wonder what she sees? Because what I see when I look at her, is a mixture of feelings, none of which I want to fucking feel. I hate what I see in her eyes. Everything I want to explore and everything I want to fucking forget.

Why is she here?

Am I being fucking tested? Again!

Fuck this.

I'm not going to fall into the same trap.

I *fucking* REFUSE.

I feel her eyes searing into my back as I walk away. The choice I *should* have made all those fucking years ago.

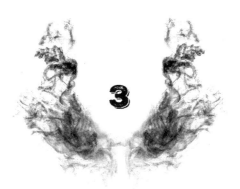

3

Dee

TOUCH BY DAUGHTER

I toss and turn restlessly. My body thrums with excitement and heat. Heat and desire at the way his voice settled inside of me, the way he came to my rescue, even if it was a little…serial killer-ish, fuck…it was hot. And this is what's wrong with me. I don't work the way normal girls do. I shouldn't be slick at the memory of him hurting someone but, damn, it was sexy as hell.

He's sexy as hell.

I wonder what it would feel like to have his hand wrapped around my jaw instead, forcing me to look at him, while his fingers explored the slippery slopes between my legs. I slide my hand under the band of my shorts and close my eyes, pretending it's his fingers parting my lips and sliding against my clit. *It's so fucking hot in here!* I throw the covers off me and welcome the breeze I feel from the cracked window as it caresses my flushed and sensitive skin.

I imagine it's his breath against my skin as he whispers all the sinful things he's going to do to me in that deep, demanding voice. I moan and open my legs wider as I push a finger into my soaked pussy, imagining it's his finger sinking in and exploring me for the first time.

I bring my other hand down to rub my clit as I continue to finger-fuck myself, moving my hips in a slow and steady rhythm, building up to the orgasm I've been chasing since stepping foot in that damn bar.

His eyes.

God, his eyes. With the amount of coldness in them when he glared at me, they should have frozen me solid right where I sat on that bar stool. But that icy stare did nothing to ease my heated skin then and it's doing nothing to ease the heat building between my legs now. If anything, the way he looked at me just added to my desire.

He looked at *me*.

He saw *me*.

Not my tits, or my ass, or anything about my body.

HE.

LOOKED.

AT.

ME.

Fuck, my heavy breathing is loud in the small apartment, my whimpers and moans are uncontrollable as they escape my mouth. No doubt the neighbors can hear every single one through these paper-thin walls and I couldn't begin to give a single fuck.

Sinn, the guy had called him.

I'm so fucking wet, I can hear it every time I move my finger in and out of my pussy. I'm throbbing and clenching, needing more, needing my finger to be deeper and bigger. Needing *him*. I add more pressure to my clit as I rub it faster and faster. My orgasm is building and it's threating to crash into me and destroy me. It's the first thing I've *felt*, really felt, in over a year.

"Sinn," his name flows across my lips as the orgasm bows my back and floods through my entire body.

I jerk and shake uncontrollably with the force of it. When I finally come down, the orgasm fading, I remove my hands from between my legs. I'm about to get up, so I can clean the mess I've made, when I change my mind. I slip my fingers into my mouth, tasting myself, and I wonder what he would think of the way I taste? I wonder what I would taste like off his lips, his tongue... his dick. I wonder what his mouth tastes like. I wonder what his skin tastes like? I wonder what he would taste like as he came in my mouth?

I used to enjoy sex, until I didn't, and I'm shocked to find myself thinking about it in this way now after so long of not having it. I never once missed it, until tonight. Until I reacted to *him*. God, I really am so fucked up.

I shiver at the memory forcing its way through my desire, demanding to be remembered. The earlier heat seems to have been sucked right out of my body. The sweat drying on my skin is cold, and I pull the covers back over me as I turn on my side and hug myself, praying for peaceful sleep to suck me under. I don't even know why I bother with the sentiment. Not one prayer has ever been fucking answered.

I'm sitting on the old couch, across from a blue, seventies style chair. Only a small, wooden coffee table separates the furniture in the small trailer. A man I don't even know is sitting in the chair. A strange man is in my house and yet it's nothing new. I'm used to my mom bringing random men and women, but mostly men, into the house. They're her friends, I guess, but they never seem to stay around for very long and they've never stayed while she's not here.

But my mom is going to be gone for another ten months. I'm still too young to understand a lot of what people say but I'm old enough to know that my mom is in jail. I understand what that means, I think. It's a place you're forced to go to when you've done something bad, and my mom seems to always be doing bad things. Drugs they say. Other kids in school tell me what their parents say, or I hear them talking about it behind my back. Despite how it sounds, I do have friends, but they're never allowed to come over to my house. Not even when my mom *is* here. I guess it's because she does drugs. I don't know much about drugs other than what they teach us in school and what they teach us is, "*say no to drugs.*" Did they not teach this when my mom was in school? She has to know they're bad because she keeps being sent to the place for bad people.

This strange man, Jim I think his name is, took us down to the river to swim. I don't really remember going but we're sitting in the living room now, in our wet bathing suits, my sister and me. So, I guess we did go. Jim is in his bathing suit too, his underwear. My sister, who's three years older than me, is sitting on the arm of the blue, seventies chair, and Jim is rubbing her back.

I wake from the dream fully alert and wide awake, the adrenaline of the memory pumping through my veins. I don't even remember falling asleep, and now, I wish I hadn't. Story of my fucking life. I haven't had a peaceful night's sleep in over a year so, I guess tonight should be no different.

This is just one of the few memories I have of my childhood. I can't even hazard a guess as to how old I was. I mean, maybe seven or eight? But that's a complete guess and it's not something I've ever brought up with anyone to verify the accuracy of the timeline. I don't want to know anything more about that moment. I don't want to ask questions or dig up more than I already have. What I *do* know of the moment, and the fact that I *can't* remember anything else, is enough for me to leave it the fuck alone. I have no desire to open *Pandora's Box* and see all the fucked-up things inside. My life, and what I know of my life, is already plenty fucked up enough for me, thank you very much.

I reach for the nightstand and grab my phone. I squint against the bright screen, immensely powerful for its small size. 3:22 a.m., which means, I only got roughly two hours of sleep and there's no way I'm going to attempt more sleep after that fun little trip down memory lane. I sigh as I get up and make way into the bathroom. I blink a few times as my eyes adjust to the dim lighting. I lean against the sink and stare at my reflection. All traces of the confident, well, somewhat confident, woman I was earlier tonight are gone. All I can see in her place is a lost little girl.

She's angry and afraid but she doesn't completely understand why. She knows she's different, that her life and her family is different from her friends' lives, but she tries to be good. She tries so hard to be good! Maybe if she does better, her mom will want to stay with her and stop doing bad things. Maybe if she does better, if she stays away from those bad things, her friends can come over. Maybe if she does better, her oldest sister will come back home and stay with her, and keep her and her other sister safe.

She just needs to be good.

A lone tear slips down my cheek as I stare at the lost girl in the mirror. I shake my head and swipe at the tear.

"You're not that little girl anymore, Dee. Get a damn grip," I mumble angrily to myself.

I turn on the faucet and splash cold water on my face. The shock of it helps clear my mind so, I do it again…and again. I brush the dripping water off my chin with the back of my arm and stand up straighter as I look, once again, at my reflection. I look like myself again, or the version I've come to know these days. My eyes are focused and not lost to the past. Well, I almost look like myself. The damn dark circles are a dead giveaway that not everything is hunky-dory. No wonder I've been falling asleep at random times during the day. A person can't survive off of a couple of hours of sleep every night. They just can't. Not without going insane in the process. Considering my night, and how I reacted to it, maybe I *am* starting to go insane.

Maybe I always have been.

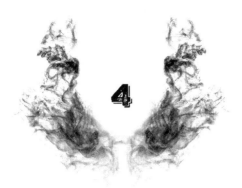

Dee

RUDE BOY BY RIHANNA

I've pretty much stared at a blank screen for an entire damn day. I keep attempting to type up...*something*, but I only end up typing random nonsense that doesn't make a lick of sense and have to delete it all and start over. Maybe because my mind is distracted with a lick of another kind.

Hmmm? Perhaps I should try my hand at being a smut author instead of a blogger with all these damn thoughts I've got swirling around in my head. I can't get those damn blue eyes out of my mind!

"Grrrr..." I snap my laptop closed and get off the bed only to pace with nervous energy. "Stop it, Dee," I chastise myself. "It didn't mean anything. He probably saves *all* the girls."

And I bet he doesn't look at them the way he looked at me. Like he could see into my very broken and damaged soul and what he saw disgusted him. Like I'm the most despicable person on the entire planet and he wants absolutely nothing to do with me. The way he stormed off, as if he couldn't get away from me fast enough, spoke volumes.

But...there was something *more*, too. I felt it. What exactly IT is that I felt? I don't know. Hell, maybe I'm making shit up in my mind. That is, after all, what I'm good at. Make believe there's something more than there is. Make believe that I'm worth more than I am. That someone else could see something *more* in me than damaged goods.

Fuck.

I guess there really is only one way to find out though. I need to see him again. I tell myself that it's only to prove myself right. But I'm not sure which point I even want to prove. The one where he wants nothing to do with me? Or the one where I think there's something more to it than just what's on the surface?

My thoughts are sheer mayhem as I shower. I don't even remember shaving my legs but apparently, I do. Good 'ole muscle memory kicking in. As I stare at my reflection, really look at myself for only the third time in recent months, I give myself a much-needed pep talk.

"No expectations," I remind myself.

Expectations are the killers of hope. Hope can be a dangerous thing, powerful but dangerous, and I try not to venture into more dangerous territory than I already do with my damaged self.

No hope.

No expectations.

If you don't have expectations, or better yet, if you expect the worst, then you won't be hurt or disappointed with the outcome, whatever it may be. Sad but true.

I give myself another once over in the mirror, tilt my chin up, square my shoulders, and let out a heavy, weighted breath. I can do this, and I can be the confident woman I once was. No one is holding me back from being who I want to be except for my damn self, and I'm prepared to fake it until I make it come true.

I walk into Sinful Delights for the second time in as many nights. I feel like a damn twenty-one-year-old again, going out to bars and clubs literally every night, except now I'm thirty-two, no group of so-called friends to party with and so much more jaded than I've ever been. I feel like all the cards are stacked against me. How can I still be in the same spot, maybe even worse off, then when I was just a kid? Time just keeps ticking by, everyone moving on to bigger and better things, while I feel like my life is a damn *Nascar* race. I'm stuck on a track, forever doomed to make left fucking turns. I push those negative thoughts out of my mind as I stop to take in my surroundings this time.

The shorter and thicker guy that escorted Billy Bob from the bar last night is posted up just inside the door. I'm assuming he's a bouncer. The dance floor, if that's what you can call the small space, is straight ahead and you have to push through the bodies there to get to the bar at the other end of the room. Off to the right, there are tables along the dance floor, the wall, and a DJ booth that sits up on a platform behind the tables.

There's a ramp immediately to my left that follows the wall and then curves around to the side of the dance floor. There's an elevated booth that has a clear view of the entire bar and that's where *he* sits. The second my eyes land on him, my heart starts to race, and my stomach is filled with all kinds of energy. Nervousness, excitement, attraction...*fear*. But not fear in the normal sense. I'm not afraid of him hurting me. I mean, not physically. I fear the way he makes me fucking FEEL everything.

He sits, regal and untouchable, right smack dab in the middle of the booth, one arm casually hung over the back of it, the other hand holding a drink on the table. He's wearing a solid black dress shirt that fits snug across his chest and arms, but the black shirt seems faded compared to the deep, shiny black of his hair.

His eyes are locked on the girl sitting in the booth with him and my heart immediately drops into my stomach, adding another emotion to the blender inside of me. Jealousy.

As if he can feel my eyes on him, he moves his head slightly and those cold eyes lock with mine. This far away, I can't make out their color, but there's no forgetting them. They're seared into my mind like a fucking brand on the back of my eyelids. His jaw clenches, his body goes from relaxed to taut with tension, and his eyes simmer with heat. Everything about his demeanor screams anger but I can't quite decide if it fills his eyes completely or if that heat has even an ounce of something else.

Fuck, he looks like a sexy, wicked, and sinful king. All he's missing is a menacing crown.

He's the first to look away, breaking the trance his eyes seem to cast me into every time he fucking looks at me. I let out a shaky breath and push my way through the crowd and up to the bar. It seems that most people like to sit at the tables, near the dance floor, leaving a few bar stools empty for the loners like me.

I slide onto a stool, careful not to flash anyone in my barely-there red dress. This one, I have to admit, does walk the line between sexy and slutty, but I felt like I had to up the ante. Like I needed to do more to get his attention.

The attention of a king.

And I mean, how the fuck do I do that other than look as hot as possible? If I was a peacock, I'd be fanning my feathers out for the world to see from outer space, but all I have are sexy dresses, heels, my curvy body, and my personality. My personality is shit lately so I'm banking everything I've got on the dress and heels. I'm closing my eyes, tossing the dice, and hoping my body secures the winning roll.

The same bartender as last night idles up to me from behind the bar, appraising me with not so friendly eyes, as she wipes her hands on a rag hanging from her belt. I barely made eye contact with her last night but tonight is different. Tonight, I'm on a mission and I'm betting she has information.

"What'll it be?" She asks, impatiently.

"Whiskey on the rocks, dash of coke," I say back, a bit of bite in my tone, but not too aggressive. Just enough for her to know I won't be walked on but not rude enough to be considered a bitch.

She looks me up and down again with her shrewd hazel eyes, well what she can see from my waist up, before she navigates her way behind the bar, preparing my order.

I watch her closely and, as I do, I can't help the small amount of envy that comes over me. She's all fluid grace and confidence. You can tell just by watching her that she knows exactly what she's doing and exactly who she is. She's comfortable behind the bar and she's comfortable in her own skin. She doesn't need a skimpy dress to build her confidence.

She's wearing a pair of high-waisted black denim jeans with rips and tears all over them, tucked into shiny black combat boots, a green belt that matches her green pixie cut and bra, sinched snuggly around her tiny waist, and a black mesh crop top hanging off of one shoulder. She's everything cool, hip, and original I'll never be.

The skin between my shoulder blades starts to tingle and the hair on the back of my neck stands on end. I can feel his eyes on me again. I subtly look over my shoulder to where he still sits at the booth, but his eyes are still on the girl in the booth with him.

Not on me.

I must have imagined it. At least he looks bored and completely uninterested in the girl sitting next to him. Even though she's totally giving off the *fuck me* vibe, leaning towards him, giving him a great view down her top I'm sure, smiling coyly, batting her eyelashes, and fussing with her hair shyly.

FUCKING GAG.

Is that what it really looks like from the outside looking in? Do I look like that when I'm flirting with a man? I fucking hope not, fuck. She looks pathetic and desperate.

The slam of a coaster on the bar in front of me makes me jump and I turn back to see the bartender eyeing me, completely unfriendly now, as she sets my drink on the coaster.

"Thanks," I mumble. She's about to walk away when I gather my courage. I clear my throat and speak up, "Hey."

She stops and turns back to me, hands on her hips and cocks an eyebrow. She's asking me what the fuck I want without ever speaking a word.

"Who's that guy? In the booth?" I gesture with my head in the direction behind me.

She slowly walks back until she's standing right in front of me. She leans on the bar, closing the distance between us, as if she's about to tell me a secret. I can't help but mimic her body language and lean in towards her, too, eager to find out more about the devastatingly handsome stranger.

"Off limits," she practically growls.

My brows furrow in confusion, "What?"

"That's who the fuck he is. OFF. LIMITS." She bites out each word, holding my gaze with her hard stare, making sure I get the message.

She must finally be satisfied with whatever she sees on my face, which honestly must just be confusion, but she pushes off the bar and gets back to work without giving me another glance.

"Well," I huff, then whisper to myself, "this place sure as hell isn't getting a raving review for their customer service."

I pick up my drink and take a gulp, letting the alcohol wash away all of my doubts and uncertainties. If I can't get information from the staff, I guess I'll just have to try a different approach. I swear I feel his eyes on me again, and this time, I turn quickly in his direction, but no, he's not paying any attention to me whatsoever.

"Alright," I whisper to myself again. "I'll make myself hard *not* to notice."

Another large gulp has me finishing my drink and I can feel the heat sliding down my throat and into my chest. I haven't picked up a drink in the past year so it's literally running right through me as I walk over to the DJ booth and up the three steps until he can see me. I smile seductively and run a hand down my hair, slick and straight, stopping my hand level with my breasts. Just like a good trained dog, his eyes take in exactly what I want him to see, and just like the girl in the booth, I lean over, giving him a better view.

"Can I make a request?" I have to yell so he can hear me above the loud speakers.

"Anything for pretty little lady," he smirks back.

I make my request and descend the stairs, waiting for my song to come on. As soon as I hear the first beat drop, I make my way into the middle of the dance floor. I don't even care that I'm dancing alone. If experience has taught me anything, I won't be alone for long.

I start to sway my hips to the sexy and seductive beat of *Rude Boy*. The lyrics are a direct hit to the rude king sitting in the booth.

A taunt.

A challenge.

A promise.

I make slow seductive circles with my hips as I turn around in a slow circle so I can eye the booth without appearing to look. Fuck me! He's *still* not looking at me. What in the world does a girl have to do? Strip down and streak through the bar? I complete the circle, giving the booth my back again, and now I'm face-to-face with someone who *is* paying attention.

He's taller than me, but not by much, with the four-inch heels I have on. I'm putting him at roughly six feet. He's got a decent build but not as broad as I typically prefer. His face is average, but then again, every face I'll ever lay my eyes on will be average compared to *his*. Either way, he'll do just fine for the moment.

He licks his lips and smirks, taking my hands in his. I let him. "Damn girl, you look fine as hell. You here by yourself?"

"Maybe," I shrug, giving him a smirk of my own.

He spins me around and then pulls me in against his chest, his hands lowering to my hips that are still swaying to the music. I run my hands down his chest, giving myself a bit more space as I drop seductively, ass to the floor, in front of him. That puts my face in line with his crotch which, obviously, is the visual every man wants. I make eye contact with him as I slowly rise back up. Unlike with the rude boy stubbornly sitting in the booth, the heat in these eyes is unmistakable.

I have to restrain myself from rolling mine. Men are so fucking predictable in their horniness. He's only thinking with his small head now and I'm so… *disappointed*. I thought I'd feel a swell of pride at finding some of my old self again, at being able to still get a man's attention, but his attention is underwhelming.

Unwanted.

Unreciprocated.

There's only one man's attention I want and, once again, he's made it crystal fucking clear that he wants absolutely nothing to do with me.

That's when I feel two large hands wrap around my arms and pull me back with so much strength that I stumble in my high heels, a small scream escaping from my throat.

But I don't fall.

Instead, my back is flush against a rock-solid stomach and chest, and the familiar scent of *him* washes over me and eases my rising panic. I'm suddenly drowning in the scent of leather and my skin is thrumming with fire and excitement from where he's touching me, where I'm being held against him. The heat of his body seeps through my thin dress, only adding to the fire dancing across my skin and pooling between my legs.

Unlike the man I was just dancing with, he towers over me. He must be six-five, easily, blocking out the light from above, the crowd that was just around me, blocking out fucking *everything*.

He's all I feel.

And I swear I can feel him in my very soul.

He leans down, putting his face next to mine as he whispers in my ear, his voice giving away no emotion, "I know what you're doing."

The scent of bourbon on his lips is intoxicating and I want to drink it down, right from the source. His hands release their tight grip and trail, softly, down my arms, sending goosebumps racing behind his touch. His fingertips find the edge of my dress and slip slightly underneath the hem, both hands mirroring each other on each side. He runs his fingertips across my thighs, tracing the line of the dress, until his fingertips are brushing the sensitive skin of my inner thighs. He's so close to my core I know he can feel the heat radiating between my legs. My breath catches at the sensation, and I can't help the delicious shiver that rockets up my spine. I press into him harder and gasp at the hard length I feel pressing against my ass.

"And the only thing you're going to succeed in," he continues, voice hot against my cheek, and fingertips hotter as he runs them under the hem, back across my legs to my outer thigh, "is getting a man sent to hell for fucking touching you." His voice remains calm, cold, collected, as if he's not threatening to kill someone…for *touching* me.

As if I belong to him.

As if I'm his to protect.

As if I'm his to control.

His fingers stop moving on both sides of my thighs, as he grips the dress and yanks it down. "Go home," he orders, harshly.

And before I can wrap my brain around the fact that he *did* see me, he *was* watching me, and his hands are now on *MY* body… he's gone again, just as quickly as he appeared.

He's gone.

I spin around so fast I almost stumble again. How I manage to stay on my feet with legs that feel like limp noodles is beyond me. I desperately scan the crowd and eye the booth where he sat all night but he's nowhere to be seen.

And I feel the absence of him way more than I should. Way more than is normal for any man I've ever dated much less a stranger. Why do I feel this way about him?

Why him?

Who the fuck is he and who the fuck does he think he is? Saving me from a piece of shit who clearly wanted to hurt me is one thing. Manhandling me, pulling down my dress, and ordering me to go home, like I'm a damn child, is something completely different. Especially when I was clearly having a good time. Ok, I wasn't really into the guy, but it's not like he could tell I wasn't. Or anyone else for that matter.

He had no right.

And then to tease me like that! And then just walk away!

"Ugh," my irritation finally pushes through my lust filled haze and I stomp back over to the bar, determined to stay until they close just to spite him.

"Go home," I mock, under my breath. "I'd like to see him fucking make me."

Instead, I sit at the bar for another two hours and let three different men buy me drinks and I flirt shamelessly with all of them. I don't dare venture out onto the dance floor again and, even though I feel his simple touch seared into my skin, and even though I scan the crowd every five minutes looking for the tall, brooding, tyrant, even though I swear I feel his eyes on me...he never makes a reappearance.

5

Sinn

On My Mind by MNQN

I swear to God, she's going to be the fucking death of me. Or whatever downfall is left for someone like me. At this point, it can't get much worse than it already is. What more do I possibly have to lose?

My fucking sanity.

Although, I suppose even that's been in question in recent years, too. Still, as I watch her walk into my bar for the third night in a row, I swear I feel whatever control I have left, s l i p p i n g. I desperately want to feel her soft skin again. I want to feel her body reacting to me. I want to hear her breath catch in her throat. I want to feel her pulse quickening. I want to smell her sweet, natural scent and taste her arousal on my tongue. I want to feel what it would be like to push my hard cock inside of her for the first time. Fuck, having her here, having to fucking look at her, having to feel my cock straining hard against my pants, is making the thoughts harder to ignore.

My eyes greedily roam over her body, over her curves, clearly displayed against another skin-tight black dress, and I can't help but imagine what it would be like to trace each one with my fingertips and then again with my tongue. Exploring her body must be like driving the *Tongtian Avenue* in China. Or, as it's more accurately called, *Avenue Toward Heaven*, because navigating her curves would be the closest to Heaven I'll ever be. It would be arduous and beautiful, thrilling, and fucking dangerous.

She's dangerous.

But I'll gladly take that danger, her version of Heaven, because I have no desire to *actually* go to Heaven. I'm not like my brother.

"Brother!" His boisterous voice booms through the bar as if just thinking about him has summoned him to my side.

I reluctantly drag my eyes away from her and meet my brother's gaze as he walks up the ramp and approaches my booth. My brother is everything that I'm not. He's all easy swagger, leather, trench coats, and gaudy jewelry. His long wind and sea tangled hair frames his ruggedly handsome face, a long mustache and beard hide half of it and yet, he emotes every single emotion so clearly. His face is always an open book to his thoughts and feelings. His smile can charm even the angriest and coldest of beasts, well, besides me. And where my eyes are blue from the coldest, deepest, and scariest parts of the ocean, his are the warm, turquoise of the *Caribbean*.

Even in our younger days I've never carried his ease and optimism. He's always been the light and goodness to my dark. He's always believed in me, how or why and to what end I'm not sure, but he's also here, in this place, because of me. Because he always tried to save me and always got caught up in the rip tide of my actions. It never mattered how many times he felt the punishment of my deeds, how many times I tried to push him away to keep him safe, he was always there. Always by my side.

He's still here.

"Well, aren't you going to give your big brother a proper welcome?" He asks, as he holds his arms out to the side, expecting a warm embrace.

I look up at him, no doubt a mix of boredom and irritation on my face, "Not likely."

"Hmmmm," he grumbles, deep in his chest.

And then he's griping the sides of the solid oak table, lifting it. I hear the table groan in protest, but he easily dislodges the bolts that anchor the table into the fucking concrete as if it was held down by nothing more than cheap glue.

I sigh and shake my head as he removes the table from between us, setting it off to the side, and then comes into my space, grabs my arms, and yanks me up and into a hug.

No one *yanks* me.

No one even fucking *looks* at me with defiance much less fucking *yanks* me. Like I'm a goddamn child or, even worse, a fucking child's doll.

It's not the fact that he's the only person bigger than I am, both in height and muscle, that allows him to *yank* me. No, I allow him to do so because he's the only one who's ever given a shit about me. He's the only one who truly loves me. And since he's the only person in the entire fucking universe that I love in return, I allow him to *yank* me, and I begrudgingly return his bear hug.

Seemingly satisfied with my effort, he returns the table to its rightful place, bolts be damned, and slides in next to me. "Tink," he yells across the bar, his voice trained to cut through the harshest stormy sea conditions cutting through the noise of the bar effortlessly, getting her attention, "a bottle of rum!"

Tink rolls her eyes and flips him off to which he throws his head back and laughs. "She'll come around to me one of these days, I'm sure of it." He smiles with ease and looks at me with a teasing glint in his eyes. "Maybe if you gave her what she wanted and fucked her brains out she'd chill out. You know, it's hard enough dealing with one miserable jackass that doesn't ever smile or have fun," he bumps me in the shoulder with his, "much less *two* miserable bastards. Especially in the same place."

"What do you want, Hook?" I ask, impatiently.

Even though I love my brother, he's always nagging me for this or that. Always scolding me or taunting me. Always trying to tell me what to do. I know he does it with good intentions, but you would think after a lifetime of trying, and failing miserably, he'd give up. Maybe he's the one who's lost his sanity?

"Oh, come on Peter, can't I just stop by to see how you're doing? To spend time with my little bro? Life isn't as serious as you make it. Ah," he turns his attention to the waitress setting his bottle of rum on the table along with a glass and a small bucket of ice. "Thank you miss...?" He leaves off, allowing the waitress to provide her name.

She glances nervously my way before dropping her eyes to the table again. "Milly," she says, sweetly.

"Milly," my brother repeats, as he takes her hand in his and brings it to his mouth, pressing his lips to her knuckles, "a beautiful name for a beautiful girl." He smiles easily at her, and she blushes the brightest shade of red I've ever seen. "I'm Henry Hook, but please, call me Hook."

I roll my eyes. "Did you come here to spend time with your brother or to flirt and get laid?"

He keeps his teasing eyes on the waitress. "Why both, of course. I'll find you later, yeah?" He asks, but it's never a question. No one has ever turned down my brother's blatant offer of sex and his streak won't end with Milly as she nods her head, bites her lip, and blushes again.

He winks at her and finally lets her hand go. Poor little Milly struggles to walk away on shaky legs and all he did was kiss the back of her hand. The effect both my brother and I have on women is comical. Although, lately, women tend to be more cautious around me, a bit more terrified of what I might do if I set them in my sights than hopeful. Still, I haven't had a woman tell me no, no matter how scared she may be. After all, you know what they say about curiosity and the kitty.

Then again, *she* doesn't seem to be afraid of me, but she also doesn't know me. Give it time and I'm sure that'll change. But do I want her to be scared of me? She seems to be taunting me, challenging me in a way I've never been challenged before, and I'm honestly not sure what the fuck to do or how to act.

"So, Brother, what's new?" Hook asks, as he pours himself a drink and settles into the booth.

I raise my arms, gesturing to the crowded bar. "Just another day in paradise," I lie. *She's* new.

He grunts, "Now I know you're lying. I know you've been a little...*murderous*, since you lost your, well...I don't need to say it. But something has gotten you even more riled up. You're sending more and more people to H2 than normal. Peter, you can't keep doing this. You can't keep playing one side."

The immediate anger at what his words stir up threatens to spill out and I clench my jaw, hard, against the rising beast. No one can see my struggle though. Beyond the clenched jaw and tightness in my body, no one knows what I'm feeling or thinking. My eyes always remain cold and distant to what stirs directly behind them.

After a beat, when I've managed to gain my composure again, I roll my neck and give my brother my best bored face. "Can't I? Please, tell me, Hook, who's going to stop me, hmmm? You?"

"You know I only want what's best for you," he says, seriously, all joking and playfulness aside.

"Getting back into Dad's good graces is what's best for YOU, Hook, not me," I say, definitively.

"Come on, Peter, I know you're not happy here, not now. Don't you at least want to try to earn your…," he trails off, no doubt looking for the right words that *won't* set me off, "your old job back?"

"Speaking of, how is our baby sister handling it?"

"You would know if you talked to her, if you met with her like you're supposed to, to help her with the new role that was just thrown at her."

I scoff. "You mean the same job that was thrown at me the same way once upon a time? And who was there for me then, besides you?" I shake my head and take a long drink of my bourbon, letting the familiar heat of the alcohol soothe my tense body. "No, I'm sure sweet little Lily has all the help she needs from you and dear old Dad."

"Look, I know we're both stuck here for now, but it doesn't have to be forever. You just have to make an effort, repent for your mistakes, show Dad that you care and I'm sure he'll give you back your--"

"Enough!" I slam the glass down on the table, shattering it. Ice and bourbon run freely along the table and then drip down the side.

Everyone in the bar is now looking our way, a quiet hush filling the space around us, and an electric excitement of what might happen hangs in the air. Sinful Delights is known for its debauchery and wildness, oftentimes with me at its center. However, I never raise my voice. That alone is cause for curiosity. But amongst the crowd eagerly gawking at us, waiting for something sinfully delightful to happen, I feel *her* eyes on me. She's watching me closely, too, but not with the same excitement as the others. Her energy, her intent, is entirely different and it makes me feel unsteady.

I exit the booth and stand, smoothing out my shirt, gaining my composure before I speak. I look down at my brother, who appears to be regretful and adamant at the same time. I know he means well, and out of everyone in our family, he truly is the only one who has ever tried to understand me but even he has failed to do so. I don't want the same things he wants. I don't, and won't, pretend to be someone I'm not in order to be whole again. If this is the price I'm to pay forever, to be stuck here, then so be it.

"I appreciate your concern, Brother, but it's unnecessary. Please, stay as long as you like and help yourself to whatever your heart desires. What's mine is yours." I dip my chin and turn to leave.

"Peter...," his voice stops my retreat, "I didn't mean for us to fight."

"I know," I say with my back still facing him, and before he can say anything else, I make my way down the ramp and through the whispering crowd as I head for the private hallway and elevator that leads to my penthouse on the top floor.

I can't fight the pull of the green eyes watching me, beckoning me to look their way, and so, I do. I lock eyes with her as I make my way to the hallway on the side of the bar. What I see in her eyes is almost enough to stop me in my tracks. Almost.

Concern.

Desire.

Both emotions so intense I can feel them in my bones. I can see the effort it's taking her to not get off her stool and come to me, but whatever she sees on my face keeps her seated.

Smart girl.

Because I don't know what I'd do to her if she came to me now. I'm in no fucking mood to play nice with *anyone*. Especially her.

Not when she reminds me of a whole other time and place. Not when she reminds me of everything I've lost. And as much as I hate the reminder, as much as I hate the memory of the past, the last thing I want to do is hurt her.

And that fucking pisses me off even more.

Dee

Night four. No sign of him.

Night five. No sign of him.

Night six. No sign of him.

Night seven...to be determined.

I'm beginning to feel *real* crazy. Like I'm a damn stalker. Like a fucking escaped mental patient. Like I'm spiraling out of control. Was he even real? Did I imagine him? Was he another one of my dreams? I mean, hell, I'm so out of it even when I'm awake, so sleep deprived, it wouldn't shock me at this point to realize I made him up. Imagined him. Fucking daydreaming wide awake.

Tonight is my absolute last attempt. If he isn't here, then I'm moving on. He was either never real or never meant to be more than a guy who saved me one time. As much as at the latter seems to be true, I can't help the nagging feeling at the back of my mind telling me I'm wrong. There's more to him.

There's more to *us*.

I'm throwing all caution to the wind. Zero fucks. Because this is my Hail Mary. This is my last chance. My last wild throw down the field hoping that he'll be there to catch it.

To catch me.

I saunter into the bar, completely familiar and comfortable with the look and vibe now. My eyes immediately go to the booth that's been empty for the last three nights, tonight seems to be no different. He hasn't been seen since the night he argued with the man in the booth, his brother, according to the grumble I got out of Tink.

I can't help but wonder what they fought about. Sinn, if that is even his name...fuck, I'm simping over this man and I don't even know his name!

I am so fucked up.

It's ludacris that I've been consumed by a stranger, but I feel like I know him somehow. There's something in him that I recognize. Perhaps it's that he seems so... *alone*, especially when he walked away from that booth. Alone and lost and angry. He's always angry. And still, I wanted to go to him. I had the strangest urge to comfort him. To protect him. Which is fucking ridiculous because nothing about that man needs protecting. And, of course, like aways, I wanted to be near him. To touch him. Fuck, I just want to be able to touch him.

I want to touch the one man who's untouchable. Or as Tink so eloquently put it, OFF LIMITS.

I pull my gaze away from the empty booth and blow a kiss to the DJ as I pass by. He winks at me in return. I slide into the bar stool that seems to have become *mine* just as Tink places my usual whiskey drink on a coaster in front of me. She still looks at me with malice, but she's come to accept me. At least, I think she has. She doesn't ever linger to chat but she also hasn't poisoned me yet so, there's that. A girl knows when to take her wins.

It doesn't take long for a man to approach me and offer to buy me a shot. I eagerly accept. They've been consistent in their pursuits every night I've been here. Thank God none of them have been like Billy Bob though. I shudder at the memory. No, all the men that have approached me since then have been nothing but polite. I mean, I won't go as far as saying respectful, because this is a bar after all, and I haven't exactly been innocent in my flirtations and lead-ons, but none have pushed their luck. And I have a sneaking suspicion it's because of a certain brooding alpha male. Even in his absence, his actions and his threats linger as a warning to all. But what exactly is the warning? A warning not to be a complete piece of shit? Or a warning not to come near me?

I shake my head, clearing that last thought. No, that's not right, because men *do* approach me. Men flirt and touch and tease and he still hasn't made an appearance. The only time he's really seemed to care is when I was being hurt and threatened. And because I am who I am, because I don't work like a normal girl should, I'm going to test this new theory no matter how much it scares me. Time to cause chaos.

I stand up and then climb onto my bar stool, kneeling on it so I'm above the crowd. I cup my hands to my mouth and yell, "Who wants to do body shots?!"

I rowdy cheer erupts throughout the crowd and they surge towards the bar. Towards me. The electricity in the atmosphere just kicked up a notch and I can't help the devious grin that spreads across my face.

I point to a man in the crowd that obviously takes care of his body. "You," I curl my finger, requesting him to come to me. He does. When he's standing right in front of me, I cross my arms, and gesture with my chin, "Lift up your shirt and let's see what you've got under there."

"Trust me," he smirks and lifts the shirt, revealing a very decent set of abs, "these will pass the test," he says all cocky and arrogant. Though, I can't fault him for it, the amount of dedication and hard work it takes to keep the type of physique he has isn't easy.

I uncross my arms and place my hands on his shoulders as I lean in to whisper against his ear and order, "Take your shirt off and get on the bar."

He grins and tugs his shirt off in two seconds, revealing a beautifully sculpted upper body. The girls in the bar all scream and shout their approval as he makes his way to the bar and hoists himself on top of it. Once he's laying back, I climb onto the bar, too, and straddle him. My head spins just a tiny bit with the motion, a sign that perhaps this isn't the best idea after all but now I'm too far in to back out. Tink is there, a mischievous gleam in her eye as well, as if she's just as curious how all of this will play out.

"Allow me," she says, as she sticks a lime wedge between the man's teeth then proceeds to spill whiskey down his chest, stomach, and into his belly button for me to slurp up.

And then I feel that tingling sensation between my shoulder blades. I look around the bar, desperately trying to spot him, but he's nowhere in the crowd or anywhere in the shadows that I can see.

"Hey," the guy beneath me grabs my hand, getting my attention, "don't leave me hanging." He smirks as he puts the lime wedge back in his mouth.

I hesitate for only a second before I lower my head, and start sucking out the alcohol from his bellybutton. I use my tongue to wipe up the rest from his hard-cut abs, keeping eye contact with him the entire time. I make my way up his chest and then lean in to take the lime wedge from his mouth. My lips press against his as I take it and squeeze the sour juice into both of our mouths.

I sit up and throw both arms up in the air and the crowd goes wild with approval. I sway a bit where I'm still seated, straddling this stranger, but I yell and cheer along with the crowd anyway. I started this; I have to see it through.

"Who's next?" I hear someone yell. Others are now climbing onto the bar as we're climbing off.

The stranger helps me down gently, but once my feet are on the floor, he doesn't remove his hands from my waist or step out of my personal space. I realize that we're eye to eye, and I'm suddenly staring into hungry brown eyes. Something inside of me stirs. A memory I just can't quite piece together. My heart rate spikes, fear is making its way through my body one inch at a time. The way he's looking at me and holding me against his body is very aggressive. Too aggressive.

He licks his lips and then brushes his thumb over my bottom lip. "You can't be such a tease and not even give me a little taste of those lips, that's just cruel. How about we find a quiet corner and you can give me that taste?"

"Ummmm," I struggle to find my words.

My earlier confidence, and need to cause chaos, have completely evaporated. All I wanted to do was a cause a little scene to see if *he* would come and get me. Hell, I just wanted him to come out and scold me at this point, tell me to go home. I don't want to go anywhere with this guy.

"No, I don't think that's a good idea," I manage to get out.

But it's no use. He's already pulling me away from the bar and I'm too drunk to fight him. I stumble along behind him, desperately trying to clear my muddled brain and think clearly. I need to find my strength to pull away. I need to find my voice. But I don't do any of that as he leads me down a darkened hallway and pushes my back against a wall.

The fear has taken complete control of my body and mind. It feels like I've been thrown into the freezing ocean with bricks tied to me, pulling me down further and further into the cold darkness. I'm weightless and heavy at the same time. I can't move.

His lips crash into mine and his tongue is forceful as it pushes past my lips and into my mouth. Further down I sink. I squeeze my eyes shut against the darkness. There's no light. There's no air. His hands are on my body now and, oh God, I can't breathe.

"Get the fuck off of her." His voice rings out like a bell in a tower, signaling everyone and everything of the incoming threat, but it's too late to try and save yourself.

The guy is ripped off of me and thrown back into the wall across from me. I immediately lose whatever strength I had left in me and sink, like a weighted body, to the floor. I can hear the loud crack of knuckles against skin and bone as my rescuer destroys his face with one vicious punch... after another... after another.

The guy is getting his face beat so badly he can't even talk to try and defend himself, and the attack came so quickly and so severely, that he had no chance in hell of trying to fight back either. I'm blinking away tears, tears I didn't even realize I was shedding, trying to see what's happening. It's dark in the hallway and all I can make out are silhouettes. One dominates the other and it can only be one person.

Sinn.

I watch, wide eyed, still frozen in shock and terror, as Sinn holds the man up by his throat as if he weighs no more than a ragdoll. And then, I faint. I must have fainted because what comes next literally only happens in movies.

Or nightmares.

Sinn punches his hand through the other man's chest and rips out his heart. He lets the man's lifeless body go and it drops like a pile of rags to the floor. The wet squish and thud of his heart hitting the floor follows.

I only remember bits and pieces of what comes next. I hear Sinn talking to someone but I don't know who and I can't make out what they're saying.

"...everyone the fuck out of here..." "...body..." "...again..." "...mermaids..." "...discreetly..." "...clean up this fucking mess..." "...yes, boss..." "...no, I'll take care of her..."

Then, I'm being lifted into strong arms and taken inside an elevator I had no idea was even back here. Déjà vu hits me, yet again, and I can't help the intense feeling that this has all happened before. I lean my head back and look up into the face of my rescuer and I gasp at the cold, blue eyes already looking down at me.

"You," I whisper. "I know you."

He doesn't say anything. He just cradles me against his massive chest and continues to hold me tightly as we start to move. I can't tell if we're going up or down though. I guess it doesn't matter. I lean my head against him and close my eyes, too tired to care what comes next.

I'm safe.

I'm in his arms and I'm safe. I let myself fall into the smell of leather and soap. An oddly perfect mix that soothes me to my very core. I let out a heavy sigh, unleashing all of my fears, all of my doubts and insecurities, as sleep pulls me under.

He came for me.

Sinn

Empty by Letdown

She's going to be the fucking death of me. She's persistent, I'll give her that. I thought if I kept myself hidden, she would give up. Move on. I want her to move the fuck on because I don't need this shit in my life.

I don't need the distraction.

I don't need the reminder of the past.

I don't need all these foreign feelings trying to suffocate me.

There's no good that can come from this. Whatever *this* is. She brings out the demon in me and that's saying something. I'm a lot of cruel and hateful things. I like control, I like to be obeyed, and I fucking love to be feared. There are aspects of hurting people that I enjoy. *More* than enjoy. According to my father, and hell, all of my family, that's not normal for someone like me.

You can't lock your friends up in toy chests, Peter! That's not how hide and seek works! Now go apologize to him and swear you'll never do it again!

I'm not stupid. I know how hide and seek works, but even as a child I enjoyed darker things, and hide and seek was a dull game. I always preferred to know where they were hiding, trap them there, and then listen to them scream themselves hoarse as they pounded on the door or wall, sometimes scratching until their fingers bled, begging to be set free. Their fear, and knowing I was in control of it, was always way more fun. Of course, my way of playing always earned me punishment from my father.

My actions are not unheard of in my family, but they are rare and mightily frowned upon. I may not feel empathy, or love, the way normal people do, but a killer...? Even *that* has never been in my nature.

And now it's happened. More than once.

The only silver lining is that this time, it happened here. This is my domain entirely, which means things are different here than anywhere else. Here, I'm in control. I create the narrative and I can change it when and how I see fit. There aren't going to be consequences for tonight like there were last time because it won't be the first time someone has...*strayed* from their path and disappeared because of it. No, I'm more concerned about the girl in my arms and the consequences I'll yet face for saving her.

I shouldn't be bringing her here. I shouldn't care about what happens to her. She's not my responsibility, period. She's in my bar and yes, I owe a duty to her but not in *this* way. So why the fuck do I care? Why the fuck am I gently lying her down in my own fucking bed?

She passed out in my arms as I carried her here and doesn't rouse one bit as I lie her down. The smell of alcohol radiates off of her. I lean in and place my nose behind her ear, smelling her shampoo... crisp, delicious apple, but there, underneath that, I run my nose along her skin and inhale something reminiscent of fresh and airy lotus. It's her scent. Both light and intoxicating at the same time. I pull the covers over her and then move to sit in a chair next to the cold, dark fireplace to watch her as she sleeps. The only light in the room is from the bedside lamp that glows dimly but allows me to see her face clearly. The rest of the room is lost to darkness, myself included, just the way I like it.

How is it possible for someone to look so pure and innocent as they sleep?

Yet, I'm not fooled. She's neither of these things. Her actions are proof of that, and she's clearly struggling with her choices, or she wouldn't be here. It doesn't matter what a person thinks about their own actions, whether or not they justify them, truly believe they're right or if they know without a doubt that they're fucked up. Some choices are easier to sweep under the rug while other things just can't be taken back.

Like taking a fucking life.

I lose track of time as I sit in the quiet room and watch her sleep. I have the urge to get up and go to her, to pull her against my body and see how well she fits against me. There's a tingle in my fingers begging me to touch her soft skin and delicately trace every beautiful line and curve of her body. There's an urge to take my lips and tongue on a mission of exploration into the different tastes and textures of her skin. To sink my teeth into that same soft skin and see how much pressure it takes before it breaks. To pinch, scratch, slap, and choke to see how much pain she can handle before she cries out. Before she begs me to fucking stop.

My cock twitches at the thought of her writhing and flinching underneath me as I give her my undivided attention like she's so desperately been seeking. Could she handle it? Could she handle the pain I like to inflict or the immense pleasure I'll grant her afterwards? Could she handle all of me?

And as I listen to her deep, even breaths, I hear the second it changes. As if my thoughts of choking her are actually real. As if my hand is squeezing her windpipe. Her body twitches, her breaths become shallow and ragged, and her heart starts to race.

I groan as my dick reacts and starts to harden. Maybe I should just give in and go to her. Who fucking cares if she's too drunk to know what's happening? I'll make sure she enjoys it. Maybe. Hell, I have no idea what she likes and doesn't like but I'm close to not giving a damn. All I need is my aching cock sliding inside of her, warm, tight, wet pussy, easing my own fucking pain.

She whimpers now, obviously having some type of nightmare, and the sound hits me right in the chest. It fucking ignites the beast inside of me and yet, it also...*worries* me.

The fuck?

I shake my head and grab my cock, squeezing the fuck out of it to temper my desire and clear my fucking head. I'm so fucking hard I can't even remember the last time I reacted this way to someone, and it's no doubt fucking with my mind. I squeeze again and clench my teeth against the pain I'm inflicting on my own dick, but it helps to clear my thoughts. I would never take her against her will, but fuck, she's testing all of my fucking limits. She's in the goddamn lion's den and she doesn't even know it.

"No!" She jerks upright, choking and gasping, as if she can't get air into her lungs fast enough.

Her chest is heaving with panic from whatever nightmare just tormented her. Her low-cut tank top gives an impressive view of her breasts as they swell and fall rapidly with her breathing. I fucking hate how she shows off her body for any and all to see, and it makes me murderous whenever she lets another man touch her. Even if it's just on her arm.

I.

HATE.

IT.

But here in my bedroom, as I sit unseen in the dark, I take the time to appreciate just how fucking beautiful her body is. How beautiful she is, even in a wild, disoriented panic. Even with dark circles under her eyes that have nothing to do with the smeared mascara from crying earlier.

Her eyes are so green they almost seem to glow, and they're framed by long, thick lashes that sweep her cheeks when she closes her eyes. Her cheeks are tinted pink, mainly because of the alcohol, and I'm sure from the fear of the nightmare. Her lips are full, the top lip slightly turned up, and larger than the bottom. She's always wearing an obnoxious shade of red lipstick and I wish I knew what color her lips were naturally, and how they would look wrapped around my cock as her bright eyes stare up at me. Her hair is a lose, tangled mess around her head and I want to wrap it around my fist, pull her head back, and taste those lips while the fear of the nightmare still thrums through her body.

She seems to finally realize that she's not safe at home, tucked away in her own bed. I silently watch her, as she looks around the room, confusion furrowing her brow and drawing her lips into a frown. It's fascinating to me how emotive she is. Her heart rate spikes again and I can feel her panic rising at not knowing where she is. No doubt, the alcohol is fucking with her memory of the past few hours.

"Oh, God," she whispers and runs her hands down her face, clearly regretful and scared to be in an unknown location.

"I'm afraid there's no God here," my voice sounds loud in the quiet room even though I barely spoke above a whisper myself.

She screams and scoots across the bed, getting tangled in the sheets and covers as she tries to get as far away from me as possible. I smirk at the failed attempt. She's been so desperate to get close to me and now, in my room and in my *bed*, she can't get away from me fast enough.

"Who's there? What do you want?" Her voice is an octave higher and shakes, showcasing her fear. Only fear or pleasure can change a voice like that.

Both turn me on.

I stay seated in the dark and continue to watch her for a few more seconds. She's trying desperately to see beyond the small glow of light and I can tell she's straining to hear for any type of movement. I finally lift my arm up and click on the tall lamp next to my chair, allowing her the opportunity to see me. The relief in her eyes is immediate as she lets out a heavy breath and her body relaxes with it.

"Where am I? What time is it?" She asks, her voice calmer now.

I glance at the clock on the opposite wall. "You're in my bedroom and it's 2:44 in the morning."

She sighs. "Figures, even shit-faced drunk I can't fucking sleep. Ugh, my head is pounding." She scoots back to lean her head against the headboard and closes her eyes.

All traces of her earlier anxiety and fear are gone. It's as if I'm not even in the same room as her. She has no idea I'm the *only* one she should fear but she seems to react the completely opposite way around me. In turn, I don't know how to react to that or how it makes me feel.

"Nightmare?" I ask.

She nods her head. "Always."

And I don't know why I ask my next question because I don't normally give a fuck. I don't care about people the way others do, so why do I find myself caring about *her*?

"What happened in this nightmare?" Maybe I'm just curious to know exactly what she remembers about...well, everything. *Sure, Sinn, keep telling yourself that.*

She shrugs and doesn't open her eyes as she answers, "There's more than one but they're all broken." She sighs and whispers the next part so low that I almost don't hear it, "Like me."

But I do hear her.

And her private admission is so much like my own that I feel the strike of those two quietly whispered words as if she ripped open my chest and tattooed them right on my fucking heart. I'm struck so forcefully that I feel like all of the air has been stolen right out of my lungs. As if it's *my* heart that's been ripped from my chest and *my* body left to bleed out on the fucking floor.

After a much too long stretch of silence, she finally opens her eyes and looks at me. Our eyes lock and I swear that fucking jolt of electricity slams into my chest and restarts my cold, dead heart. I see every damaged and broken piece of her.

I see the sadness.

The darkness.

The pain.

And I see the lonely truth she tries to hide. I see it and I desperately try to ignore it because the only reason I can see her so fucking clearly is because she's a direct reflection... of ME. It's the same goddamn thing I saw and felt *that* night. The night I lost everything.

A knock on the door breaks our charged, silent stand-off and I get up far too eagerly to answer it. For once, grateful for the interruption.

I can feel her curious gaze on my back as I move toward the door. The electricity in the air is palpable and I'm having a hard time with...*everything*. Fucking everything!

I wrench the door open and practically snarl in Slightly face, "What?"

"It's all taken care of, Boss," he dips his head in a slight bow, not entirely out of fear, although I can smell the pungent scent of it on him. No, he bows his head in respect.

"Good. Send Tink up with water and ibuprofen." I slam the door in his face before I can get a confirmation or any other type of distraction.

I place my hands on the closed door and lean into it, hanging my head, and giving myself a second to regroup. Even though I was just relieved about the interruption, I also desperately want more time alone with her. I fucking swear, my mind is too goddamn twisted when I'm around her. I can't think straight. And the loss of clarity and control only adds to my burning temper.

"What's your name?" Her voice is no longer a faraway whisper. She's no longer stuck in her own head, in her own world of nightmares, but maybe worse… she's' stuck in mine.

I let out a frustrated sigh, I'm not used to people questioning me about anything, but I turn around to face her. As soon as I do, as soon as those big, sad yet curious, green eyes lock with mine again, all of my frustration is gone.

"Peter Sinnclair, but you can call me Sinn."

"I thought so," she says. "About the Sinn part, I heard someone call you that, but I didn't know your full name. I'm Wendee Wright but you call me Dee."

"I know who you are," I say in as bored a tone as I can manage, which is extremely hard to do since I'm nothing even close to bored when she's around.

She looks taken aback, eyes go wide and eyebrows shoot up in surprise. "You know who I am?"

"Don't flatter yourself. I know everyone who comes into my bar, especially the clingy, stalker ones."

I immediately regret the words as soon as they leave my mouth. Why I even said them, I have no fucking clue. They're not true and the hurt in her eyes is instantaneous. She recovers quickly though. All openness she had in her face seconds ago is gone. She's shut down and is just as cold and blank as I am. Well, maybe not that frigid, but close.

"I see," she says, as she throws the covers off of her and climbs out of my bed, still a little unsteady in the high heels, but she manages to finally get her footing.

I can't help the direction of my gaze, as my eyes slowly sweep up her long, smooth legs before they disappear into the short, pleated skirt, barely covering her intimate parts. The thought of her parading around downstairs like this, *in my fucking bar*, with practically no clothing on, irks me beyond my own understanding. I want to bend her over the bed, lift up that slip of a skirt, rip off her panties, and whip her ass with my fucking belt. I want to watch her delicate ass cheeks redden and welt as my belt leaves marks on her perfect skin. I want to punish her for dressing like this and fucking teasing me. Driving me insane and making me feel things I don't know how to feel.

I want to hear her scream in pain.

And when she finally cries out for me to stop, I want to slide my hand up the back of her thigh and find her soaking fucking wet for me. I want to drag my fingers up her slick pussy, teasing her clit with slow determined strokes, building her up to a writhing, pleading need, until she's crying out for a release. Then I'll push my hard, aching dick inside of her and fuck her until she's begging me to stop.

I want to hear her scream in pleasure.

Fuck that, I want to take her so far over the fucking edge of pleasure that she won't even have a voice to cry out with.

Once again, I'm left standing feet away from her, clenching my fists and fighting hard against the urge to do all of that and more. How can she come so close to breaking down all of my walls, all of my defenses, all of my control, without even fucking touching me? All she has to do is be here and I'm losing my own battle of wills. I can feel my resolve wanning. I can feel my frozen barriers cracking.

"Why do you hate me so much?" Her voice breaks through my internal battle until I'm once again back in the room with her.

Her hands are crossed over her stomach, one hip pushed out, as she stares at me with none of the concern or desire I saw in her eyes the night I fought with my brother. She's a mask of coldness now and it's shocking to see. It is just a mask though, it's not who she is, not really, but it's still a shock to see. And I don't fucking like it.

Her voice betrays her. It shakes on the way out, the only small piece of emotion she lets slip. "I see it in the way you look at me. The way you're looking at me now," she gestures to my rigid stance.

She has no idea what I'm feeling is the exact opposite of hate. Or is it? I have so much hate in my heart there's not room for anything else so maybe it is hate. But is it her that I hate? Or the reminders of everything she brings with her? Is there a difference?

"And I just don't understand why. You don't even know me."

I hear what she's saying. I'm trying to process her words, how she's clearly perceiving me right now and this entire situation, and I'm trying to understand it all. Not just her words, but how I do actually feel. When she's not around, I have no fucking problem remembering why I'm so goddamn angry. I have no fucking problem being the monster that I am. When she's not here.

But when she's here...

When she's here, I don't know what the fuck to believe. I don't know who I am.

So, we stand in another charged silence, facing off. Neither one of us moving. Neither one of us backing down. Neither one of us know what the fuck we want to do.

Another knock on the door interrupts us. Again, I'm relieved for the intrusion as I turn to answer it. It's Tink. She looks just as amused as I do about everything as she holds up a glass of water in one hand and a bottle of ibuprofen in the other. She doesn't say anything, just glares at me. I move aside so she can come in and give the items to Wendee. I don't want any reason to have to get closer to her.

Tink's eyes go to the rumpled bed and I don't have to see her face to know she's pissed. She probably thinks I slept with her, which in turn, will piss her off more than she already is. Tink is a lot like me when it comes to the main emotion in her heart, but she wasn't always this way. She's become this angrier version of herself because of me. I don't begrudge her anger. After all, how would you feel if you spent the majority of your life watching the person you're in love with fuck everyone else but you? No, I don't begrudge her, but I also don't understand why she's stayed here, with me, and why she's continued to be so loyal. Love is cruel and malicious. It makes people do the absolute worst things.

"Here," she shoves the items into Wendee's arms and then turns back around and marches back to where I'm still standing by the door. "What are you doing, Sinn? Why are you putting up with her? She needs to move the fuck on. She's not fucking special and you need--"

My hand is around her throat, and she's pushed up against the wall, feet dangling a good foot off the ground, before any more words can come out of her mouth. I hear Wendee gasp but I ignore it. She needs to see me like this. She needs to know exactly who I am.

"You would dare tell me what *I need* to do? Who the fuck do you think you are to have such a right?" I'm squeezing her throat completely closed so there's no way for her to answer and, since it was a rhetorical question anyway, I don't need her answer.

My voice goes low and deep, my anger is barley being contained as I lean in and growl, "You were no one when you came here and I can make you no one again. I can make you disappear with a snap of my fingers, Tink, don't ever fucking question me or push me, ever, again," I bite out each word.

I make sure she sees the hate and the warning in my eyes as I look into her wide, scared, yet defiant, eyes. She's never once done anything to go against me, and I don't think she will now, but she needs to know I won't tolerate her even thinking about it.

Her eyes start to water as they stare back at me, and I'm satisfied that she understands the threat. I slowly lower her down and the second her feet touch the floor she's wrenching out of my grasp and stomping away as fast as she can go without outright running.

I grind my teeth and pop my neck, easing some of the tension in my head and shoulders before I turn back to face Wendee. I'm not sure what exactly I expected to see in her expression, but she's back to giving me a blank face.

"I'm gonna go," she says coolly, setting down the glass of water and pills on the nightstand.

"You can't walk home at this hour and in this," I gesture both to her outfit and to her intoxication, "state. You can stay here, take the pills, drink the water, and get some rest. You can go home once you're feeling better."

She shakes her head and walks toward the door. The door I'm still standing next to. She stops in front of me and pulls her head back to look at me. Even in her tall ass heels, the top of her head barely reaches my chin. The next thing I know, her hand is coming up towards my face.

I panic.

No one *touches* me.

Not even when I sleep with women, I always fuck them from behind so they *can't* touch me. They *can't* look at me. My heart drops to my stomach and I instinctively reach out and wrap my hand tightly around her wrist.

"Don't," I growl.

She gasps again at the sudden forcefulness and then her eyes stare at my hand where it's holding her wrist in front of her face. My blood-stained hand.

"That's blood," she says quietly. "Last night was real. What I saw," she swallows, "was real."

I don't say a word as she slowly pulls her eyes away from my hand and back up into my eyes. This time, I absolutely expect to see her fear, maybe even disgust. Nothing could have prepared me for what shines through her eyes.

Gratitude.

Her green eyes sparkle through the tears forming in her eyes and then one lone tear escapes down her cheek. I swear I feel my heart studder at the sight of that tear. The gratitude and the tear, they don't make any goddamn sense. I'm so damn taken aback, so shocked and focused on her eyes, that I don't even realize she's leaned in and is tiptoeing, struggling to reach my face, and then I feel it.

The barest touch of her lips against my cheek, dangerously close to my lips. Just a whisper of a kiss, nothing more, and yet I felt it rock through my entire body. A pebble being dropped into a calm and unsuspecting pond, no matter how small, will still cause a ripple effect. She's the pebble and I'm the fucking pond. Except I'm not a goddamn pond. I'm the motherfucking rioting ocean. I'm the beast of an iceberg that sank the fucking *Titanic*.

"Thank you," she says softly, before she pulls her arm out of my grasp and walks away.

She leaves me standing in my bedroom like a frozen iceberg, helpless only to watch, as the ship called Wendee peacefully passes me by.

What in the actual fuck just happened?

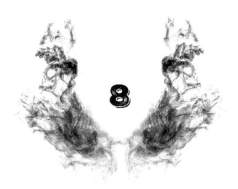

Dee

PUSH//PULL BY SAM SKY, LAUREN BABIC

Sinn was right. I shouldn't be walking home at this hour without being completely alert and in control of my mind and body. I think the entire situation with Sinn helped sober me up a bit though. Then again, that's probably just my own false confidence talking and trying to justify my reckless decision to walk home.

Alcohol is the best at making you feel like you can do things you normally can't, or shouldn't, do. Why do you think so many people drive drunk? Do you really think that many people get behind a wheel with no care in the world of hurting, or even killing someone because of it? No. There's no way that's true. They do it because they truly believe they're fine. Alcohol is muting their senses, like common sense, and telling them they can do anything. Just like it's telling me I'm fine to walk home.

Luckily, I do make it home unscathed and stumble into my tiny apartment, kicking off my heels. I should have at least taken the ibuprofen and water Sinn offered me, but I wasn't thinking straight. See, alcohol at its finest. But I do take some now. I manage to down three glasses of water and messily make myself a peanut butter and jelly sandwich before I throw myself down on my bed.

My thoughts are a riot of chaos, and I don't think it has anything to do with the alcohol. I acted like an ass tonight and I almost ended up in a very bad situation. The way I felt in that hallway comes rushing back. I hate that I let myself freeze. I should have fought, I should have screamed, I should have done something! Anything would have been better than fucking freezing like a deer in headlights.

But he came for me.

My fucked up and reckless plan worked.

He came for me.

Not only did he rescue me, again, he actually *killed* that man. His threat from before, on the night he told me to go home, rings in my mind.

The only thing you're going to succeed in is getting a man sent to hell for fucking touching you.

In the moment, I took his threat as no more than words he spoke to let me know he didn't like another man touching me, not that he would *literally* kill someone for it. Did he kill the man I danced with? Why does he care who touches me when he seems to fucking hate me? I don't understand him at all. One second, he's rescuing me and the next, he's looking at me like I'm his worst enemy. His mixed signals are fucking me up. I don't know what to do or how to act.

Maybe Tink is right. Maybe I should just move the fuck on and forget about him. That would definitely be the easier and smarter choice. Then again, when have I ever done anything that was easy? When have I ever done anything that was good for me? Answer...

never. Life has never been easy and, in this moment, I see clearly just how much of it has been my doing. I'm drawn to the darkness for some reason. I'm drawn to the danger and the thrill of, *what if*. Because what if I can have Sinn? What if I walk away and have to live with the regret and wonder of what if?

I touch my wrist where his hand gripped me tightly, the sensation of his large hand still burning on my skin. There was nothing nice or soft in that touch. It was punishing and threatening, but instead of fear it sent a shock of excitement rushing through me. His hand on my skin was so cold it burnt. Like the stupid shit I did as a kid, putting salt on ice and holding it to your skin. It's cold and hot all at the same time as your skin literally burns underneath.

Sinn is salted ice.

Ready to burn me up completely.

And there's nothing more thrilling than the thought of letting him burn me, so I can finally feel alive. Maybe that's why he' so addicting. Every time he's near me, I feel alive. How would it feel to be completely consumed by him? Is the feeling worth my own destruction? Because there's no doubt in my mind that Sinn will absolutely fucking destroy me.

The bus is dark and quiet as we get closer to school, the complete opposite of how we departed seven hours ago. A mix of young juvenile male testosterone and emotionally naïve female estrogen. Dicks and hearts mixed together in a chaotic and frenzied energy of inexperience and excitement now exhausted and tapped out.

We're coming back from a basketball trip and, as small as our school is, we can all fit inside one large bus. It's both a blessing and a curse growing up in such a small town. Everyone knows everything about everyone and everything. There's absolutely no hiding a fucking thing in a town this small. There's also no coming between us when it comes to outsiders. We're a close-knit group, all of us, for the most part, but we're still kids. We're still cruel, and there are still fights, rumors, gossip, and bullying. Just because there are fewer of us doesn't mean we're any different than other kids.

As we reach the gym, the bus parks in front to let us out and everyone rouses from either sleep or hushed conversations to gather their things and head home to enjoy what's left of the weekend. As the doors open and everyone climbs out of the bus, heading to their vehicles, I stay and help carry the equipment back into the gym. This is one reason why I'm one of the coach's favorites. The other reason is because I'm naturally athletic, pretty good at everything I put my mind to, and I throw myself into every sport possible; basketball, volleyball, track, plus our yearly fiestas, which consist of dancing Folklorico in a two-night event. I'm also in the Honor Society, a part of the Knowledge Bowl team, and yearbook team. To say I stay busy as often as possible is an understatement.

The innate desire to do and be good has stayed with me from a young age. As a sophomore in high school, the desire hasn't changed. At this point, I think it's a crucial part of who I am. Yet, all of my efforts have gone completely unnoticed by the one person I've tried to impress.

My mother.

All of the goodness I've tried to do, tried to be, hasn't changed a fucking thing about my home life. I'm still a ghost in my own home. At this point, I'm starting to wonder if I had it all wrong this entire time. Maybe I need to do the bad things to be seen?

Maybe if I'm just like her, she'll want to be around me. Maybe if I have the things she desires, she'll see me.

I walk out of the gym to see half of the cars have already left. I'm the only one in my class that isn't driving yet. I've taken the driver's ed class along with everyone else, I have my learner's permit, but no vehicle to use. I also don't have a parent responsible enough to remember to come pick me up. I only live a mile from school, I could just walk home, but it's almost 1:00 a.m. and it's fucking cold outside and I'd really rather not. Not to mention it's embarrassing. I spot Jake's truck still idling in the parking lot. He lives in the same direction I do and could easily drop me off on his way home. I just have to ask. Letting out a heavy sigh I walk toward his vehicle.

I knock on the passenger side window and it lowers immediately. Jake's a grade above me and, although I wouldn't say we're a school quite big enough to have jocks, if we were, he would definitely be one.

"What's up?" He asks.

"Hey, I was wondering if you'd be able to drop me off on your way home?" I ask, shyly.

A cruel smirk pulls at his lips as he turns toward me. "And what would I get out of it?"

"Ummmm, I think I have a couple bucks I could give you for gas money...," I start to rattle off nervously, as I fish through my jacket pockets, which is ridiculous because he literally has to drive right by my house on his way home.

"I had something else in mind," he says, as he unzips his jeans. "Get in."

I feel all the blood rush into my face and my cheeks burn up. I swallow the fear that's crawling up my throat at what he's suggesting. I've never even kissed a boy much less done anything *sexual* before. Not to mention, everyone would know about it come Monday morning. I can just hear what they'd say now.

"I didn't know you had it in you, Dee."

"Not such a good girl after all."

"I knew she'd turn out to be just like her mother."

"Slut."

"Whore."

"Hey, Dee, I'll drive you home next time."

"How bout I give you a different kind of ride."

And on and on it would go. It will follow me for the next two and half years of high school. And yet, as I'm standing in the freezing cold, body shivering, I'm contemplating doing it. If everyone thinks I'm just going to end up like her, why don't I just give in to the bad stuff and give everyone what they want and expect? Being good has gotten me nowhere. Being good has gotten me right here, standing in the cold, contemplating sucking a dick for the first time just so I can get a ride home.

"I said get in," he orders.

I'm about to pull on the door handle when coach's voice yells out across the parking lot. "Dee, you need a ride? We can take you."

"Never mind," I mumble. "Coach is gonna take me."

He snorts, "Fucking prude." Then the window is being rolled up in my face and he backs out quickly, causing me to jump out of the way.

My body jumps in bed from the intensity of the dream, waking me from another... well, I can't really consider this one a nightmare. Nothing bad happened but it was a turning point for me. An awakening so to speak. It was the first time I realized that even boys in high school are toxic. It was the first time I was treated like nothing. Like less than nothing. Not a human with feelings. Not a friend who needed help. Nothing more than a vessel to be used, abused, and thrown aside for the next person to pick up off the floor.

Shortly after that experience, I started to realize how selfish and cruel people are. How all they see when they look at me is how they can use me. Manipulate me. Degrade me. And because I have no one in my life protecting me, there will never be any consequences.

And these selfish and cruel people have things I need. I'm at their mercy and there won't always be a coach around to save me. In fact, no one has saved me since.

Thus starts my spiral into the world of toxic men.

And my reality then only echoes my reality now.

I have no one.

I have nothing.

But that's not entirely true, is it?

He saved me.

Not once, but twice. And that reality is what caused me to tear up and thank him. No one has saved me in a very long time and I almost forgot what it felt like. I forgot what it felt like to be seen as more than a body. More than a person to use. More than a means to an end. More than a victim.

Sinn sees me for me. Ok, maybe not exactly. He doesn't know how broken I really am, but he does see someone worth saving. And that speaks so much louder than all the words he's never said. It speaks louder than the anger he portrays. If he truly, genuinely hates me, which I can't fathom why he would, then he wouldn't save me.

He wouldn't *kill* for me.

That's enough for me to settle my battling thoughts on what to do. I need to fight for this, for him, because no one has been worth it until now. Is he truly worth it? There's still a small sliver of doubt in my mind, but I push it aside. I will get through his walls. I will see what he's hiding on the inside. Because we're all hiding something. There's not one goody-two-shoes out there without at least one skeleton in their closet. Trust me, I've seen more than my fair share. And there's nothing he could possibly be hiding that I can't handle.

I hope.

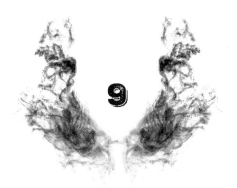

Sinn

FIRE BY TRAPT

I debate whether or not to go down to the bar tonight but then decide it's a futile attempt to try and avoid Wendee... and these feelings. Besides, I've already neglected my work for too many days when I was trying to avoid her and what good did that do? Absolutely nothing. It actually made it worse. My absence caused her to act reckless and foolish, and it allowed me too much alone time to sit with myself and my own dark, twisted thoughts. Which is never a good thing.

So, I get dressed in black slacks and a dark blue button up. Blue and black are the only colors I wear because they're the only colors that define me. They also do a great job of hiding blood. I smirk at the thought of blood blending into my clothing and no one being the wiser as I reach for my bottle of *Salvatore Ferragamo's, Intense Leather.* I spray once on my chest before buttoning up my shirt. I run a hand through my hair, combing it in its usual neat, but carefree style. I freeze mid motion as I stare at myself in the floor to ceiling mirror, realizing what I'm doing. I'm making an effort with how

I look. Not that I didn't before, but now I'm acutely aware of the fact that I *want* to look good. For *her. Son of a motherfucking bitch,* I shake my head.

It takes longer than I'd like for her to show up. It's nearly 1:00 a.m. when she finally walks in and, as much as I want to be frustrated, I can't help but feel relieved. I wasn't sure what was going to happen after the events of last night; the hallway escapade and then the thing with Tink. I wasn't sure what she would think in the light of day once the alcohol had cleared out of her system. Things are always different when you're sober and the light is shining on all the devious deeds previously done in the dark.

But here she is.

Dressed in a navy-blue dress with a plunging V-neck, mirrored in the back, with a banded waist and a skirt that loosens and flows over her hips, all the way to the floor. Compared to some of the other outfits she's worn, this one is mild. But when she walks, a slit on the left side exposes her leg from ankle to thigh. The slit is dangerously high, which causes my fucking blood pressure to rise just as fucking high. This dress is so much sexier because of the peek-a-boo effect and it's definitely having the same effect on my cock.

I watch her with the intensity and focus of a Navy SEAL sniper who has his enemy in his scope. She doesn't even glance in my direction as she walks past the booth toward her seat at the bar. Only this time, she doesn't sit down. She orders a drink from Tink, who begrudgingly delivers it, and then she's walking back across the dance floor, and up the ramp.

Towards me.

My heart pounds in my chest to the beat of her steps as she approaches.

BOOM.

BOOM.

BOOM.

BOOM.

I swear the whole fucking bar should be able to hear my heart beating in my chest with the intensity in which I *feel* it. It's a bass drum inside of my chest and it beats only for her.

Wendee.

She approaches the table, her shoulders pulled back and chin tipped up, feigning confidence, but her voice is a little unsteady as she speaks.

"Sorry to interrupt but I was hoping I could join you."

She lifts her eyes up to meet mine as she says the last word. YOU. I was hoping I could join...*you*. The insinuation is clear. I stare back at her, dark blue eyes locking with bright green ones. That invigorating buzzing energy is immediate between us. We're like two magnets being drawn together. Only sheer stubbornness and uncertainty have kept us apart but there's no denying the sexual tension between us.

And we've barely even touched.

What's going to happen when I finally give in and claim her? Because it will be me and me alone doing the touching. I don't care how different she feels to me. No one touches me.

She finally blinks and seems to second guess her decision to come up here as she looks at the woman sitting in the booth next to me and then down at her drink.

"You're clearly busy. I was wrong to--"

"Leave," I growl in a low voice.

Her head shoots up as she looks at me again. I haven't taken my eyes off of her since she stepped into this bar. I watch her throat bob in a hard swallow, and she nods her head as she takes a step away from the table.

"Not you," I clarify. Her eyes shoot back up to mine, surprise and relief clear across her features.

I finally slide my eyes away from hers and acknowledge the woman sitting beside me for the first time since Wendee walked in.

"Leave," I repeat, not kindly.

The woman doesn't argue or fight, but she gives Wendee a death glare as she leaves the booth. I take a note of it and of her face before she leaves. That will be the last time she *ever* looks at Wendee that way. I'll address it later. Right now, my attention is on the beautiful, frustrating, and intriguing woman standing in front of me. Now that she's here, and I've allowed her to stay, she doesn't seem to know what to do. Hell, I don't know what the fuck to do.

"Well, are you going to stand there all night or would you like to have a seat?"

She blushes but slides into the booth next to me, on my left, the opposite side the other woman was just sitting on. Her scent wafts over to me and I greedily inhale her air into my lungs, wishing I could hold onto it forever. I keep my right hand on my drink but lift my left arm over the back of the seat and lean my body slightly towards her. It's a large booth but she settles in just within my reach. It's entirely too fucking close and not nearly close enough.

She clears her throat, "Thank you for letting me stay."

"I have a feeling you'd just keep trying if I denied you." *And I don't want to deny you.* Even though it's silent, that admission unsettles me. She unsettles me.

She gives me a shy smile, "You'd be right."

"Why?"

She shrugs. "I don't know, exactly. There's just something about you. Something...*familiar*. I know it sounds crazy but I feel drawn to you."

"Is that all? You're *mystically* drawn to me?" I raise one eyebrow in mock humor as I take in her embarrassed and unsure expression.

She meets my eyes again and hers betray her expression. There's definitely something *deeper* motivating her. Something she's feeling and not saying but, since I'm not one for talking in general, I don't push her for the truth.

She reaches for her drink and takes a sip. I decide to change the subject for both our sake.

"I didn't think you'd be drinking again so soon after last night," I observe.

She groans. "Last night was a mess, *I* was a mess." She shakes her head. "It's just Dr. Pepper, no alcohol. No alcohol for a while. Last night...," she trails off.

A lot happened last night. I'm not sure what part she's going to bring up. The fact that she watched me murder someone would be at the top of my list if I was in her shoes.

"You saved me, twice now, but I'm confused. Don't get me wrong, I'm incredibly grateful by the way. I really can't thank you enough."

The memory of her lips brushing against the corner of my mouth comes back full force. It's so fresh in my mind, so intense, that it feels as if she just leaned in and did it again. Only this time, I want to turn my head and capture her mouth with mine. I want to taste her and drink *her* down instead of my bourbon. Which is in-fucking-sane because I don't kiss. I don't touch. I PUNISH. I fuck and get off. *That's it.*

"But I don't understand how you can want to save me when you seem to hate me more than anything in the world and--"

"I don't hate you." The words are out of my mouth before I can think them through. I don't hate her? Until this very moment, I wasn't sure if I did or not.

"You don't?"

I shake my head.

She furrows her brows, clearly thinking about our previous encounters. "But the way you look at me sometimes...I don't know, but I swear it looks like hate, or even disgust."

"I hate what you remind me of and I hate the way you make me feel." Another admission I didn't see coming.

"Oh," she licks her lips, her chest is rising higher as her breathing is getting heavier. "How do I make you feel?"

"You make me *feel*," I try and explain. "That's enough to piss me off because I'm not the type of man that *feels* anything."

"Oh," she repeats. She drops her gaze to her glass and spins it around on the table, needing an outlet for her nervous energy. "I love the way you make me feel," she whispers. I'm not sure if she meant to whisper it out loud or not but her admission definitely piques my interest.

I reach my hand out until my fingers are lightly grabbing her chin, turning her face towards me. She gasps at the touch, seemingly just as shocked as I am, but her eyes remain downcast.

"Wendee." it's the first time I've said her name and it gets her attention. Her luminous green eyes raise up to meet mine. They're full of uncertainty, hope, and *need*.

She licks her lips again and they stay slightly parted, as she lets out a breathy, "Yes?"

"How do I make you feel?" I ask, as my thumb lightly traces her luscious bottom lip.

"Alive."

That one word seems to flow from her lips, onto my fingers, and travel up my arm and over the rest of my body. My skin is tingling all over from the sensory overload of just sitting next to her. Her scent. Her warm breath against my fingers. Her skin under my touch. All of it has my cock growing, even without the need to hear her whimper in pain.

Alive.

Fuck. She makes me feel alive too.

"Does this make you feel alive?" I ask, as I trail my finger down her chin, her neck, and follow the material of her dress as it lays against her chest. I gently trace the edge of the material over her breast and watch as her nipple peaks under the lightest touch.

"Wendee, I asked you a question."

"Yes," she admits in a heavy whisper.

I keep my fingers moving south. The slit in her dress is exposing her entire leg, almost clear up to her hip. My fingertips meet her soft skin and I make lazy circles on the top of her thigh, moving slowly to the inside. Her breath hitches, making my cock twitch, as I reach the sensitive skin close to her center.

"Are you wearing panties?"

Her eyes shoot up to mine, wide and confused, but also excited and full of desire. Fuck she's as easy to read as an open book with illustrated pictures.

"Yes," she repeats.

I remove my hand from her thigh and sit back against the booth, appraising her. "Take them off and place them on the table."

"What?"

"You heard me and I don't like to repeat myself. Take. Them. Off."

She darts a look around the bar. We're out in the open, but no one can see what happens underneath the table, only what happens above it. And, at the moment, no one is paying us much attention.

She reaches into the slit of her dress and lifts her ass, pulling the panties off, and then all the way down her legs. She wads them up and throws them on top of the table.

I reach for them and stretch them out. "Lace thong, in my favorite color, black. And a royal-blue dress. Were you thinking of me when you got dressed tonight, Wendee?"

"Yes," another whispered admission.

I move my hands to the center of the panties and rub my fingers over the wetness. "They're soaked. Are you already wet from me barely touching you?" The thought of her soaking wet pussy has my cock aching and pushing forcefully against my zipper.

Fuck.

I never even knew I could get this fucking hard but everything about her has me pulled as tight as a fucking bowstring.

She doesn't say anything but I see her clenching her thighs together, desperate for friction. I lift my arm back over the top of the booth. "Come here," I order her.

She hesitates, bites her lower lip, her cheeks already flushed with the heat of her desire and fuck, she looks so fucking sexy. I shouldn't want to touch her, not like this. Not this intimately. This isn't how I do this. Then again, Wendee hasn't made me do anything I normally do.

She slides closer to me but stops about half way. "Don't be shy now. All the way." I stay where I'm sitting, completely relaxed and unassuming, when in reality my insides are a mess of excitement and anticipation, and my dick is a fucking vaulting pole inside my pants.

She slides along the booth until her body is touching mine. I reach down and grab her right leg, hooking it over my left. I grab her hand and place it on her leg. "Make sure this leg stays here. Don't move it." She nods. Her chest is really rising and falling with heavy breaths now, as if she just got finished running a mile and not simply sitting next to me.

Because of the slit in her dress, her bare pussy is now clearly exposed to me. All I have to do is look down. Even lost to the shadows I'd still be able to see her, though not as clearly as I'd like, but I keep my eyes on her face, watching every little thought and emotion that passes over it.

I glide my fingers slowly up her exposed thigh until I reach the heat of her core. My finger immediately sinks into soft, warm wetness, and I have to fight against the groan that wants to escape my lips at how impossibly *good* she feels as I sink a finger inside of her.

"Mmmm," she leans her head back and closes her eyes, mouth parting as she pushes her hips up higher so I can get deeper.

I add another finger. "Oh, fuck, Wendee," I can't help but close my eyes for a second as I focus on how it feels to slide inside of her. "You're so fucking tight." I can just imagine how her tight pussy will feel hugging my hard cock as I push it inside of her.

She's so wet her pussy is making squishing noises as I slide my fingers in and out of her. I continue to stretch her tight pussy wider, and then I add my thumb, rubbing her swollen clit.

"Oh, God," she pants.

I growl, removing my fingers from inside of her and slap her sensitive clit. She yelps and jumps at the sudden sting of pain.

"I never want to hear you say that name when you're with me. There's no God here, Wendee. Only me. Only *Sinn*. Do you understand?"

"Yes," she breathes out a moan as my fingers find their way back inside of her.

I lean my head in and whisper into her ear, "Do you like how this makes you feel? How my fingers make you feel?"

"Yes." She starts to rock her hips, meeting my fingers in a sexy rhythm as they slide inside of her.

"Do you want to come on my fingers, Wendee?"

"Yes, Sinn, please," she begs.

I pull back so I can watch her face again. Her head is still thrown back, she's panting her pleasure to the ceiling, and anyone who looks over now will clearly know exactly what the fuck is happening in this booth. That gives me immense satisfaction to know that I'm claiming her. That everyone in here sees that she's mine and mine alone to touch. I want to unleash my aching cock and pull her on top of me right here, right fucking now. But this isn't how I do things. This isn't me.

"Wendee, look at me," I order.

She opens her eyes and obeys without hesitation. Fuck, that was a bad idea. Her eyes are so alive. She's on the verge of pure bliss and I'm the one bringing her to her climax. I want to see her face as I push her over the edge. I want to swallow her moans of pleasure. I want to experience every facet of her in every position and every way possible. I curl my fingers, where I know I'll hit that sensitive spot inside of her, and I add more pressure to her clit.

"Fuck, Sinn, that feels so good. You're going to make me come."

I have to force myself to pull my fingers out of her pussy and not give her the release she wants. She whines at the absence of my fingers and her eyes look confused. They're still lost to pleasure, but definitely confused.

"Why did you stop?" She asks, breathlessly.

The fact that I want to make her come, the fact that I want to watch her face as she crashes, and the fact that I want to fucking touch her, and kiss her, and claim her, has me so fucked up and so fucking confused. I have to stop this before I cross a line I've never crossed before. I have to do *something* because I want her in ways I've never wanted anyone before and that fucking scares the shit out of me.

I grab her face with the hand that was just knuckles deep in her juices and speak through clenched teeth. There's no faking the anger I feel. Anger with myself for doing this and hurting her.

"Because whatever you think I am, I'm not. I'm not your savior, I'm not *good*, and I'm not fucking nice. Don't romanticize me. You have no idea who or what I am," I seethe in her face, griping her chin harder, before I push her away from me and slide out of the booth.

I don't look her way again as I pass the booth, push through the crowd, and head to my penthouse. Once I'm inside the elevator I take her panties out of my pocket and stare at them.

"Fuck!" I bunch them up inside of my fist and punch the metal wall hard enough to dent it.

The elevator doors open, and I stumble into my penthouse feeling drunk on rage and pent-up desire. I lean against the wall and unzip my pants, pulling out my cock. I un-bunch the panties from my fist and place their wetness on my rigid, aching dick. I want to feel her wetness coating me and this is the closest I'm going to fucking get. So I grab them, along with my dick, and start pumping.

Dee

I'LL MAKE YOU LOVE ME BY KAT LEON, SAM TINNESZ

I'm left sitting in shock, in the booth, alone. Never in my life has anything close to this happened to me before. I mean, I'm definitely used to getting hurt. Not being called again after having sex? Sure. Being cheated on and lied to? Absolutely. You know, the *typical* plays from a fuckboy playbook. But I've never had a guy flat out refuse to give me an orgasm and walk away from me *before* sleeping with me. This is definitely a first and I don't know what the fuck to think.

My body is still buzzing from his touch. I can feel his fingertips trailing a line of burning ice down my breast and along my thigh. I can feel his warm breath against my neck and smell the leather and bourbon, mixed with my arousal, and it's sooo fucking heady. It hits me so deep in my chest, in my stomach, between my legs, it's as if I'm drunk all over again but I'm one hundred percent conscious and sober. Sober drunk. Is that a thing?

He's so damn confusing! He let me interrupt him, when I don't think he tolerates interruptions from anyone...*ever*. He told me that he didn't hate me but he hates the way I make him *feel*. Not feel any particular way, just feel, in general. And I don't know if he meant to be that open and honest with me or not but that seems like a pretty big deal to me.

From someone who understand *exactly* what he means by that admission, I know there's more to it than what he's pretending to convey. If he's anything like me, I make him feel the same fucking way he makes me feel.

ALIVE.

And his voice, when he sank his fingers inside of me, echoes in my mind, imprinted in my memory.

Oh, fuck, Wendee. You're so fucking tight.

My thighs clench at the memory of his fingers inside of me. His voice radiates through me. A person can hide a lot of things, but if you're not careful, if you're not in complete control, something can give you away.

A look.

A word.

A touch.

A tone.

And his tone of voice, as he got lost in the moment along with me, is enough to give me the confidence I need to get out of this booth and go find him. I'll make him confront the feelings he's so desperate to bury. The feeling of his fingers digging into my jaw as he practically growled his warning in my face should be all I need to back the fuck off, but I'm not like most girls. This is the world I'm used to. This cut-throat and dangerous world is what I know.

I may be broken but I'm not stupid. I see all the anger he holds at bay, and the last thing I want is that anger focused on me, but if that's the emotion he needs to feel in order to let go, then so be it. There's something in the way he looks at me, the way he's saved me, that tells me he won't actually hurt me.

And then there's the mystery of my panties. I look high and low for them before I leave the booth, but I can't find them. He *took* my panties. That's the nail in the coffin. The last piece of information I need to get my feet moving.

I climb into the elevator and take a guess, hitting the button for the top floor. As the doors close and I begin my ascent, my heart starts to race frantically, and the fear, uncertainty, and excitement all start to swirl together inside of my stomach.

He's not going to hurt me. He's not going to hurt me. He's not going to hurt me. He's not going to hurt me.

Maybe if I think it enough it will become the truth.

As soon as the doors quietly swish open, I'm met with a mountain of muscle and a cold, dangerous energy that sends a shiver of dread up my spine. There's a light coming from somewhere behind him, further into the penthouse, but the entry way we're standing in, is lost to shadows. All I can see is his menacing, and very large, silhouette. His hands are clenched tightly into fists at his side, the same posture I've come to know intimately. It's as if it's reserved specifically for me.

I tentatively step out of the elevator but don't make any moves to advance toward him. Not yet.

"What the fuck do you think you're doing here?"

Ok, Dee, you can do this. You came here for a reason and now it's time to walk the walk. "I think you want more than you want to admit."

He doesn't respond, just stands like a solid, fearsome statue, if a statue could exude threatening living energy. I take a deep breath and continue, taking a small step towards him. Slow and steady, voice calm and low, as if I'm sneaking up on a vicious bear, trying to see how close I can get, before I ultimately get its attention, and get attacked.

"I see the way you look at me," I trail my fingertips in the same line that his took. I take another step. "I heard the way your voice betrayed your words as you sank your fingers inside of me." I move my fingers up my own thigh until my hand disappears under the dress. "I felt the way you touched me, Sinn, and I don't think you were ready to stop any more than I was." Another step.

"You have no idea what I want," his voice calm, controlled, giving nothing away now.

"Then tell me."

"I already told you." His voice is a low, warning growl now, "I'm not good, or nice, and nothing you say or do is going to change that."

"I know," I say, confidently, though I'm not sure exactly where my confidence is coming from. "I don't have any fantasies about who you *could* be. I see exactly who and what you are. I've witnessed your cruelty, and how far you're willing to go firsthand. I have no illusions of saving you or changing you. In fact," I take another small step and I'm now in his orbit. I'm dizzy with desire, his energy is surrounding me, I can feel it alive on my skin. I want so desperately for him to touch me again. "I'm drawn to you because of all of those things. I want you *exactly* the way you are."

He's on me in an instant, faster than I can follow with my eyes. One hand is fisting my hair, wrenching my head back, causing me to cry out in shocked pain, as the other hand grips my jaw again. His touch is brutal. There's nothing soft or delicate this time and, even though this is what I asked for, this is what I knew would happen, I can't help the small bit of fear that climbs into my throat, making me want to scream for help.

ALIVE.

It makes me feel so fucking alive. My body and mind are awake, living openly and freely in every second I'm in his crushing hold. In his deadly orbit. And I enjoy it way more than I fear it.

"You say you want this but I don't think you fucking understand. I want to hurt you, Wendee. I want to hear you whimper and scream in pain. I want to see *my* marks and bruises on your perfect, delicate skin. I'm a monster, Wendee. The worst fucking kind."

My chest is heaving, my neck is pulled back at a painful angle, but still, I feel the slickness between my legs. My voice is strained as I manage to whisper, "Show me."

He growls and releases me so suddenly that I stumble. I manage to right myself and watch as he walks to the end of the entryway and hits the switch, flooding us in a bright, blinding light. I blink, until my eyes adjust, and then my focus is back on the man in the room with me. No, the predator. In his own words, the *monster*.

His eyes are glued to me, and now, with the light, I can see everything I couldn't see a minute before. I can see the excitement in his eyes, the anticipation for what's to come. His eyes take in every inch of my body before he finds my eyes again.

"Do you enjoy dressing in provocative clothing?"

Okayyyy, that is not at all where I thought this conversation was going, but I remember his earlier statement about not repeating himself, so I answer. "Yes."

"I see the way men react to you. And women, too. Does it make you feel powerful?" He cocks his head, seemingly genuinely interested, as he starts to circle me.

I feel like a helpless bunny being hunted and cornered, with a spotlight flooding the space, chasing away all of the shadows, leaving me nowhere to hide.

"Yes," I repeat.

"Take it off," he demands.

I let out a shaky breath. *Whatever he does to me, I can handle it. This is what you wanted, Dee, well, ready or fucking not.* I find the small zipper on the side of the dress and unzip it. Then, I pull the straps off of my shoulder, and the dress falls easily down my body. Since you can't wear a bra with this dress, and I no longer have on panties, I'm left standing naked in front of a fully dressed Sinn as he continues to slowly circle me. It's as if he's contemplating the best way to attack.

I hear the clink of his buckle and then the low whoosh of the belt as it slides free. My heart starts to race even more, making me worry that I may just pass the fuck out if it beats any faster.

Sinn makes his way back in front of me. A belt has never looked more terrifying than it does now, dangling threateningly from his fist.

"Last night, when you were in my room, I imagined what it would be like to punish you for the way you dress. For allowing everyone to see your body so freely." My eyes are on the belt and he bends it in half, holding it in his fist, ready to swing. "Now, I get to."

He walks around me again, until he disappears behind me. "Bend over and take off those heels."

"Oh, God," I whisper, and immediately jump and cry out in surprise as his belt lands a hit on my right ass cheek.

He's suddenly right behind me, grabbing me by the throat from behind, pulling my head back. "What did I say about using that name when you're with me?" His voice sounds angry as it rumbles out of his chest and reverberates through my back.

I can't help but arch against him and gasp as my ass comes into contact with impossible hard dick. Fuck. He really is enjoying this. "You said...not to...say it," I struggle to say around his hold on my neck.

"Don't do it again. I won't tolerate it a second time. Now, bend, the fuck, over." He releases my neck but doesn't step away from me.

I bend over, and with my heels on, my ass is lined up perfectly with his crotch. He pushes his hard length against me and I close my eyes, shuddering at the feel of him. Then he's gone, and the crack of the belt rips through the air, as he lands a second blow to my ass cheek, in the same spot as the first. I yelp again, more in surprise than pain. It takes me a second to remember that I'm bent over for a reason. He wants the heels off. I start to fumble with the buckle at my ankle. My fingers are shaking so badly it takes me way too long to finally unleash the damn little hook.

As I'm reaching for the other one, another slap lands on my ass cheek, harder and louder this time. I can barely register the sting of this one before another one immediately follows.

Smack.

This one *does* hurt, and I whimper as the pain not only stings, but radiates through my ass cheek.

"Mmmm, that's more like it," Sinn says, still standing behind me. "The other shoe, Wendee."

I'm breathing hard now, my cheek throbbing but not completely hurting...*yet*, but I'm not sure I can handle any more hits though. My fingers are trembling so badly that I really struggle to undue the little buckle. No hits come and I focus on unlatching the buckle. Once I finally get it released...

Smack.

Smack.

Smack.

Three savage hits in rapid succession. This time the pain is unbearable, and I cry out, falling to my knees. My ass cheek is splitting in pain. It feels like he broke skin and I swear, there as to be blood running down my leg. In fact, I can *feel* it. I reach between my legs and feel the dripping wetness on my inner thigh. I pull my shaking hand away and look down. My fingers are glistening.

But not with blood.

Sinn's black boots come into view. I'm still crouched on the floor where I fell, more dazed and reeling from the realization that I'm wetter than I've ever been in my life.

"Get up," he orders, voice low and deep.

I try to comply. I try to get my feet under me, but my legs feel like Jell-O, and I don't think there's any way they can support me right now, even if my life depended on it. Which it might.

Sinn's large hand wraps around my upper arm aggressively, and he hauls me to my feet, guiding me roughly through the living room and into the kitchen. "I hope I haven't broken you already, we're just getting started," he says, as he pushes me face first onto the island countertop.

His hand pushes down on my head as his large body leans into me. I feel his hand slide up the back of my thigh. Gathering the sticky wetness on my skin before he runs his fingers along my slit.

"When I imagined this last night, I had hoped to feel you wet for me but this, damn," he moans, as he sinks two fingers inside of me and I echo the moan with one of my own. His moan is the sexiest thing I think I've ever heard and it makes my pussy throb even more than it already is from his fingers sliding inside of me. "This is so much better than I imagined. You're fucking *drenched* for me and I can't wait to fill you up with my cock."

His fingers are relentless as they punish me. I'm so wet and so horny from the last orgasm he denied me, it won't take me long to spill over the edge.

"Please," I beg, as his fingers bring me closer and closer to my release.

"Do you think you've earned it, Wendee?"

"Yes," I practically yell. "Yes!"

"You did take the belt surprisingly well." He removes his fingers from inside of me just long enough to smack my sensitive ass, causing me to whimper from the loss of his fingers and from the pain. "And we do need to get you loosened up for my cock." He pushes his fingers back inside of me and then removes his hand from the back of my head to spread my legs wider. He starts to rub my clit with one hand as his other hand continues to fuck me.

I try to grip the countertop, to hold on to it for purchase, as I feel the pleasure building quickly at his relentless attention.

"Your body is so talkative, Wendee, I can feel your pussy pulsing against my fingers. You're going to come all over them right now, aren't you?"

"Oh, fuck. Yes, I'm going to come," I cry out, as I jerk and spasm against his hand, my body is uncontrollable as the orgasm rips through me.

Once again, he's left me dizzy and completely unhinged from reality. It feels like I'm weightless, flying amongst his galaxy, and I don't ever want to come down.

Sinn

Fuck. I never thought making a woman come would be so fucking satisfying. But as I slide my fingers out of Wendee's beautiful, soaking wet pussy, all I want to do is making her come again. And again. And again.

I want to kneel down and lick her from front to back. I want to make her come again on my tongue and then on my dick. I want so desperately to taste her, but I'm already so far gone from anything

I've ever felt that I don't dare. I don't dare taste her and let myself become addicted to her. I need to draw the line. I need to hold my ground and do this how I've always done it.

No kissing.

No touching allowed.

Only fucking from behind.

I unzip my pants and pull my cock out for the second time tonight. I've been rock-fucking-hard since Wendee sat down in the booth and then forced to stuff my cock back in my pants when the elevator started to come back up. I never expected to see Wendee standing there, confronting me with barely-there confidence. Still, she was bold enough to do it and there's no way I could have denied her as she practically *begged* me to fuck her.

I rub my fingers over myself, coating my cock with her wetness as I prepare to ravish her. I slide the head of my cock along her dripping opening and grit my teeth at how fucking good she already feels. I can feel the heat radiating off of her and I'm dying to push inside of her.

"We need a condom," she orders, as she feels my dick sliding against her.

"No, we don't," I assure her. "Do you trust me?"

"How can I? I don't even know you."

"I'm asking you to trust me."

"And you trust *me*?"

"Yes."

She hesitates, I slide my dick against her again. "Okay," she whispers.

"I've felt how tight you are, Wendee, and even though we worked you loose a bit, I'm not fucking small, and this *is* going to fucking hurt before it feels good. Do you understand?"

Even though my body is practically vibrating with the need to slam into her, ablaze with a ravenous hunger I've never felt before, I won't take her without her consent. Even though we're already here, it's already implied what the next step is going to be, I refuse to take her without her verbal consent.

"Yes," she whispers breathlessly, "please, Sinn, I want it."

"Fuck," I push the head of my cock into her opening, and I'm immediately met with resistance. Even with sliding in effortlessly because of how wet she is, she's still extremely tight.

"Fuck," she echoes the word back to me.

I pull back out of her, and before I can think through what I'm doing, I'm flipping her over. The need to see her face as I push into her for the first time is overwhelming me. I need it like I need fucking oxygen to breathe. I pull her hips to the edge of the counter, lining up perfectly with my dick. She pushes up on her elbows and looks down to where my cock is about to be buried inside of her.

"Holy shit, Sinn, I don't think I can take all of it." Her eyes are wide with fear and her throat bobs in a hard swallow.

"You can, and you will," I say, as I push myself into her, never taking my eyes off of her face.

She gasps as my thick head sinks inside of her, forcing her body open for the rest of me. I don't slam into her like I planned. She's tighter than even *I* imagined and it's hard to get inside of her. I also don't want to completely hurt her. Something I'll have to examine at a later date. Right now, I'm just focused on getting every last inch of my aching cock sheathed inside of her.

I pull back, leaving the tip inside before I push a second time, harder. A whimper leaves her lips, her eyes are a mix of pain and pleasure. I'm holding her hips in a bruising grip as I pull out and push again, this time, getting all the way inside. She winces and places her hand on my chest, attempting to hold me off.

I freeze under that touch. Her palm is flat against my chest, and even through my shirt, because I'm still fully dressed, I can feel her touch burning my skin.

No touching!

She doesn't notice my shock or seem to notice that I've stopped. Maybe she thinks I stopped because she asked me to, when in reality, it's because she touched me. Period. But she's too focused on my dick inside of her.

"Fuck, you're so fucking big. I need a minute."

I grab her wrist and pull her hand away from my chest, then grab the other one and hold them both in one hand above her head as I push her flat against the countertop. I use my other hand to hold her hip, and I pull almost all the way out of her before I slam into her again. Her body is more prepared for me but still tight and resistant. I keep pulling out and pumping inside of her in long, hard strokes. I watch as the pain erupts across her entire face, her mouth opening wide and crying out every time I sink deep inside of her. Her eyes are watering but she doesn't ask me to stop. I'm so fucking hard and turned on, I have to concentrate on not spilling inside of her like some inexperienced school boy.

"Good girl. I knew you could take it," I congratulate her, as I ease up.

I pull out and give her shallow strokes, only about half of my length, but she's still straining to open to my width. I continue to work in slow shallow strokes, and it doesn't take long before her pussy is throbbing around me. Her beautiful, full breast are bouncing up and down with my strokes, and her legs have wrapped around my waist, gripping my tightly. Possessively. And it sends a shock of rightness through me. This feels right. *She* feels right. Her face has gone from pain to pleasure as she throws her head back, pleading and begging for me not to stop.

"Fuck, don't stop. Please don't fucking stop. Right there."

Seeing her writhing in pleasure under me is turning me on just as much as the pain did. She's so fucking beautiful. I release her wrists and palm her breast. Her hand comes down on top of mine, searing through my skin like molten lava, urging me to squeeze it harder, as her other hand squeezes her other breast.

"Wendee, look at me." She doesn't hesitate. She opens her eyes and meets my gaze. "Come for me, Wendee." My voice sounds strange to my ears.

It's full of gravel and heat and *feeling*.

I don't have time to think about it before I'm lost in the wonderous moment of Wendee's pleasure releasing on my cock, over her beautiful face, and all through her body. I pinch her nipple, hard, and she cries out, arching her back off the counter as her body jerks with the force of her orgasm.

I snake my arms around her back and pull her in against my chest and step away from the island. This is too close, too intimate, but I desperately want to feel her bare breasts as they rub against my chest. I want to feel them on my skin so badly that I almost rip off my shirt. I've never wanted to feel someone so completely before. The thought makes me more frustrated, as her arms instinctively wrap around my neck, and I pound inside of her. I lift her up and drop her down the entire length of my dick. She still cries out as I sink, balls deep inside of her, but her cries aren't as intense as they were before.

Her head is thrown back and her breasts are bouncing in my face. I lean down and grab one with my mouth. I suck and flick her nipple as I continue to fuck her, hard. She's a mess of moans, whimpers, and cries. I'm coming undone by the feel of her, by the sound of her, by the smell of her, by every fucking thing about her.

And I want fucking more. This isn't enough. I don't think I'll ever get enough of her.

I bite down on her breast, pressing harder and harder, and harder, until she cries out again and I taste her sweet metallic blood on my tongue. It's all I need to throw me over the edge. I push her down on my dick one last time as I release all of my rage and desire deep inside of her tight little pussy. I groan as the orgasm practically explodes out of me and I'm surprised it doesn't cut her in fucking half.

I stagger to the island and set her on the counter, leaning my forehead against her chest. We're both glistening in sweat and trying desperately to catch our breath. I feel her fingers sink into my hair at the back of my neck, her touch so soothing and relaxing, that I sigh in contentment and sink further into her hold. I immediately realize what the fuck just happened and pull my head off of her chest. I grab her wrists again and drag her arms away from me. She doesn't fight me or question me.

I slowly slide my still semi-hard cock out of her, and she winces again when her body finally releases me. As I tuck myself away, I notice a small amount of blood on my cock and more on her thigh, as well as the small trail of blood trickling down her nipple. Seeing her blood like this doesn't excite me nearly as much as it should. I want to ask her if she's ok, but I can't bring myself to ask, scared of what her answer will be. Scared that I did, in fact, push her too hard, too fast. A twinge of fear runs through me, tightening my chest.

Fear that this is going to be the one and only time I'll have her. Fear that I've lost her before I've even claimed her. Fear that I've damaged her more than she already is. Maybe even to the point of breaking her beyond repair.

I don't make eye contact with her as I walk over to the sink and turn the faucet on. I hold my finger under the stream of water until it turns hot. I grab a clean cloth from under the sink and soak it under the stream of hot water, then squeeze out the excess water so it doesn't drip everywhere, but when I turn around, she's no longer sitting on the island.

I walk out into the living room and see her in the entry way, bending down for her discarded dress, and a pang of something awful and heavy punches my chest. It's a foreign feeling. It feels exciting and terrifying all at the same time and I'd rather ignore it than address it.

I walk over to her as she's stepping into the dress. "Here." My voice comes out softer than I'd like. I clear my throat, getting control of my voice so it comes out more like my usual cold, emotionless self. "For the blood." I gesture to her body.

"Thanks, but I'll be ok until I get home. I'll clean up there," she says, avoiding my gaze and pulling the dress over her body, zipping it into place.

"You're leaving." I don't ask it like a question, because it's clear that she is, but she answers anyway.

"I told you; I know who you are and I don't have any naïve fantasy about changing you. I know what this is between us. It's not my first rodeo."

I clench my jaw, my jealousy immediate at the mention of her with other men, but I don't know what to say. She's right. I am who I am and she's not going to change me.

She already has.

She bends to pick up her heels and winces. I think I did hurt her more than she's letting on. She finally turns to face me and scoffs.

"I mean, you didn't even get undressed." She gestures to me with the hand holding her heels. "If that's not the definition of a meaningless fuck then I don't know what is." She turns and walks to the elevator. The doors open immediately, and she steps inside. Right before the door shuts, she makes eye contact with me and, I swear, I see so much more than she's saying with her eyes.

I see longing.

Or maybe that's my own inner emotion fighting to break free. I want to rush after her. I want to carry her back inside, take care of her, clean her up, and soak in a hot tub with her. I want to feel her hands on me. I want to feel her skin on mine. I want to taste her lips, her skin, and her pussy. I want to drown in her. I want to be so many fucking things for her. But I don't know how to be anyone else. So...

I let her go.

Tink

I See Red by Everybody Loves An Outlaw

She doesn't see me where I sit alone, in the dark, at *my* bar. This *is* still my fucking bar. Well, not the entire building, but the actual *bar*, where I serve liquor, belongs to me. It's *my* domain. But this entitled little bitch has come in here lately like she owns the damn place. It's only going to be worse now that she's slept with Sinn.

The thought of him sleeping with her makes me see fucking red. Anytime he chooses someone over me is another razor blade slice to my heart. But he doesn't know that. No one does. Maybe that's my mistake. Hoping that in time he'd come to see me, truly see me, if I just stay by his side. If I continue to be here for him and be exactly what he needs, when he needs it. And I thought maybe I'd have a chance soon since he's been uncharacteristically distant with women.

Ever since *that* night.

I still don't know exactly what happened that night. I don't think anyone besides Sinn knows the details of what happened. But it changed him. It changed him deeply. He's never been one to completely let loose, like Hook. Sinn has always been reserved, with a tendency to enjoy the darker things in life, but he's never been like this. This cold and emotionless. Numb.

Until she walked in the bar a week ago.

It's as if he came back to life. Still, not the way he was before, but it's *something*. I hate that it's because of *her* and not me.

At least I get to witness her walk of shame.

Because a walk of shame is exactly what it is. I know Sinn, probably better than he knows his own damn self, and I know what he is and *isn't* capable of. And feeling anything for this whore is something he definitely isn't capable of. He barely feels anything at all, and there's no way this ridiculous girl is going to change that. Besides, she won't be here for long anyway. They never are.

Especially if I have anything to do about it.

But the hard truth is, Sinn has been acting different lately. Different because of *her* and I won't take any chances. I wait a few minutes, until I'm sure she's gone, before I slither out of the dark. I pull the hood from my dark hoodie over my head, covering my face, and slip out of the bar. The weather is still warm at night so, I'm hoping I don't draw more attention to myself by being covered up, but then again, no one here actually gives a shit about anyone's business but their own. Still, I can't help but feel like a conniving, sneaking serpent, and I shiver at the thought of what Sinn would do to me if he found out what my intentions are. Good thing he trusts me and would never suspect me of doing anything I shouldn't.

I walk soundlessly, keeping to the shadows, as I make my way down to the docks. They're not far from the bar, only a few blocks, and I make it there quickly. Instead of heading directly for H1 or H2, I head towards the sandy beach instead. It's almost 3:00 a.m. but there are always people walking around, especially near the docks. It's like they're subconsciously drawn to them. So, for my mission tonight, I steer clear.

I walk far out onto the beach, where no lights from the docks or streets reach. To where the darkness feels thick and alive. I'm guided by the slightest glow of a crescent moon but it's enough. I make my way to the water's edge and act quickly, before I can hesitate. I pull out the small knife I took from the bar, the one I use to slice up fruit and would love to slice *her* up with, and I swipe it deeply across my pointer finger. I need a cut I can easily explain if I'm asked and cutting my finger while slicing fruit for drinks is entirely appropriate, and will garner no questions. I squeeze my finger, urging the blood to drip faster, as I lean over the water and let my blood drip into the lapping waves at my feet.

Once I'm satisfied that I've given enough of my blood to the ocean, I take a few steps away from the chilling water's reach, take a seat, and train my eyes on the water in front of me.

Then I wait.

And wait.

And wait.

And wait.

I've always been a patient person. I've waited patiently for years, upon years, for Sinn to see me. I don't plan on giving up now and I sure as hell am not going to sit back and let some meaningless girl come in and distract him. I would normally just wait it out, like I have with other girls that have temporarily caught Sinn's attention, but as much as I hate to admit it, this one's different. I don't know how or why but she is. I can just feel it in my gut and a woman's intuition is very rarely wrong.

So, I wait. I sit here and wait so that I can take action. It takes longer than I'd like but eventually the water level changes and is no longer lapping close to where I sit. I remove my shoes, fold my jeans to mid-calf, stand up, and follow the receding water line. The wet sand is cold and clings to my bare feet as I walk in a steady decline towards deeper water.

When I finally come to the water's edge again, Serene is there, bobbing in the water that's waist high. Her white hair almost glows, even in the slight moonlight that filters down on us, framing her delicate and hauntingly beautiful face, and down to her waist. Her eyes do glow, reflecting the light like a predator in the night, allowing her to see perfectly clearly, whereas I'm almost blind due to the darkness. And she *is* a predator, though Mermaids often get portrayed as the beautiful, peaceful, and magical beings in fantasy stories. They are magical and beautiful, but peaceful, they are absolutely *not*.

"Why have you summoned me?" Her lovely voice sings out, dancing along the waves.

So many souls are fooled by their beauty and their voices that sound like angels singing, that they don't notice the sharp claws or the dangerously sharp and pointy teeth behind the luscious lips, until it's far too late.

"I need a favor."

"And why shall I do anything for you, Little One?"

"I bet you've grown rather accustomed to the additional meals Sinn has been providing you lately, but he'll be back to his normal self soon, and those meals will stop coming."

"A few extra bites to eat is always a good thing," she shrugs, "but we do just fine dining on our own."

"Well, what if I could guarantee some extra pieces of dessert would keep finding their way to you?"

"And how could *you* guarantee this, Little One? If I'm not mistaken, Sinn is the one in charge here, not you."

It's my turn to shrug. "What he doesn't know won't hurt him."

Serene laughs, and the waves around her rise up, as if laughing with her. When she stops and the waves finally settle, she addresses me again. "It's quite bold what you're suggesting, going behind his back, but what danger you put yourself in means little to me. If you can pull it off, we have a deal, but if you can't, there will be blood to spill in my waters, one way or another, and I've already got the taste of yours. Do you understand?"

I don't mistake her threat. It will be my blood that will spill in these waters if I fail to keep my end of the bargain. I hesitate before agreeing. Is it worth it? Do I want to be in debt to the Mermaids? Fuck no, I don't, but I don't see any other way to get what I need. I need Hook and he only comes to land once every six months. I don't have that kind of time.

"I understand," I agree, reluctantly.

Serene smiles brightly, showing off her sharp teeth, in no doubt what's meant to be a threatening promise if I fail. "Very well, what shall the favor be?"

"I need you to carry a message to Hook. I need to speak with him, *urgently*. Tell him to meet me here, in this exact spot, tomorrow night."

"Is that all, Little One?"

"Tell him it's about his brother and don't let him refuse."

Serene dips her chin. "It shall be done. Now, go." She dismisses me easily.

I don't waste my breath thanking her. I turn and start walking back up towards the beach. It seems further away now that I'm making my way back across the ocean floor, picking my way carefully around hauntingly beautiful seashells that catch the light of the moon. I'm almost to shore when ice cold ocean water slams into me from behind. I stagger forward under its weight, losing my footing, and falling face-first into the water.

I get my feet back underneath me and push past the surface, gasping for air and shivering from the freezing temperature of the water clinging to my clothes and hair.

"Fucking bitch," I mutter through chattering teeth as I stumble onto the dark, empty beach, picking up my discarded shoes before making the miserable walk back to the bar.

The following night, I do the same thing. I sneak out of Sinful

Delights like a thief in the night although tonight is the best night I've had in a week.

She didn't come in.

It put me in a great fucking mood, but I can't say the same for Sinn. He was even more on edge and angrier than ever. He met with several patrons, yelled at each one of them which he never does, and even threw his drink across the room sending shattered glass and bourbon everywhere.

I cleaned up the mess.

Like I always do.

And what did I get for my generosity? Not a fucking thing. Sinn never even looked my way, not once. Not even when I personally delivered a new glass of bourbon to his booth and asked if he was ok. He grunted, grabbed the glass out of my hand, and demanded I bring the entire bottle of bourbon to his table. Which, of course, I did because I'll always be there for him. I'll always be there to provide what he needs. And one day, I'll provide more than bourbon.

Sinn stayed at his booth past closing, staring at the door with an intensity I've never seen from him before. I don't think he even blinked for the last hour. He was clearly waiting for her. But she didn't come. She didn't fucking come and I'm always here. Why can't he see that?

I started to worry that I wouldn't be able to sneak out to meet Hook on time but Sinn finally went up to his penthouse and I ran out of the bar before the elevator doors even closed. I ran the few blocks to the docks and veered off towards the beach before getting too close. I sigh in relief, as I see Hook's silhouette standing at the edge of the water and I finally slow my frantic pace.

I step up alongside him, panting, "Thanks for coming."

He cocks an eyebrow as he side-eyes me. "It's not every day Serene is summoned to be a messenger. I imagined it must be urgent indeed."

"It is," I say, my heartbeat and my breaths slowing.

He turns to face me. "I don't have long. Smee is loading up the Jolly Roger for transport as we speak. Tell me."

"Sinn has been acting differently."

Hook laughs sarcastically. "No shit. He's been acting like a devious ass ever since that night. That's old news, Tink, My Sweet."

I roll my eyes at his attempt to flirt or sweet-talk me. Hook is attractive and...*happy*. He's the exact opposite of his brother and that's why I've never been remotely attracted to him. I'm drawn to everything cold and dangerous about Sinn. I know, I'm crazy, but I just think underneath all of that ice there's more depth than even he realizes. I know he's capable of more and I want to be the one to bring it out of him.

I sigh. "He's been acting even worse. There's this girl—"

Hook laughs again, this time, throwing his head back and laughing fully, from the bottom of his belly, a loud and mocking laugh. "Oh, Tink, did you seriously call me here because you're *jealous*."

Anger rages through my veins, I cross my arms, and resist the urge to stomp my foot like a pouting child. "Nooo," I say defensively, even though I don't fully believe the attempt at denial any more than Hook does, but he lets it go. "This girl is...different.

Sinn has been distracted by her. He seems almost obsessed with her. He's been interfering when anyone hurts her, even a little. He's there, saving her. Since when does Sinn save anyone from what happens in Sinful Delights." I throw my hands up in frustration. "That's the whole idea behind the fucking bar."

"I don't see how this really means anything—"

"He killed someone for her."

That gets his attention.

"You must be mistaken. My brother is a lot of things, but a killer isn't one of them," his voice is dangerously low, threatening.

"I had to help clean up the fucking blood, Hook. He ripped out a man's heart for touching her. Slightly and Cubby had to bring the body down here and throw it into the ocean for the Mermaids to destroy any evidence."

Hook runs his hands down his face. "You're certain it was Sinn?"

"Yes."

"Tell me about the girl."

I shrug. "I have no fucking clue. She showed up a week ago and she's just like all the others."

"Well, that's not true is it. Not if she's causing Sinn to...," he swallows, unable to say the words himself, "and you said she's different so you must have a theory."

I sigh again. "I think she might have something to do with that night. I don't know anything for certain, it's just a gut feeling, but I don't know why else she would get under Sinn's skin the way she has. That's the only thing that makes sense to me, but I know absolutely shit about that night to be sure of anything."

"I see. But I don't understand why you're concerned. She'll be gone soon enough just like all the others before her. Just wait it out."

I shake my head. "I don't know if she will. She's not showing any signs of remembering. I know it's rare, but I think she's completely lost. Not just a little confused or guilt ridden. If she doesn't remember, she could end up stuck here, unknowingly and Sinn hasn't made any attempt to guide her."

"So why did you call me? What is it you think I can do about all of this? Sinn barely talks to me these days much less listens to me."

"I want gold dust," I admit quietly. Nervous about asking for it and what he's going to say.

Hook turns back to face the ocean. The sound of the water lapping at our feet seems incredibly loud in our sudden silence. Hook doesn't move a muscle and he's quiet for a long time, making me question this entire plan, but he finally breaks the silence.

"You want to make the Green Fairy. You want to force her to remember."

"Yes," I whisper.

He pulls at his beard now, clearly conflicted about the idea. "I don't know, Tink, it's dangerous. Forcing people to remember can cause permanent damage. Things can go very wrong, not to mention, Sinn has been doing this a long time. I trust him to help her."

"You haven't seen him and the way he's been acting this past week like I have. You don't understand. Everything is different with this one and I'm worried who Sinn will become if he stays on this destructive path."

What I don't say is that I don't give one single fuck if it's dangerous or causes any damage. In fact, I hope it fucking does. I hope she gets and stays fucked up from the gold dust and Sinn loses any and all interest in the bitch.

"I need to see for myself before I agree. I'll make this transport and be back tomorrow night. I'll come to Sinful Delights and decide after I've talked to Sinn."

I sigh in frustration but it's better than a flat-out *no*. "Fine."

"I'll see you tomorrow night. Until then, behave, Tink," he lectures.

I put my hands up in mock surrender. "I'll be on my best behavior, cross my heart and *hope* to die."

"You're impossible," he says, as he shakes his head and walks away, leaving me standing alone on the dark, empty beach.

I linger for another few minutes, contemplating everything that's happened tonight and in the past week. Am I really just being jealous? No. I've seen Sinn with multiple women and, although it does fucking hurt like a motherfucker, I've never really been concerned. Not like I am now. Whether Hook believes me or not, this *is* different.

And I'm not going to let some ignorant bitch change him.

I'm not going to let her take him away from me.

Sinn

She didn't come to the bar last night. I was a mess of anxiety and fucking disappointment. Not to mention ager. At myself. I did this. I showed her a glimpse of the monster and she couldn't handle it. It doesn't matter how much bravado you think you have, thinking one thing and seeing it, no...*experiencing* it, is an entirely different ballgame.

I hurt her.

That's the only thought that kept crossing my mind watching the minutes tick by slower than a turtle walking through molasses as I waited for her to show up. I finally gave up after closing and went to the penthouse but all I did there was more fucking sulking. Like Wendee, I've never been a good sleeper and last night I didn't even attempt it. I tried to pick up a book and read, to get lost in someone else's story, but I couldn't focus on the words in front of me. I kept reading and rereading the same lines, over and over, and I still couldn't process them.

Wendee.

She's the only thing that's been on my mind for far too long and now I've fucking ruined everything. I ruined her. I might as well continue the ruination. I step out of the elevator and emerge from the hallway to see Tink behind the bar, prepping for another busy night.

"I'm going to Salvation Lights," I announce gruffly.

Tink looks up at me, her hazel eyes reflecting everything I want Wendee's to reflect. I know how she feels about me. She thinks she does a good job at hiding it, at acting tougher than she really is, but I know her truth. She *thinks* she knows mine. But just like Wendee, she doesn't. She's never experienced the beast inside of me first-hand. No one who does ever comes back for seconds.

"Will you be there all night?" Tink asks, her nonchalant attitude is a smokescreen I see through easily.

"I don't fucking know, Tink. I'll be there as long as I feel is necessary."

I know she's only asking because she wants me near her always. Because she likes to keep an eye on me and see exactly what I'm doing. Because she's fucking jealous. But I fucking hate being questioned and she knows that, too.

I head out of one bar and cross the quiet street to another. Unlike Sinful Delights, Salvation Lights is practically glowing. The neon sign above the door is large and bright, illuminating the golden doors and the sidewalk below. In less than an hour, the streets will be buzzing with people and both Salvation Lights and Sinful Delights will start to fill up for a night of...*fun*.

I pull open the doors to Salvation and step inside. It's the exact same layout as Sinful except flipped. The booth I sit in is on the right and the DJ booth is on the left with the bar straight ahead. It's also full of bright lights, gold and white everywhere, very elegant and...clean. There are no dark corners or shadows to hide in here. No debauchery. It's uptight and boring.

Since I'm feeling more devious than normal, I'm on a mission to see how many poor unsuspecting souls I can turn to the dark side tonight. How many goodie-two-shoes can I convince to give into their dark desires?

"Hey, Boss," the twin brothers behind the bar echo in unison as I approach.

"The usual?" Michael asks. I nod. He then turns and nods to John, who busies himself getting my drink.

Michael and John are two more of my Boys that have been with me for years. Not as long as Tink, Slightly, or Cubby, but they're on the short list of people I trust to do their jobs and do them well. I know they're loyal to me and have yet to catch them in anything nefarious. They basically run Salvation when I'm not here, which is more often than not lately.

I take my drink to the booth and settle in. Even here, my mind is only on one person. I keep staring at the door as if she'll miraculously walk in. Maybe after her night with me she's had a change of heart. Maybe she'll want the protection and good energy Salvation emanates. Maybe I'm just fucking grasping at straws.

It doesn't take long for the bar to fill up. All the patrons here are shining bright and squeaky clean, dressed to the nines, and the air is filled with light-hearted cheer and laughter.

What a fucking bore.

I leave my secluded booth and make my way toward a group of five women huddled together by the bar. Two of them see me approaching and quickly whisper to the others. All eyes dart my way, giggles and nervous energy surrounds me as I stop in front of them.

It's honestly rather annoying and not at all what I'm attracted to, obviously, but I know how to be sweet and charming just as well as I know how to be cold and dangerous.

I plaster a fake, but disarming smile on my face. "Ladies, you all are looking spectacular this evening. I'm extremely honored that you chose to walk into my bar tonight." I place a hand on my chest, over my heart, and give a slight bow in their direction. "Are we celebrating anything special?"

More giggles assault my ears but instead of grinding my teeth I smile wider. If anyone was really paying attention, they'd notice that the fake innocence and joy never reaches my eyes. But no one really cares. They see what they want to see. People, no matter how good they're pretending to be, or how good they genuinely think they are, they're all selfish in the end, only truly caring about themselves.

"Actually, it's my birthday," one of the women in the group announces with a shy smile.

"Well then, I believe a celebration round on the house is in order. Michael," I yell, getting the bartender's attention. "A round of drinks for these lovely ladies and something special for the birthday girl. Shall we?" I usher them to the bar.

A round of free alcohol and the information that I not only own this bar but the bar across the street has them eating out of the palm of my hand. Of course, I'm not ignorant in how I look either. I know that I'm attractive and women are often eager to throw themselves at my mercy, a clear mistake they don't realize until it's too late. If only they had paid attention and saw the truth flashing in my eyes instead of what they chose to see.

Tsk, Tsk.

Needless to say, thirty minutes later, I'm escorting five ladies into Sinful Delights and they're all *eager* to be mischievous. Really, sometimes it's too easy to appeal to, and manipulate, the base instincts in others. Especially sex. Sexual desire is primitive and often the base need that's hardest for someone to ignore and control.

As soon as I step one foot into Sinful Delights, I feel her. Relief floods through me as my eyes immediately find her sitting in *my* booth, *with my brother*. What the fuck is Hook doing here? He only comes to land once every six months. He was just fucking here a week ago.

I immediately forget about the five women surrounding me as I stalk up the ramp that leads to my booth. As I approach, Wendee's head tips back and a loud, joyful laugh erupts from her throat. The sound reaches out like a hand that grips my fucking heart and squeezes tightly. I've never heard anything more beautiful in my entire fucking life. It's even more beautiful than her cries of pain and the sound bounces around inside of me like a ping pong ball, hitting my heart, my stomach and my dick, making it twitch in response.

I stop in front of the table. Hook has Wendee's hand in his and the rage that rises up inside of me at the sight of him touching her, is instantaneous, powerful, and dangerous.

"What the fuck is this?" My voice is low and deep, on the verge of fucking murder. Which, apparently, I'm good at when it comes to her.

Wendee's eyes flick up to mine. The sparkle of happiness dances in her eyes, but they immediately darken as they look at me and I don't know if I like the heat of desire I see more or if I'm disappointed that the happiness has seeped away. I suddenly want *both* of those looks directed at ME, not my fucking brother.

"Brother," Hook's voice is full of laughter, his eyes also sparkling, but with his normal flirting and playfulness. I know exactly what he's doing with Wendee and I'm close to wrapping my hands around his neck and fucking choking that look out of his eyes. "So nice of you to join us. I was just getting to know, Dee, here."

Dee. He speaks as if he's known her longer than I have.

"He was reading my palm." She swallows nervously, as she looks between me and my brother. Her eyes land on him again and some of the joy comes back into her eyes as she smiles then laughs lightly. "It was absolutely ridiculous."

"What?" Hook exclaims in feigned offense. "I swear, my palm reading abilities are far superior than any others. You just wait and see, it's all going to come true," he winks.

"Out, now," I command, my eyes still on Wendee.

She glances down at the table like a scolded child, not wanting to make eye contact with me or my brother now, as she scoots out of the booth.

"Peter, come on man, we were just having some innocent fun," Hook tries to explain.

As she steps out of the booth, I notice she's wearing a black romper with blue flowers on it and matching blue heels, and I can't help but wonder if she's wearing black or blue matching underwear and what they look like. Her hair is in loose ripples framing her face and down her back, almost all the way to her beautiful ass. The ass I know must be bruised and sore. The memory of her falling to her knees with my belt marks on her skin makes my cock twitch again. Her lips are painted with her usual devilish red and I want to take my thumb and smear it across her face. I want to see her natural lips. I want to taste her without the fucking lipstick ruining her flavor.

I take a seat at the end of the booth, keeping my legs out and not slipping them under the table. Before Wendee can take another step away, I grab her wrist and pull her to me, sitting her down on my lap so she's sitting sideways, her legs between mine. I don't miss the wince as I sit her butt down on my lap. I love it and hate it all at the same time. I wrap an arm protectively around her waist as my other hand comes to rest on the top of her bare thigh. I can't help but dig my fingers into her soft skin possessively.

She gasps in surprise, and I have to concentrate on keeping my own shock off of my face. This is unheard of for me. I don't even know what the fuck I'm doing or what I expect to happen now. I'm acting on total impulse and I've never felt the need to be so possessive before. I've never wanted to claim someone so openly or desperately. No, I've never wanted to claim someone *ever*. I've never wanted someone this close to me.

Hook's eyebrows shoot up, his own shock on full display. "Well, this is a new development."

"You don't ever visit twice in one week, or even in a month. What are you doing here?"

Hook shrugs and takes a drink of his rum. "Maybe I'm tired of only having fun once every six months. Maybe I want to be like you and have fun more often."

"You've been following the same schedule for as long as I can remember. You follow the rules, Hook, so don't lie to me. This isn't about *fun*."

"It definitely could be. Dee and I were having a lot of fun before you showed up with your shitty, dictator attitude. What happened to, *'what's mine is yours,'* Brother?"

"That doesn't include Wendee. You can have anything or anyone else in this bar but don't fucking touch her again. I won't tell you a second time."

Hook whistles. "I had no idea she meant so much to you, Brother. I swear I meant no offense. I came in and she was sitting here alone, waiting for you. I thought I'd give her some company as we waited for you together. It was nothing more than that."

"And it never will be."

"I hear you, Peter, loud and clear." He slides out of the booth. "I'm going to go find some fun elsewhere and give you two some alone time." He chuckles. "Never saw this coming," he mutters as he walks away.

Once he's gone, I'm left alone with Wendee, still sitting tense and nervous in my lap. I'm suddenly drowning in her scent and the feel of her in my lap. Her presence is overwhelming and intoxicating and I want more of it. I want more of her gasps and her cries of pain...and now, her laughter.

I move her hair over her shoulder, my fingertips brushing her neck as I do, sending a shock of desire and need through me, as I lean in and whisper in her ear.

"Wendee, you're shaking like a leaf. Why?"

"I don't know," her voice is tiny, barely a whisper.

I'm terrified that she's shaking because she's actually scared of me, scared to be near me. I think about everything that's played out between us and my heart sinks in my chest. She has every right to be scared of me, but I don't want her to be. She got a glimpse of the monster that lurks inside of me that first night she was here, the night in the hallway, and then again with how I handled Tink. Hell, the way I talk to everyone, even my brother. Not to mention how I treated her in my penthouse. Even though I held back, I still shined a light on what lurks underneath.

But she's still here. She came back when no one else has. Not after being the center of my attention. Not after I've *hurt* them. And I know I hurt her so I'm struggling how to absorb the fact that she's here, in my fucking lap, when I didn't think I'd see her again. I find myself wondering once again, why is she here?

"Are you scared of me?" My voice is still a low whisper against her skin.

Of course she's fucking scared of you. I hold my breath as I wait for her response. I don't want to hear the truth, but I need to know. Just like everything with her, my emotions and thoughts are a twisted fucking mess of what I want and what I don't want. The lines are blurring and I'm fighting myself at every turn. Like right now, I'm dying to press my lips onto her skin but fighting the urge because it's not who I fucking am.

"No," she says, quietly.

"You should be."

"I know."

The fact that she isn't scared of me, not in the way everyone else is, does something to my insides and it fucks with my control. Fuck it, I lean in and press my lips to her neck. She immediately lets out a heavy sigh, releasing some of her tension, but I can feel the frantic beat of her heart through the vein in her neck. That pulse pounding against my lips excites me and I flick my tongue out, tasting her skin, tasting her nervous excitement. Fuck, she's the perfect mix of salty and sweet and I want to fucking devour her. I move my lips gently across her skin and smile as I feel the goosebumps erupt in their wake causing her to shiver in my lap.

I move my hand from her thigh and dance my fingertips up her arm until I get to her shoulder where an inch of fabric stands in the way of my lips and her skin. I hook my finger under the strap and pull the material of the romper and the bra strap down her shoulder. My lips follow, and I leave a gentle kiss against her shoulder before I scrape my teeth along her soft skin, eliciting a delicious moan that sends my mind reeling.

"Where were you last night?" I ask, voice cold, as I think about her being in the arms of someone else and put her strap roughly back in place.

"Home."

I grip her chin tightly, jerking her face toward me. I need to see her eyes. I need to watch every emotion as it graces her face because she might be able to lie to me with her words, but she can't lie to me with her eyes.

"Don't lie to me, Wendee. Were you with someone else?"

Her eyebrows furrow in confusion. Hell, I'm fucking confused as to why I fucking care. "No," she states, plainly.

"Then why didn't you come here? It's the first night in nine days that you haven't been here."

"I uhhhh..." she clears her throat, "I needed to rest."

I keep ahold of her chin, still needing to see her eyes, but I ease my hold. "I hurt you."

She keeps her eyes locked on mine, no fear in them as she answers the unasked question. "Yes."

I expected her to lie to me. To deny the truth. To play it off and pretend like everything is fine because she thinks that's what I want to hear, just like everyone else around me does. But she doesn't lie to me, and fuck, I want to kiss her beautiful, honest mouth. I drop my hand from her chin before I can act on the urge to lean in and hold her mouth to mine.

"Why did you come back if I hurt you?"

She shrugs a delicate shoulder. "You hurt me while doing something I wanted to do. I've been hurt in much worse ways. Besides, I told you, I want you exactly the way you are."

"I know you're telling me the truth but I feel like there's more to it than what you're saying."

"I could say the same to you," she challenges.

I change the subject, not liking how well she reads me, and how honest I am with her. I've never spoken this much to *anyone*. She has me fucked up and I need to regain control. "I should punish you for making me wonder where you were last night." She sucks in a breath. "Does that scare you or turn you on?"

She bites her lip but doesn't break eye contact with me. "Both."

I clench my jaw and return my hand to her thigh sliding my fingers along her skin and then over the thin material of her romper until I feel the heat between her legs. "If I was to feel you right now, would you already be wet for me?" I ask, as I move my fingers up and down her slit.

"Why don't you find out?" Her eyes flash with another challenge.

I stand without warning, sending Wendee out of my lap, but I hold on to her, so she doesn't stumble. I reach down and take her hand in mine, another fucking thing I never do, then lead her down the ramp, through the crowd that's now staring, pointing, and whispering as we pass, and through the hallway to the elevator.

I drag her inside then turn to punch the button to the top floor, but before I do, I feel her hand slide over my hard cock. I react instantly, grabbing her wrist, and shoving her into the wall. I hold both of her arms tightly to her sides as I tower over her.

"No touching," my voice comes out even angrier than I intend, and I see the flash of fear in her eyes, before it's quickly replaced with determination.

"What kind of fucked up rule is that? You can do whatever the fuck you want to me but I can't even touch you?"

"You don't have to understand my rules, just follow them."

She scoffs. "And let me guess, I'm not allowed to even *look* at another man but you can fuck whoever you want, whenever you want, right? The typical double standard all men have?"

"I'm not all men," I seethe in her face. I want to say, *I'm worse.*

"So, I can go down to the bar right now and take someone home? Just not your brother, is that what you're saying?"

I wrap my hand around her neck, the other I lay flat on the wall next to her head, caging her in. The thought of anyone else getting to see her the way I saw her, coming undone beneath me, makes the monster inside of me fucking furious.

I speak calmly, surprising even myself. "I already showed you what happens to any man that touches you, Wendee. Don't fucking test me. You're mine and only mine. Only my hands will touch you. Only my dick will fuck you."

I squeeze, showing her exactly who's in control, and she gasps for air but doesn't try to pry my hands off of her. She still has fierce defiance in her eyes as I stare down at her. Fuck, I want to force my tongue into her mouth and kiss her while she's struggling to breathe around my hand squeezing her throat shut.

I release her but don't step away from her. She gasps and coughs, trying to get air into her lungs through the burning of her throat. Once she stops coughing, she locks eyes with me again.

"And you get to fuck whoever you want?"

Her confidence to constantly push me is amazing. Even if she does fear me to some degree, she doesn't ever let that fear hold her back. She astonishes me and floors me with her beauty and her bravery. She's the only woman who has ever challenged me in *any* way. The only woman who's captured my attention past a quick fuck. The only woman I want so many things with. Things I can't even speak out loud because of how absurd they are. The only woman forcing these unwarranted changes in me.

"No," I acquiesce. I don't elaborate that I haven't slept with anyone else in years or tell her that I don't want anyone else besides her. I definitely don't tell her she's all I fucking think about.

Her eyes widen in surprise. "Oh."

We stand in charged silence, staring at each other for what feels like eternity before I see the devious spark light up her green eyes and her lips curl at the corners as she begins to slide down the wall. Her hands remain by her sides as she sinks to her knees in front of me, eyes still stubbornly locked on mine.

My eyes narrow and my nostrils flare at the sight of her kneeling before me. My cock is hard and ready, eager to be let free, and I'm eager to feel her sweet little mouth envelope me. I clench my jaw, my hands in tight fists by my sides. I don't trust myself to either grip her hair and yank her back to her feet or unzip my pants and shove my aching cock deep into her tight little throat.

After a few seconds of waiting and me not moving to restrain her or expressly tell her, NO, she reaches up and grabs a hold of my zipper. The sound is loud in the quiet elevator as she slowly unzips my pants, still never taking her eyes off of mine. Her hand slides inside, then struggles a bit to find the opening of my boxer briefs, but once she does, she grabs ahold of my dick and pulls it free.

I hang thick and heavy in front of her face. Heavier than I've ever felt before, and I don't know if it's because I'm that fucking turned on or if it's the weight I feel sinking in my chest as I'm about to be touched for the first time since... fuck, I can't even remember. Before I can change my mind, her hands wrap around me and I'm already fucking fucked. Just her small hands trying to wrap around my sensitive cock feels like fire shooting straight into my gut. Then she starts to pump me, spinning her hands as they slide from base to tip. I groan at the sensation, fucking amazed and blown away by how good just her hands feel as she's jacking me off.

Then her wicked little mouth is on me. I hiss as her lips wrap around the tip and her tongue slides against my sensitive skin. She slides down the length of me until I feel the back of her throat, only taking in about four of my nine inches. Then she pulls out and does it again and again, all the while gathering spit with her hand and spreading it over the rest of me. She uses her mouth and hand, in sync, to devour my entire cock.

The sensation has me throwing my head back and moaning like I've never experienced head before in my life. Fuck, the way she's sucking, licking, griping, and rubbing is unlike anything I can remember. Then she adds in her own moan as I hit the back of her throat and it vibrates around my dick and sends a shockwave of pleasure and desire rocketing up my spine.

I look back down at her and her eyes are closed, she's moaning her own pleasure around me as she has her way with me, and it's one of the most arresting sights I've ever seen. She's clearly enjoying bringing *me* pleasure and it's hot as fuck to witness. As if she can feel my eyes on her, she rolls her eyes up to meet mine, and I see the familiar challenge in them right before she leans in and pushes my dick down her throat.

My hands move to capture her hair and hold it back, my fingers sinking into the back of her head as I begin to participate. She pulls my dick out for a second, so she can grab a breath, and then she's diving back onto me. This time I help her effort and push down her throat as I hold her head in place. I groan again as I feel my dick push against the tightness in her throat. She gags against the intrusion and pulls her head back. I let her have her reprieve, but I want to hear her choke on my dick again and again.

There's a line of spit hanging from her lips to my cock and more dripping down her chin. She grabs it and uses it to lube my cock and continues to pump her hands around me.

I hold her hair in one hand and use the other hand to hold her jaw. "Open your mouth and stick out your tongue."

She complies immediately and I slip my cock inside of her mouth, in awe at how it looks disappearing inside of her. My eyes graze over her face as I continue to pump inside of her. Her red lipstick is smeared and her mascara is starting to run with the tears that are coming out of her eyes. But her eyes. Fuck, her green eyes shine with triumph and are the clearest, most beautiful emerald I've ever seen. She's worth so much more than any jewel in the whole fucking world.

She's fucking priceless.

I refocus my efforts to thrust inside of her mouth. I pump my hips in a steady rhythm as she greedily takes my cock. I push down her throat again but I'm always met with resistance before I can get the last two inches in. She's struggling to fit my width and length inside of her mouth just like her pussy did and I make it my own personal challenge to succeed in making her take all of me, in both holes, effortlessly.

She's gagging around me again as I hold her head on me. Tears are leaking from her eyes but she moves her hand to work my balls, even as she struggles to breathe. My balls immediately tense at the feeling of her soft, wet, warm hands and the orgasm is just suddenly there.

"Oh, fuck, Wendee…fuck!"

There's no controlling it or stopping it as I spill down her throat. The force of it makes my body jerk and I have to release my grip on her head to hold onto the wall to keep from falling to my knees next to her. I groan as the pleasure rips through me like I've never felt.

"Fuck," I growl.

It's like a knife opening me up from navel to throat. I feel exposed and vulnerable for the first time, ever, and I'm not even the one on my knees. It feels like I might as well be.

Wendee licks and sucks my dick clean, thoroughly drinking down every last drop of my cum, as I come down from my high.

She's still on her knees, smiling up at me like she just won some kind of fucking prize, when *I'm the one* who got off.

I should be the one looking triumphant.

I should be the one feeling like a king.

But as I look down on her, I see my undoing and my salvation all twisted up together, in the mystery that is…

Wendee fucking Wright.

"Get up," I order, as I finally remember to breathe and move.

I tuck myself back into my pants and realize we're still in the elevator on the ground floor. Anyone could have called the elevator and found Wendee sucking my dick. The thought of getting caught sends a thrill through me. At the thought of anyone seeing that Wendee is clearly fucking mine, as if I haven't already made that clear. Then again, maybe I need to make it *crystal fucking clear* so no one, not even my brother, puts his hands on her again.

I punch the button for the top floor, then turn to face Wendee. She's leaning against the wall, a satisfied smirk on her face. I stalk over to her, tipping her chin up with my finger, my thumb rubs her bottom lip, smearing her red lipstick even more before I sink it into her mouth.

"I'm just getting started with you."

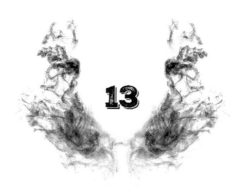

13

Tink

BAD AT LOVE BY HALSEY

As promised, Hook shows up at Sinful Delights the following night. Unfortunately, so does she. I thought that maybe she had bitten off more than she could chew when she spent alone time with Sinn.

I've never been with him in any type of intimate setting. I have no clue what he's like behind closed doors or what he does to women, but I've heard the rumors. I've seen the after effects. Plus, I know how he is when he's *not* behind closed doors. He's vicious and emotionless and heartless. He's down right cruel and I see how it excites him. I'm not sure exactly why I even want to experience his cruelty any more than I already do. I don't understand why I'm so obsessed with him, but I am, even as I've watched all the women come out of that elevator broken. I watched *her* hobble out of here, the same way I've watched all the others, but unlike them, she fucking came back.

Relentless and annoying fucking bitch.

And now I'm forced to watch her sit in his booth, like she has any right to fucking sit in it, and laugh and flirt with Hook. Honestly, what a fucking whore. One brother isn't enough? I'm not jealous *exactly* of Hook giving her his attention. I mean, I don't want anything to do with Hook, I want Sinn, but Hook does usually give me attention. Even if it's to tease me or piss me off in some way, he's always seen me in a way that Sinn never has. He's seen me as a woman and not an employee. But not tonight.

Because of *her*.

What the fuck is it with this goddamn girl?

I'll be happy once she remembers why the fuck she's here and she can move the fuck on. We can all move the fuck on.

I see the second Sinn comes back into the bar. He's escorting five giggling and annoying women. "Of course," I sneer and roll my eyes.

But it's honestly the least of my worries. I watch him storm up the ramp and confront his brother and that bitch. He does *not* look amused, and it amuses the fuck out of me. I smirk as he orders her to get out of the booth.

"That's right, bitch," I mumble under my breath, "get the fuck out of…"

The words die on my lips as I have to watch him grab her.

And sit her down in his fucking lap.

And wrap his arms around her.

What in the actual motherfucking fuck! He's never done anything like this with anyone. I just don't understand why her? What is so special about her? I mean, ok fine, I can admit that she's absolutely beautiful, but so what? He's had plenty of beautiful women. What has this witch done to him? I swear, it has to be witchcraft or something because none of what's transpired over the past week has been normal.

Hook is walking toward the bar. I move to the end, seeking more privacy, and he veers to meet me. His eyes are sparkling with amusement and he chuckles as he approaches.

"Well, I can see why you're so worried, Little Pet, he's definitely acting different."

"I'm not your fucking pet," I seethe.

Little One.

Little Pet.

Why is everyone always referring to me as little? As if I'm not as important as anyone else. No one fucking takes me seriously but that's all about to change. I'm making shit happen and they will all see me for who I am and what I'm capable of soon enough. I'm not anyone's little anything. But I push that aside for now as I focus on the topic for this evening and why Hook is here in the first place.

"Now do you see what I mean? This isn't normal. This isn't Sinn."

"You're not wrong. I'm not sure I've ever seen him with a woman publicly before. Like…," he pulls at his beard, "ever."

"We need to do something. I need the gold dust," I whisper.

"I'm not convinced it calls for that, Tink."

"What do you mean?! Look," I lift my chin and look behind him.

Hook looks over his shoulder and we both watch as Sinn leads her to the elevator. To his private penthouse. I'm fucking fuming.

"Good," Hook laughs. "Lord knows the bastard needs to get laid. Maybe this is exactly what he needs."

"Ugh, is that all you think about? This isn't about him getting laid, Hook," I argue. "This is about how he's been acting since she showed up here. He's been sending people to H2 like crazy."

"That's nothing new."

I sigh, he's not wrong. "Ok, fine, but…," I lean in and drop my voice, "*killing* people is new. And he's doing it because of *her*. She's bad news, and I know you want your old brother back just as much as the rest of us do. We want the Sinn before *that night* and killing isn't exactly the right direction to getting him back. She's only making it worse, Hook. She's making *him* worse."

Hook shakes his head. "I'm sorry, Tink, I just don't see this as a bad thing."

I scoff and cross my arms.

"In fact, him showing *any* type of emotion, other than pure rage, is a *good* sign. We need to be patient, not make any rash decisions, see how this plays out."

"So, what you're saying is, you're not going to help me?"

Hook shrugs his big shoulders. "I don't see the need for it at this stage. I'm sorry, Little Pet."

"Fine." I uncross my arms and lean into the bar. "I'll just go to The Crocodile for help then. He won't be as squeamish about pissing off your brother."

"Tink, wait a minute..."

I push off the bar and walk away as he calls after me in protest.

"You need to think this through. Don't go and do something you'll regret. Don't piss him off, Tink!"

I'm not sure who he's warning me not to piss off, Sinn or The Crocodile. Maybe both. But fuck if I'm going to sit around and watch Sinn go down an even darker path because of this nobody. No, I'm going to save him whether he thinks he needs saving or not. He's obviously not thinking clearly and this is why he trusts me.

To be loyal to him.

"I'm doing this for you, Sinn," I lie to myself.

A lie I almost believe as I get back to work, pouring these pieces of shits their drinks, and trying not to think about what's happening in his penthouse.

14

Dee

WICKED GAME BY GRACE CARTER

Our living room has been turned into a slumber party room but not because my sister or I have friends over. No, friends are still not allowed to come over, much less spend the night. This slumber party has nothing to do with blanket and pillow forts and little girls' giggles filling up the space with joyful innocence. Hell, it's not even teenagers gushing about crushes and practicing makeup together. I'm not quite there yet anyway, still in the tomboy phase, but I am old enough now to realize the fact that our life is *not* normal, and yet, *this* is just another normal night in the Wright family home.

A small twin size bed is pushed up against the wall in one corner next to the couch, and a couple of blankets are hanging from the ceiling blocking off the hallway to the rest of the trailer, where the bedrooms and bathroom are. The kitchen is still accessible but is basically useless. The bay windows in the kitchen and all the windows in the living room have all been covered up with black, plastic bags, duct taped in place, to keep the cold out.

Our mom opens up the small wood burning stove to throw another log inside then sets a cooking pan on top and pours in a couple cans of ravioli for dinner, while my sister and I play *Monopoly* by candle light. It's not an uncommon occurrence to go without real heat and electricity. It's almost like camping, just inside instead of outside in a tent.

At least there are no unwanted guests tonight, and I'm happy and content that we're together, just us, as a family. Well, we're still missing my oldest sister, Dani. She left to live with our aunt in another state when she was sixteen. I was only five at the time. I'm twelve now, my other sister, Kizzy, is fifteen. Is she going to leave me once she's old enough, too? I don't think Dani is ever coming back. I don't blame her, and I won't blame Kizzy, if she decides to leave either, but... I'm terrified of being left here alone.

Why have we been left behind? Why can't we get another life, too? Kizzy and I bounce around from aunts' and uncles' houses, to grandparents', but no one ever seems to want to keep us longer than a year or so. However long it takes for mom to come back again. Then, we're dumped back onto her doorstep like a bag of smelly, dirty laundry. It doesn't matter how good I try to be.

No one wants me.

"I need to pee," I announce, as I place the dice on the gameboard. "No cheating!"

"I'm not a cheater, Dee." My sister rolls her eyes. "Hurry up," she says, bossily.

I grab a candle and then slip past the hanging blankets into the freezing cold hallway. I can't run or else the candle flame will blow out, so I have to endure the cold for a few seconds longer than I'd like. I make my way toward the end of the trailer and into the bathroom. Sitting the candle onto the small countertop, I pull down my pajama bottoms and hover over the toilet seat. I don't dare let my butt cheeks touch the plastic. I'm not about to have my butt frozen too the seat or have my cheeks freeze right off. Ok, I'm being a bit dramatic, but in below freezing weather, with no heat other than the wood burning stove in the living room, I'm not taking any chances here.

At least we have running water at the moment and can still use the toilet. There are times when the water gets turned off as well, with all the other utilities, and then we're forced to literally use the bathroom in the freezing snow and ice outside. I'll take my wins where I can.

My body is shaking uncontrollably as the cold penetrates my skin and grabs a hold of my bones. My teeth are chattering violently and I'm making motor sounds with my mouth as I pull my pajama pants back up.

I wake up shivering, and I'm not sure if it's entirely from the dream or if I'm cold in real life. As I slide my arm against a cold, silk sheet, I realize it's probably a mixture of both. It takes me a few seconds to remember where I am.

Sinn.

Just the thought of him causes my heart rate to spike. I remember his room from waking up in it last time. The lamp next to the chair, where he sat creepily watching me, is the only light in the room. It's not nearly enough light to illuminate this large bedroom, if that's what you can call it. It's larger than my entire studio apartment.

I slowly roll to my other side and my breath is immediately stolen out of my chest. Sinn is asleep next to me. Well, on this ginormous bed, he's not actually next to me. He's on the opposite end of the bed and just out of my reach. My body is suddenly flushed with heat and the earlier cold shiver that woke me up is nowhere to be found. I shiver for an entirely new reason.

Even in his sleep, he looks controlled. He's still fully dressed, his all-black attire is a harsh contract to the rich, red of the silk sheets we're laying on. He looks...sinful.

So sinful.

My eyes eagerly peruse his body. His shirt has been unbuttoned from the top, leaving a teasing peek of his muscular chest. He has one arm behind his head, one arm resting against his stomach that's rising and falling in even breaths, and the leg closest to me is slightly bent. His head is tilted ever so slightly toward me, and I take this time to really stare at him, to explore every painfully beautiful inch of his perfect face.

He does looks more at ease in his sleep, but I wouldn't go as far as saying he looks *peaceful*. Or harmless. There's nothing safe about this man, and yet I've never felt safer. His harsh eyebrows have relaxed and are not pulled into their normal scowl. His eye lashes are dark and thick, laying against his chiseled cheek bones and they flutter ever so lightly as his eyes move behind his closed lids. I wonder if he's dreaming. And what he dreams of. Does he dream of me? Or is he tortured by his own personal hell, like I am, every damn night?

I want to reach out and brush his midnight hair off his forehead. I want to trace his beautiful, full lips with my fingertips. I want to continue unbuttoning his shirt to reveal what's hidden underneath and explore every inch of him thoroughly. But he barely lets me touch him. The only part of his body he's allowed me to see is his dick, and fuck me, it's beautiful and terrifying. I never thought a penis could be beautiful until I saw his, and it's terrifying in the way that it hurts me *and* brings me pleasure. It's terrifying in the way I've already started to crave it.

Just the thought of his large, hard dick, has me clenching my core, and then I groan. I'm so fucking sore. Once my mind has zeroed in on that soreness, I feel it throughout my body. My body aches. It feels like I did a damn *Crossfit Games* workout and not just had sex. I roll back over to the side of the bed and push myself into a sitting position. I realize that I'm once again, naked, while Sinn has remained completely clothed. He has some seriously fucked up control issues.

I manage to stand, my stomach protesting with a sharp pain as I stretch my body. Fuck. Maybe I needed more than just one day of rest between nights with this beast. I feel like I've been stabbed in the stomach with a fucking knife. Close enough, I've been stabbed with a punishingly, beautiful dick. That thing is a weapon of pleasurable destruction.

I shuffle quietly around the room, picking up my clothing so I can get dressed and get back home. I never intended to stay here last night, but after hours of relentless attention from Sinn, I literally passed the fuck out. I'm thankful he allowed me to take up space in his bed once more. Like I said last time, I know what this is and what this isn't. This isn't a, *let's cuddle and have pillow talk afterwards*, type of arrangement. It's not my first go-round, but I'd be lying to myself if I didn't admit that somewhere deep down inside of me, I do wish that it was different.

I want Sinn in a way that I've never wanted anyone else. My upbringing has pretty much dulled me to normal feelings and normal human connections. I have no problem being alone because I have been for most of my life. But even now, as a jaded and cold adult, I can't help but want what I've never had. What would it be like to truly connect on a deeper level than just sex with someone? What would it be like to have someone who understands me? Who sees me for who I am underneath all of my scars? What would it be like to have someone actually choose me? Put me first and care about me?

Maybe that's just a fairytale.

A dream I'm desperate to have amongst the all-consuming nightmares.

A lie.

I take one last lingering look at the man I feel a connection to, a connection I know is only one-way, before I walk out of the bedroom and quietly close the door behind me.

I make my way to the elevator and down to the dark and eerily silent bar. It's so strange to see a place in a way that it's not meant to be seen. It's like having a magician showing you the truth behind the illusion. It takes the magic away.

I wonder if I'm currently the magician and Sinn is the onlooker. He's currently entranced, in awe of something he sees and wants, but what happens once he's seen all my truth? What happens once he gets all he wants out of me? He'll tire of me and throw me back into the crowd. Just like all the others have done in the past.

The streets and sidewalks are oddly empty as I exit the bar. There's a hush over the city like I've never felt before. Then again, when was the last time I was out on the streets at 4:00 a.m.? It's past clubbing time and not quite time for the early business men and women to be bustling about. Maybe this is the time when the city does actually sleep. Well, everyone but me obviously.

My heels click loudly against the concrete as I walk as quickly as possible. The sound seems to echo off of the buildings and empty alleyways I pass, like a fucking calling card to a creep or psychopath waiting for exactly this situation to happen. The alleyways look more ominous than usual, and an uneasy dread swallows up my aching stomach. I glance over my shoulder as I quicken my pace, the tingling feeling of eyes watching me raises the hair at the back of my neck. Am I being watched? Followed? I adjust my apartment keys so that I'm holding them between my knuckles. I should have just stayed at Sinn's for a couple more hours. Seriously, my decision making is shit.

I finally make it into my apartment building and let out a relieved breath. The familiarity of the building eases my tension as I walk into the elevator and the doors lock me safely inside. The elevator pings on the fifth floor and the doors rattle open. Unlike the elevator at Sinn's, this elevator is a little worse for wear. I half walk, half jog down the hall to my apartment door. I feel safer inside but I still have that lingering, dreadful feeling that I'm being followed.

My hand shakes as I try to get the key inside the lock. "Come on, Dee, get it together," I mumble to myself.

I hear the lock click and I push the door in, hurrying inside. As I turn to shut it behind me, a large hand slams against it, keeping it open. My heart leaps into my throat, cutting off my scream and turning it into a pathetic little yelp as I jump back and away from the door. A giant yet familiar silhouette fills up the doorway and then steps inside. I'm immediately surrounded by the smell of leather, bourbon, and sex.

He swings the door closed and it slams behind him as he continues to stalk toward me. I keep walking backward, away from his threatening energy, until the back of my thighs hit my bed, and I fall onto it. The only light coming into the space, is from the street lights through the open window, making it impossible to make out any details of his face or body. All I can see is a reflection from his eyes and feel his anger radiating off of him. And it's directed at *me*.

"Do you have a final death wish, Wendee?" His voice is a whisper but it rattles with his anger.

I have to strain my neck to look up at him. He's impossibly tall and this position only makes it extremely clear how large and terrifying he is. How easily he overwhelms me.

"No," I whisper shakily up at him.

He reaches a hand out and grabs my jaw, his hand almost covering my face entirely. His one hand alone could smother me and suffocate me. "Then why the fuck do you keep insisting on walking through the city, at night, where anything can happen to you?"

"I—"

"Are you that eager to get away from me?"

I can't quite make out the look in his eyes, they're too hidden by shadows, but I can see them darting frantically between mine. They're seeking *something*, an answer to a question, but I have no idea which one.

"No, I just... It's just that...," I stammer, caught in his harsh grip, and trying to process how he's here. *Why* is he here? "I didn't want to overstay my welcome."

"So, you thought you'd just leave in the middle of the goddamned night? Alone," he says, through clenched teeth. "You thought that was a good idea?"

I swallow down my fear and manage to shake my head.

"This is the *second* time I've had to follow you home and make sure you got here safely. Do you have any idea the type of monsters that are out there just waiting for someone like you to walk right into their trap? I may be a certain kind of monster myself, Wendee, but make no mistake about it, despite what you've seen and what you might think, I'm not the worst kind out there."

He grips my chin a little tighter before he lets go. He stalks back over to the front door. I think he's going to storm out of here just as quickly as he stormed in, so I'm caught off guard when he only turns the lights on. He turns around to face me again and he looks so out of place in my tiny apartment. His body and his energy are taking up too much space, too much air, and I feel like I can't breathe. He's so angry I can feel it coming off of him in waves as he stands across the room and glowers at me. His fists are clenched tightly at his sides. The familiar Wendee stance.

I know he told me he doesn't hate me, and I should believe him, but seeing him like this sure makes it hard to see anything else. But if I look hard enough, if I look past the cold exterior, I see the fire in his eyes. It's hidden deep within his icy blues, but it's there. A fire so fucking hot it's bound to burn me alive. And I don't know which option terrifies me more.

Freezing to death?

Or burning alive?

But one thing is certain, this man may be saving me from the Billy Bobs and the monsters of this world, but he is *not* my savior.

The air between us is a live wire. It's practically crackling with electricity. Hate and desire and fear and excitement and fuck, *all of the feelings,* dance in the air between us. I've never felt anything like this in my entire life and I can't help but be drawn to it. *To him.* It feels like for the first time in my sad, pathetic life, I'm LIVING.

My heart is racing and I have no idea if it's because I'm fucking terrified of what I see in his eyes or if it's because it excites me.

He's safe.

He's dangerous.

He's everything that I want and nothing that I need.

His hands clench and unclench at his sides and then he walks towards me. He's back in front of me in three long strides. His hand comes to my face, his fingers thread through my hair softly, almost lovingly, before his hand tightens. He grabs a fistful of my hair and yanks my head back roughly, causing me to cry out in pain.

"I wonder how I should punish you," he says softly, as his thumb caresses my cheek and moves tenderly over my parted lips.

"Please, Sinn," I beg, as tears start to well in my eyes. I can't handle any more punishment tonight. My body is sore, no doubt bruises are forming on my body as I sit here, once again in his merciless hold.

"Please what, Wendee? Please make you beg me to stop the pain? Or please make you beg me to stop the pleasure?"

"Neither, Sinn, I can't handle any more right now. Please," my voice cracks as a tear slips down my cheek.

He moves his thumb to catch it and he wipes it off my face before he brings his thumb to his mouth and licks. He closes his eyes for a brief second, lets out a heavy exhale, and removes his hold from my hair.

"Get undressed," he orders.

"Sinn, please," I plead.

He brings both of his large hands to my face and holds me steady, but gently, as he leans down and gets eye level with me.

"Do you trust me?" He asks, almost desperately.

Like he *needs* me to trust him. For the first time since I've been with him, I see a glimpse of vulnerability in his blue eyes. Something loving and tender, but oh so fragile. I have the intense urge to lean into him, to press my lips to his, and show him that I see it. That I see *him*. I see him trying and I know he's trying for *me*.

"Yes," I whisper and lick my lips.

His eyes drop to my lips, and all of the vulnerability is gone in the blink of an eye, quickly replaced by heated desire. He wants to kiss me, I know he does, but he's refusing to cross that line. He has his rules and he's fighting to maintain them. But I was able to touch him in the elevator after he vehemently said, *no touching*. I just need to pick and choose my battles, and this is one I'm not willing to push.

Not when my body won't be able to handle the consequences of my actions.

He pulls away and repeats, "Get undressed." Then he heads into the bathroom.

A few seconds later I hear the bathtub faucet turn on. *Is he running me a bath?* I kick off my heels and stand, slowly starting to undress, still a bit hesitant as to what exactly is coming next. I'm just unhooking the bra when Sinn appears in the doorway. Once again, I have no underwear on because I couldn't find them when I was searching for my clothes on his bedroom floor earlier.

I feel Sinn's gaze rake over my naked body and it sends a chill of pleasure rippling through me, causing goosebumps to erupt down my arms. I've never been so easily affected by a mere gaze before, but fuck, this man is so intense that everything he does to me is heightened and all-consuming. Even if all he does is look at me.

Despite my earlier pleading, I feel the slickness starting to build between my legs. It's like my own body is betraying me, throwing itself at the mercy of this crazy, gorgeous, sex king. His nostrils flare as if he can smell my arousal and I'm suddenly embarrassed. I feel my cheeks heat as I stand before him, naked and vulnerable. I'm once again on full display to him while he's never even taken his fucking shoes off around me.

He stalks toward me and before I even realize what he's doing my feet are off the floor and I'm cradled in his arms as he carries me into the bathroom. I don't even have time to protest before he's gently putting me down inside the tub. I let go of him and grab the sides of the tub, slowly lowering myself into the water. It's hot but feels amazing, and I notice it's tinted purple with the scent of lavender filling the air.

"Did you use one of my bath bombs?" I ask, as I look up into his scowling face and try to smother my smile.

"I thought you'd like it," he sounds hesitant. Almost as if he's second guessing himself.

"It's perfect, thank you." I close my eyes, lean my head against the tub, and sigh as I sink all the way down letting the hot water rush over my shoulders and breasts. There are some sharp stings as the water runs over new bite marks and open wounds scattered on my skin, but they dissipate quickly.

I can already feel my tight muscles relaxing. All of the tension I held since I left Sinn's place is slipping away. Even the deep pinch of pain in my abdomen is subsiding as everything else loosens up.

"Mmmm," I moan, temporarily forgetting that I'm not alone.

The sound of my moan is loud in the silence of my small bathroom and it pulls me out of my relaxed and oblivious state. My eyes shoot open, and I'm met with icy blues intently watching me. He clears his throat as if suddenly remembering he's not alone either and he starts to unbutton his sleeve cuffs. I'm mesmerized as I watch him pull the sleeves up and over his biceps, revealing strong and muscular forearms. This is the most skin I've ever had the pleasure of seeing, and it sets my heart racing. How in the fuck can forearms be so damn sexy?

I watch in utter astonishment as he sits on the edge of the tub, picks up my loofah, dips it in the water, then grabs my body wash and proceeds to squirt a generous amount onto the loofah. He rubs it together and the suds are instant. His hand dips into the water and gently wraps around my ankle, bringing my leg out of the water.

I have to remind myself to breathe as he starts to wash me.

Sinn.

The king of fucking sin.

He's not only here, in my pathetic excuse of an apartment, but he's in my bathroom, *bathing* me. I want to pinch myself to see if I'm dreaming, but I don't dare move and ruin this. Whatever *this* is.

So, I keep watching him as he slides the loofah over my calf, over my knee, and up my thigh. My heart speeds up a few notches as he gets closer and closer to my center, but he's being the perfect gentleman and continues on to my arms.

He hesitates as his eyes travel over the bruises forming on my wrists, bruises caused by his hands holding me captive in their strong grip. He flips my arm over and places the barest caress of a kiss onto the underside of my wrist. I swear I'm going to faint from this version of him. I think this is the sexiest I've ever seen him. And the scariest. Because now I know he's capable of showing emotion other than anger, control, and desire. He's showing me that he cares. In his way, he does actually care about me.

He's refusing to meet my eyes, his eyes stay stubbornly locked on my body, trailing the line of the loofah, as it slides across every inch of my skin. His jaw in clenches tightly, but his regular scowl is gone. He looks as relaxed as I've ever seen him, besides when he was asleep. And fuck, he's so damn beautiful it actually hurts to look at him. My chest constricts and I mentally kick myself. *No, Dee. Do not get feelings for this man. Don't fucking do it.* He leans over me to wash my other arm, I look down at where his hand and loofah are touching me, and that's when I finally see them.

Scars.

His arms are practically covered in scars. They're all long, thin, and vary in length, and the shade of white against his tan skin, tells me they've been healed for a very long time. A huge ball of sorrow soars up from my chest and threatens to clog up my throat. I can feel my eyes watering and I blink rapidly, holding them back. I know he doesn't want or need my sympathy. Hell, he probably hates the thought of anyone pitying him. I know I do. I'm not sure he's ever been this vulnerable with anyone before and I'm not going to ruin this moment. I'm not going to ignore this small amount of trust he's giving me. So, I get a hold of my damn self, and I ignore the questions I'm dying to ask.

Who did this to you?

How?

Why?

He moves the loofah over my breasts, pulling my attention back to what he's doing. His free hand follows the loofah and slides gently over my slick breasts, causing my nipples to peek under his touch. He takes that as an invitation to take one between his fingers and pinch.

I gasp at the quick shot of pain and the lightning strike of pleasure that shoots straight to my core. "Sinn," I breathe out, and then his eyes are finally on mine. And what I see in them, is something I've never seen before.

Tenderness.

I've wanted to kiss him from the moment I laid my eyes on him and his gorgeous lips but never more than I want to in this moment. Then his words echo in my mind.

You don't have to understand my rules, just follow them.

So, I keep my hands to myself, remain laying in the tub, and keep my eyes locked on his. I don't want to miss one second of what I see in them right now.

The loofah slides down my stomach and then I feel the rough material against the sensitive skin between my legs as he continues to wash me there as well. I've had plenty of people touch me, hell, I've had plenty of faces between my legs, but I've never had anyone wash me before. It's oddly intimate, especially when the eye contact is this intense, and I'm not quite sure how I'm not a blushing, embarrassed mess. But he doesn't make me uncomfortable. Not in that way.

I gasp again as the rough material of the loofah is replaced by his strong fingers. He slides his middle finger down the center of me, parting me, then he expertly slips two fingers inside, eliciting the loudest moan from my lips as I angle my hips higher.

The tenderness is gone from his eyes as they darken and heat with desire. "Are you always this eager for sex, Wendee, or is it just for me?"

"Just you," I admit, as I hold his eye contact, trying not to pant as his fingers slip in and out of me in a slow, steady rhythm.

"Don't lie to me," he growls, as he removes his fingers from inside of me and begins to rub my swollen clit.

I shake my head, fighting hard against the urge to close my eyes and tilt my head back. "I've never lied to you, Sinn. I haven't had sex in over a year. Haven't even wanted to...until I saw you."

A muscle in his jaw twitches and his nostrils flare, his eyes still stay locked on mine, and fuck, what I would give to know what he's thinking right now. I grip the sides of the bathtub and start rocking my hips against his hand, the sound of the water sloshing around us and my heavy breathing seems to echo off of the walls. I don't know if it's the intensity of the situation or the pleasure quickly building between my legs that makes me continue talking like an idiot, word vomit spilling out of my mouth that has no place in this situation. In what we are.

"You're so fucking gorgeous, it's not fair. I've never wanted to touch anyone as badly as I want to touch you, and I haven't even gotten to see your body, also, not fair." I'm starting to pant as the orgasm builds inside of me with the help of his fingers moving deftly between my legs. "But the way...you make me...feel...Fuck, Sinn, don't stop."

"I make you feel alive," he repeats my words back to me.

"You make me…feel…everything. Fucking everythi…," my last word is cut off as I finally throw my head back and cry out in pleasure.

Sinn's hand is wrapped around my jaw in an instant, pulling my head back down. "Eyes on ME, Wendee. I get to watch you come undone."

"Fuckkkk." My body bucks uncontrollably, sending water over the edge of the tub, no doubt soaking Sinn's pants where he's still seated on the edge.

He doesn't even seem to notice as he holds my gaze and draws out every last wave of my orgasm. My body continues to spasm with the force of it, and when he finally removes his hand from between my legs, I'm left trembling in his hold.

He leans in, whispering in my ear, "That look is for me and me *only*, Wendee. You are no longer allowed to touch yourself unless I tell you to. Your orgasms are mine to give or mine to deny. Do you understand?"

He pulls away far enough to see my face. I think I'm still too lost to pleasure to really understand what I'm agreeing to, but I'll do anything this man asks of me. It's like he has the master key to my entire being and only *he* has the power to unlock me.

I nod.

"Say it," he demands.

"I understand."

He reaches behind me and under my legs, pulling me easily out of the water, cradling me to his chest. There's no doubt that his clothes are one hundred percent soaked now but he still doesn't seem to mind. He grabs the towel off the rack and then walks me back to my bed. He sits me on the edge and then proceeds to dry me off. Once he's done, he wraps the ends of my wet hair in the towel and pulls the covers back. I climb into them, and the cold sheets against my naked skin makes me shiver as he pulls the covers over me.

Sinn leans over me, for a second I think he's going to kiss me, but he veers off to the side, brushing his lips against my cheek as he whispers, "Don't forget. *Mine*."

"You shouldn't do this," I say to his back as he's walking toward the door.

He stops and turns, facing me, "Do what?"

"Be nice to me."

"Why?" His question is a harsh growl.

"Because I don't want to fall for you when you're just going to leave anyways," I admit on a quiet whisper.

"I'm not the one that's going to leave, Wendee. You are." Before I can ask why he thinks I'll leave, or even try to argue that I'm not, that I don't want to, he reaches the door, opens it, and then hits the lights.

His silhouette fills up the doorway for a brief second before it's gone. The click of the door is the last thing I hear before I'm left alone in the darkened silence.

Sinn

MY DRUG BY ANTHONY MOSSBURG

"What the fuck am I doing?" I run my hand through my hair in frustration and confusion as I walk quickly down the sidewalk, heading back to Sinful Delights.

I peel my wet sleeves back down my arms but don't bother buttoning the cuff. I'll just be taking the fucking soaked shirt off in a few minutes anyway. And to answer my own question, I have no fucking clue what I'm doing. Something about Wendee hooks me deep into my core and I just...*act*. I act on pure fucking impulse and my impulse is to protect her, touch her, and fuck her. And the one impulse that's turning my whole goddamn world upside down...the urge to take care of her. I don't even think about what I'm doing before I'm headed into disaster and have to just commit to the action. Either that or admit I'm fucked.

I was pissed when I woke up to the sound of Wendee sneaking, or trying to sneak, out of my penthouse. The fact that I fell asleep at all, as I lay on the bed watching her sleep, has me disconcerted. I never let my guard down. I never let anyone take me unaware or get the upper hand against me.

Then there's Wendee.

I was left in a vulnerable state because of her. My body and mind betray me at every turn. I felt a peace and quietness like I've never felt before as I laid next to her and watched her sleep. It's as if her presence alone soothes my tumultuous soul. She quiets the storm in my mind just by being near me. Because when she's near me, she's all I see. She's all I hear. She's all I fucking feel. I can feel her digging into my skin and embedding herself into my fucking soul. What would happen if I gave in completely? What would happen if I held her in my arms instead of keeping her at a distance?

No, Sinn. It's not an option. She's going to leave, just like all the others. Not that I gave a damn about anyone before her but it's inevitable. I can't get close. I can't let her in only to have her torn away from me. Or even worse, have her *choose* to walk away from me. *So, get your fucking shit together, man.*

I storm into the penthouse, a hurricane of emotions rolling through me as I head straight for my bathroom. I strip out of my wet clothes and stare at myself in the full-length mirror that takes up half of one wall. I know what people see when they look at me, when they see only what's on display. Only what I allow them to see.

A six-foot-five threatening force of fucking nature, if nature was a rock-solid body, lithe with both muscle and grace, and a flawlessly sculpted face. A face that can chill even the biggest and hardest of men with one look from my icy-blue eyes just as easily as it can melt the panties right off of every female with a perfected smile.

No one ever gets to see the real me; the me underneath the anger and the façade of normalcy. No one sees me underneath the scars that mar half of my body, and it's been so long since I've even attempted to show anyone the real me, that I'm not even sure who that might be anymore. Maybe the angry version of me *is* the real me after all.

I glance down at my exposed arms. The scars are clear as day against my skin. There's no way Wendee didn't see them as I bathed her earlier. I was expecting her to gasp in horror and shy away from me or frown and pretend to care and have pity for me. Both reactions would have been normal and both reactions would have pissed me off. But she didn't react at all. She acted like she didn't even see them, which I know is not the case. You can't NOT see them. So why didn't she react?

She's nothing like I expect. She's nothing like anyone else I've ever met. She's not afraid of me. She's not running in fear for her life after getting a glimpse into my darkness. She challenges me and pushes me. She's making me do things I just DON'T DO.

And yet, here I am.

I think back to the elevator when I allowed her to suck my dick and I groan at how good it felt sliding into her mouth. Her hands never roamed, they stayed on my dick, no doubt she was playing it safe and taking what she could get without pushing me too hard, but I wanted her hands to roam. Because if they felt that good on my dick, how good would they feel on the rest of my body? And then just minutes ago when I fucking bathed her and I gave her an orgasm without once hurting her and it fucking turned me on.

I didn't need to hear her cry out in pain to get me hard. My dick has been saluting me since I walked into her apartment and set eyes on her. Hell, just the thought of her gets me fucking hard. It doesn't even matter that I came two more times after the elevator incident. I'm insatiable for her. I crave her. Just her. Just her coming undone from my touch, my dick. And I haven't even tasted her yet.

"Fuck," I run my hands through my hair as I walk to the shower and turn on the cold water.

I stride underneath the cascading waterfall, but not even the frigid water can ease the burning of my skin, or dull the ache in my throbbing cock. I don't even want to address the ache in my chest. Instead, I reach for the soap and lather it in my hands before I begin to stroke myself. I imagine the feel of her soft skin as my hands glided smoothly over her soaped up breasts. Her nipples peeked at my touch *immediately,* and I wanted so badly to wrap my lips around one and suck it into my mouth.

I squeeze harder, stroking faster.

My fingers found her opening like they've been sinking inside of her tight, little pussy for years. And even underneath the water, she was so fucking wet.

I lean over and drop a generous amount of spit on my cock, spreading it over the length of me as I try to imagine I'm sliding into her wet pussy instead of fucking my own damn hand. I've never been this fucking horny or desperate for someone. I don't know what I'll do if I can't have her again. I push the thought away as I replay the image of her face as she came on my fingers.

I want to steal all of her moans and cries with my mouth. I want to drink them down and keep them with me forever. I want to memorize her face and her bright green eyes as she looks at me while her entire world comes crashing down around us. Because in those seconds she lets go of everything and I get to see her without any masks. I get to see *her.*

"Wendee," I whisper her name like a goddamned prayer, as the orgasm rips through me, and my seed spills out and washes down the drain.

"Fuck," I grunt.

I am so motherfucking fucked.

16

Dee

Another night, another outfit, and I'm quicky running out of things to wear. I grew up extremely poor. With no father around and a mother that sold our food stamps for cash so she could buy drugs, I hardly had decent food to eat, much less clothes and frivolous shit. That trauma, the mindset of constantly being in survival mode, has followed me into adulthood. I have a hard time spending money on things I don't absolutely need. There's also the small fact that I'm still poor when it comes to the money situation, so I don't really have a choice, trauma or not.

I sigh in defeat as I choose a pair of dark blue, waist-high, jeans and a lacey white crop top to wear instead of cycling through my dresses again. There's one dress in my closet that I haven't worn yet. It's a beautiful gold and black spaghetti strap dress that hugs my curves and flows to the ground elegantly, with two slits, one up each thigh. It's stunning and one of the prettiest dresses I own but for some reason, every time I even look at it, I get the worst feeling in my gut. Just looking at the dress makes me nauseous, and I have no fucking clue why. And since I'm not really planning on throwing up on

Sinn to impress him, I choose the jeans even though they make me uneasy in an entirely different way. I feel like dressing in jeans is so far beneath what Sinn finds attractive. I mean, the man is always dressed to impress and seems to hold himself, and others, to a higher standard. But he's seen me at my absolute best, if he can't handle me in jeans then I guess it's best to find out sooner rather than later.

Since I can't wear black underwear with the white top, I opt for a white lace set, grateful that I *have* spent money on some nice underwear. And, if my underwear keeps disappearing, I'm going to have to invest in more. I've never had to worry about it as much as I worry about it now with Sinn. In the past, I really could care less what a man thought of my underwear. No, these purchases were for me and me alone. Every woman enjoys feeling sexy and items such as lingerie, underwear, and a great outfit all contribute to that in their own way. Looking and feeling sexy and confident makes me feel powerful. Power is armor and in a man's world, in the world I grew up in, power is a necessity.

I tug the jeans over the white lace thong and they hug my body like a second layer of skin. The spaghetti-strap top shows off both my cleavage and a line of my stomach just above my bellybutton. The top is dainty and beautiful. I add a pair of red heels to match my red lips and it gives the jeans an entirely new, dressed-up look. I decide to pull my hair into a high ponytail. I've always worn it down, and honestly, I prefer how I look with my hair down. It also adds as a shield of sorts. I can hide behind it if I need too. But pulling it up and out of my way, I'm completely exposed.

There's no hiding me.

There's no hiding the bite mark.

Sinn's perfectly straight teeth are imprinted on the top of my left shoulder where he bit down as he was pounding inside of me from behind, breaking my body with both the force of his thrusts and the orgasm ripping through me.

I rub at my sensitive wrists, still feeling the sensation of his large hand clamping both of my wrists together easily. He's so big and so strong, I can feel his incredible strength every time he restrains me, or lifts me up as if I weigh no more than a feather instead of my one hundred and sixty pounds.

Just the memory of him, how he feels, how he dominates, how he utterly consumes me, has me clenching my thighs. My body has been strung out since I woke up. I've never been the type of girl to need pleasure or a release every day, but that's all changed since the day I met Sinn. It's like my body isn't mine anymore and I'm living with, and exploring, someone else's. This new body *needs* a release. My hand was sliding south when I woke up, prepared to reenact last night's bathtub scene, when I remembered the deal that I made with Sinn.

That look is for me and me only, Wendee. You are no longer allowed to touch yourself unless I tell you to. Your orgasms are mine to give or mine to deny. Do you understand?

It's not like I made a damn pinky promise, and he'd never know if I *did* give myself an orgasm, but I still couldn't bring myself to follow through. *I* would know that I lied, that I went back on my word. And I don't know why but I don't want to lie to him. Besides, I can never give myself the mind-blowing, body breaking, type of orgasm Sinn gives me. It will be worth the wait.

I make myself wait until 11:00 p.m. to leave my apartment. I don't want to literally be the first one to show up at the bar and put all of my eagerness and desperation on full display. I need to act like I have some damn self-control and a shred of dignity left. I mean, *fake it 'till you make it*, has worked me so far.

I walk into the familiar atmosphere of Sinful Delights and it's as if all my bravado and self-control is checked like a coat at the door. I can't stop my eyes from immediately finding the reason why I'm here. Once again, he's not alone in the booth and I fucking hate what that fact does to my body. It's like an incinerator switch gets flipped on and I'm instantly filled with a raging, scorching fire of jealousy.

And I don't know why.

He's not mine. We're not even dating. We're literally *just* fucking. Actually, that's not even the right term, Sinn is fucking me. I don't even have the right to say what happens between us is mutual. He never even undresses. Hell, he hasn't even kissed me for Christ's sake! Why am I acting like he's more than he is.

Because you want him to be.

As always, as if he can sense my attention on him, Sinn looks directly at me. I quickly avert my eyes. One, I hate that he caught me staring, and two, I don't want him to see the hurt and jealousy I know are clearly written on my face.

I keep my eyes averted as I make my way to the bar. Instead of going to my usual seat, I head to the opposite end of the bar, as far away from Sinn's booth as I can get. I'm not sure why I'm acting this way. Him having another beautiful woman, obviously flirting and eager to fuck him, is nothing new.

Tink isn't behind the bar tonight, which is a first, so I order my usual whiskey on the rocks with a dash of coke from the new guy behind the bar. I remember him from my first night here. He's the tall, skinny one that Sinn ordered to escort Billy Bob out of the bar.

"Thank you," I say with a smile as he places a coaster and my drink in front of me.

He nods his head, but his eyes aren't looking at me. They're trained over my shoulder. I smell his leathery scent seconds before his massive body is looming over me.

His deep, sensual voice rumbles through his chest as he leans his head down and whispers in my left ear, "Are you purposely trying to provoke me, Wendee?"

"What? No, why?" I ask, confused.

I feel his hand snaking around my ponytail, then he grips it in his fist and pulls my head back. The force of his pull staggers me backwards where I'm met with a hard chest pressed against my back and a hard dick pressed against my ass. I gasp at the sensation, a shock of desire rockets through me and my ass involuntarily grinds against him. I hear his low hiss as his free hand grips my waist firmly, suppressing any more movement.

"For starters, this fucking ponytail," he pulls harder, stretching my neck into a painful angle, "this fucking top leaving my mark on full display," a deep seething rumble reverberates through his chest and into me, "and these *fucking jeans.*" His hand slides from my hip and he makes room between our bodies as he grabs a handful of my ass in a bruising grip. "I've never wanted an ass to sit on my face more than I want yours to. RIGHT. FUCKING. NOW."

His words send a crude and hot imagine blasting across my closed eyelids. Him, finally naked beneath me, as I ride his face and take his cock into my mouth at the same time. He's never gone down on me, which I assume is one of his RULES. Like the infuriating no kissing rule that I'm tempted to break and accept whatever consequences come after.

"Then take it, Sinn. I'm yours to take however you want," I manage to barely breathe the words out with my throat at this angle.

My admission shocks me. Not two minutes ago I was reminding myself of exactly what we are to one another. Which is little to nothing, and yet the words I just spoke...they're not a lie.

I'm his.

At least my body is. I can still say with certainty that my heart has remained locked inside of my chest, but for how long? Is this ice king going to be the one to finally rip my heart from my chest and crush it in his hands for good?

I open my eyes and I'm met with a fucking wildfire. A wildfire of blue flames looking down at me. Most people associate heat and fire with red and orange but the hottest part of any flame is its blue center, and these twin flames staring down at me are no doubt going to burn every inch of my skin and singe my fucking soul.

A throat clears loudly next to us followed by a smooth voice that breaks our trance on one another. "Now, this looks like a party I could get into."

Sinn's eyes turn back to ice so quickly that I wonder if I imagined the heated fire within them. He releases my ponytail but possessively wraps both arms around my waist, tugging me against him.

I'm stunned when I finally turn around to face the owner of the voice that interrupted us. He's nearly as tall as Sinn and his brother, which is *not* common, but his build is leaner. He stands casually with both hands in the pockets of his tailored black slacks. His suit jacket is a ridiculous, dark maroon crocodile print, that oddly looks...*real.* The material shines like a wet reptilian body even in the dim lighting of the bar. The jacket is buttoned over a white button-up shirt and black tie. He's giving Sinn a run for his money for the Mr. Boujee award. I almost want to roll my eyes, but I instantly lose the urge when mine lock with his.

Dangerous.

If I thought Sinn's deep arctic blues were cold, it's only because I've never seen these eyes before. They're so light blue they're almost white, and white would be the perfect color to describe the emotion I see staring back at me.

None.

Absolutely none.

These eyes are void of anything remotely human. There's no anger, no mischief, no curiosity, no boredom, there's no trace of anything alive in his eyes. It's like I'm staring into the eyes of a corpse.

A cold shiver of terror cuts like a sharp knife down my spine.

"Well, aren't you going to introduce me, Nephew?"

Nephew? I feel Sinn stiffen against me, but he doesn't hesitate or faulter, and I look up into his face trying to see his eyes, but I can't sense any type of fear or apprehension coming from him. His only tell is his stiff body against mine but I doubt anyone else would be able to notice his discomfort.

"Wendee, this is my uncle, The Crocodile."

The man laughs. He throws his head back, one hand coming to cradle his chest, as he laughs with unrestrained emotion. But when he finally stops and meets my eyes again, that emotion he so easily portrayed, doesn't reflect in his eyes. The contradiction is unsettling.

"Please excuse my nephew for his boorish introduction. The Crocodile is a nickname, nothing more. My name is Samuel," he says with a polite bow, "and it is an absolute pleasure to meet the woman that has my nephew so indecently distracted."

I feel my cheeks heat at the mention of our very public display of...*affection*...just moments ago.

Sinn comes to my rescue, getting straight down to business. "To what do I owe this unexpected visit, Uncle?"

"I've been summoned."

Sinn's body tenses further beside me and I'm afraid if he gets any more rigid he's likely to turn into stone where he stands. I glace quickly between the two men, trying desperately to read the situation. Samuel is smirking, relaxed and at ease, while Sinn's jaw is ticking, his hands are griping me tighter than is comfortable, and his beautiful full lips are pursed together in a tight, straight line. If I could get a good look into his eyes, I'm sure I'd see his familiar anger shining through.

"By whom?" Sinn's voice is a hard, low whisper.

Samuel's eyebrows shoot up, showing his surprise. He may have mastered his facial expressions and how to emote using his body language but it's not genuine. His eyes remain cold and dead.

His head cocks slightly, eyes narrowing on Sinn. "You don't know," he states with a hint of mockery in his tone. "Well, isn't this whole situation riveting! Come, let's have a seat and chat. After you," he steps aside and sweeps his arm forward.

Sinn's releases me, his eyes never leaving his uncle's face as he takes a few steps in the direction of his booth.

"Don't be rude, Nephew. Wendee is more than welcome to join us. In fact, I insist. Allow me." He steps closer to me, now that Sinn has vacated his spot next to me.

I look from his offered arm up to Sinn, searching for a clue as to what to do and how to act. Unlike Henry, this new family member scares the shit out of me, and I don't want to be anywhere near him. I have the feeling Sinn would agree. This entire encounter has me on edge and I want nothing more than to shrink away and disappear, letting them handle whatever it is that needs handling.

Sinn does NOT look pleased. He looks even more pissed off than the first night he came to my rescue, and I'm terrified of what's going to happen next. I stay rooted to my spot until I see the slightest nod from Sinn. I hesitantly take Samuel's offered arm and am immediately rewarded with a dazzling, practiced smile. I smile weakly up at him, my heart is hammering so hard in my chest that it's competing with the bass of the music the DJ is playing, and I'm sure everyone around me can hear it. I let Samuel escort me across the dance floor and up the ramp to the booth.

Sinn slides in on one side leaving me enough room to sit next to him on the end and he reaches his hand out to me. I quickly reach for him, unhooking myself from Samuel's side, relieved when he allows me to walk away. Sinn pulls me into the booth, his arm going around my shoulder as he pulls me into his side protectively. Samuel then slides into the booth on the other side of the table across from us.

"So, Wendee." He leans on the table, clasping his hands together and leaning toward me as if extremely interested in getting to know me. It's innocent enough but I can't help the nervousness racing through my body. "Tell me, how long have you known Peter?"

Peter? It takes me a second to remember that Sinn *is* Peter. "Oh, ummmm, I dunno. Like a week or so."

"Ten days." Sinn's deep voice startles me. Everything is startling me. "She's been coming here for ten days."

"I didn't know you were keeping track," I tease. The fact that he knows exactly how many days I've been in his bar is actually kind of thrilling. Or at least it would be under different circumstances.

"Ten days," Samuel whistles. "You two seem to be pretty close for only knowing each other for ten days."

I feel my cheeks heat again as the blood rushes to my face. Sinn remains quiet. I do the same. Besides, it's not like he asked a question.

"Has Peter told you about this place?" He gestures to the room around us. I assume he means the bar.

"Ummmm, no, not really. All I know is that he owns this bar."

"I see. So, you have no idea who Peter really is or where you really are." Again, he states these facts. There's no question in his tone.

The image of Sinn burning Billy Bob's face and ordering him to be taken to a dock runs through my mind. Then there was the guy in the hallway and the blood that stained Sinn's hand proving that what I witness was real and not dreamed or imagined.

I swallow down my rising fear. "Oh shit. Don't tell me you guys are like a mafia family or something?"

There's an intense beat of silence as I look between Sinn and his uncle, holding my breath, waiting for the other shoe to drop. I knew Sinn was some kind of dangerous...*boss* of some kind. I knew he wasn't normal, and I chose to get close to him anyway. His red flags were flying high in the sky, but my eye sight remained locked on the ground and the man that saved me. Not once but twice.

The silence is shattered by Samuel's loud and amused laugh, which causes me to jump in my seat. *Fuck! Calm the fuck down, Dee! Sinn won't let anything happen to you.*

When he finally stops laughing, Samuel addresses me again. "No, no, we're not a mafia family, don't worry."

I let out a relived sigh, "Well, that's good."

"We are a rather...*infamous*, family though. Some of us more mischievous than others." He nods toward Sinn with a sly smile on his lips. "I find it very interesting that Peter hasn't told you anything about his past or...how you play a huge role in both his past and his future."

"Wait, what?" I scrunch my brows in confusion and stare at Samuel, trying to process what he just said. That can't be right. He must have me confused with someone else. "What do you mean I play a role in his past and his future? I literally just met him *ten* days ago, like he said."

"Are you entirely sure about that, Wendee?" Samuel asks.

"What?! Of course, I'm sure!" But even as I say it, I know it's a lie. There's a memory that's locked up deep inside of me, a memory I've suppressed with only the tiniest bits and pieces coming through randomly and chaotically.

Darkness.

Helplessness.

Pain.

Blood.

Brick.   Ocean.

Cigarettes.

I rub at my wrists, a familiar tingling sensation burning through them. Sinn's eyes. I've seen his eyes before. I knew it the first night I saw him in this bar but chose to ignore the warning.

"Sinn?" I turn to face the man I feel the safest with and for the first time in his presence I'm not sure I want to be here. Who is he? Does he know me? Has he known me longer than he's let on? Is he a part of the memory I've tried so hard to forget? The one that torments me in my sleep. Is he a danger to me? Did he hurt me and I just can't remember? Oh God...

"Sinn?" I repeat when he doesn't acknowledge me. "What's he talking about?" Sinn's angry gaze remains locked on his uncle. "Sinn, look at me damn it! What's he talking about?"

"You caused him a great loss and only your soul can pay the price to get it back."

"Enough!" Sinn's voice booms across the bar. He finally levels his cold, rage-filled, stare on me. "Leave us," he growls.

"But—"

"Now, Wendee!" He yells.

I flinch at his verbal attack. He's never yelled at me before. I'm seeing a whole new side to Sinn and I'm terrified to admit that maybe this is his *true* side. I really don't know him at all. I scramble out of the booth, but I hear Samuel's next warning before I'm out of earshot.

"Tick tock, tick tock, Peter. Time is running out for you to tell her the truth and to return to your full self."

The truth? The truth about what?! Fuck! What kind of horror did I survive that I can't remember? I know I experienced something unspeakable, something that my mind has locked away in order to protect me. Was it at the hands of Sinn? But why would I be drawn to him if he hurt me? Wouldn't my body's natural instinct be to run in the opposite direction? Then again, I'm not normal, am I?

Looking back on all of the times Sinn has looked at me with so much animosity and anger I could never understand why, but now it's starting to make sense. He *knows* me. And he's been manipulating me from day one. But why? Fuck! Why can't I remember?!

I hastily wipe at the tears that have free-fallen without my notice as I make my way to the bar. I take the first empty seat I can find and Tink is in front of me. Her face is politely blank but there's something in her eyes, something between excitement and caution. I know she's never cared for me, but she's never been flat out hateful or hostile toward me, and right now I could fucking care less about some petty female drama. I have way too many thoughts and questions flying around in my mind. I can't even focus on anything.

"Drink," I mumble. "The strongest drink you have, please." I continue to wipe my face clean of tears, running my fingers roughly under my eyes, hopefully wiping up any black smudges.

"Here, this should do the trick. It's exactly what you need," Tink tells me, as she sets a bright green drink down in front of me. It's practically glowing.

"What is it?"

"Something I like to call, The Green Fairy. Trust me, you'll thank me afterward."

"What is that floating in it?" I ask, as I pick up the glass and examine it.

"Just a little gold dust. Completely harmless, I promise. Now, drink up."

I stop asking questions. I have too many motherfucking questions and not one fucking answer. "Bottoms up," I cheers the empty air, tip the glass back and chug.

Maybe I'll find some answers at the bottom of this glass.

Sinn

MAN OF STEEL BY BRANTLEY GILBERT

To say that I'm pissed off is the understatement of all fucking understatements. I can't believe that The Crocodile showed up out of the blue and started meddling in MY business. And not just *showed up*, no, apparently, he was fucking summoned. Summoned! By one of my own! Someone has clearly gone behind my back and the betrayal I feel is *poisonous*. No, it's more than that.

It's murderous.

What reason could anyone have to summon my uncle? I haven't a goddamned clue, but I will fucking find out. But right now, I need to find Wendee.

She doesn't know the truth, and after that little charade The Crocodile just pulled, I can only imagine what type of nonsense is running through her mind. I saw the fear in her eyes as she looked at me. It was the first time she's ever looked at me that way and it gutted me. It was like my heart was being scooped out of my chest with a dull and rusted old ice cream scoop.

The Crocodile is an expert at weaving his web of misdirection and deceit. Honestly, he should be called The Spider or The Fucking

Snake instead of The Crocodile. But, just like a real crocodile, he's dangerous and cunning. Even worse, he's patient. He'll sit back and wait, and wait, and wait, until it's the absolute perfect moment to strike. And once he sinks his teeth into you, he pulls you under and you'll never be free again.

Even though he's right, she is the only solution to my current problem, I can't let Wendee become his next victim. I just can't. But it's not my choice no make, it's Wendee's. On one hand, I'm being extremely selfish by choosing to keep the truth from her, and on the other hand, I'm giving up...*everything*. But none of that is important right this second. Only Wendee is important. And right now, I feel like something is wrong. Terribly wrong.

I storm up to the bar, looking at everyone in a new light. A light of betrayal. Who did it? Why? Hook was just here when he shouldn't have been. Was it him? My own fucking brother? My blood!

"Where is she?" I demand, as Tink approaches from behind the bar.

"I don't know. Why? Is something wrong?" She asks, feigning innocence.

If there's one thing I know about Tink it's that she's not fucking innocent. I know she hasn't been happy with how I've been acting lately, and I know it has everything to do with Wendee. But is her jealousy strong enough to make her betray me like this? She's been with me a long fucking time and she's seen me with more women than just Wendee. Surely, it can't be her. Can it?

I hate being uncertain and not being in control of every miniscule detail around me. My anger is raging harder than a category five hurricane, but right now I'm in the eye of the storm, my worry for Wendee overriding even my deepest-rooted anger.

"I swear to GOD," I say, in a dangerously calm tone, the use of His name on my lips is a weapon. A threat. And everyone is going to know just how fucking serious I am right now. "When I find out who summoned him, they're going to wish for the torture of Hell over what I'm going to fucking do."

I watch the fear wash over Tink's face, the hard swallow her throat makes, and I can hear the frantic beating of her heart. She's fucking terrified. But is she terrified because I'm on the verge of total destruction, uncaring of the innocent souls who get caught in my path, or is she terrified because she knows something?

One way or another, I will find out. And whoever did this, will pay the appropriate price. A price of blood and pain.

I push off the bar and storm down the hallway and toward my private elevator. Wendee is still here. I can *feel* her. I need to find her and convince her to listen to me. She needs to know everything. She needs to know the truth. Fuck! I should have told her sooner. If I had, The Crocodile wouldn't have been able to rattle her. She never would have looked at me that way.

Scared. She was scared of me.

When I'm the one person in this godforsaken place that she doesn't need to fear. She never needs to fear me. She never needs to fear *anyone* as long as she's here with me. My selfish needs and wants kept my mouth shut and now my back is up against a wall, and I'm forced to play defense. I just hope she listens to me.

I punch the button to call the elevator and the doors swoosh open instantly. "Wendee!" My voice comes out in a strangled panic and my heart constricts in my chest at the sight of her. I crash into the elevator and fall to my knees in front of her.

She's sitting on the floor, her knees pulled up to her chest, her hands griping her head, and a waterfall of tears cascading down her cheeks.

"Make it stop," she whimpers. "Oh, God, please make it stop. Make it stop. Make it stop," she repeats over and over, shaking her head and squeezing her eyes closed.

"Wendee," I reach out and gently touch her knee. When she doesn't protest or recoil away from me, I reach for her face. "Wendee, look at me," I manage to control my own rising panic and I speak in the hard, commanding voice I recognize.

It seems to get her attention because she brings those haunted green eyes up to mine. The tears stop as recognition seeps through. "You," she whispers. "It was you."

"Wendee, what's wrong? Are you hurt? Tell me what's wrong." My eyes quickly dart over what I can see of her body. I don't see any wounds, there's no blood, but something is clearly wrong.

"I remember. I remember *everything*," she moves her arms slowly, eyes wide and horrified, as she holds her hands out to me, palms up.

How is she suddenly remembering? Did The Crocodile do something to her? These are questions that can't be answered in this moment, but answers that I need to have, as soon as she's calm and can explain what's happened.

I take both of her wrists in my hands and rub my thumbs across the soft, sensitive skin, trying to give her some kind of comfort. The tears start flooding down her cheeks again, her body is violently convulsing with her guttural sobs. "I...waited for... you," she stammers through her sobs. "I thought...you'd come... back. You never... you never came...back," her voice breaks.

Fuck! I can't stand to see her like this! I swear I can feel her pain as if it were my own. I can feel all of her fear, all of her shattered hope, and I swear I feel something inside of me breaking, too. This brings back all of the emotions and memories from *that* night. The night I lost myself, lost control of my anger, and broke the rules. For *her*.

"Wendee, please, stop crying," I beg, in a voice I no longer recognize. I'm losing my grip on the cold, detached, and domineering version of myself and am being replaced by something foreign. Something I don't fully understand. "It's going to be ok. Everything is going to be ok," I try to reassure her.

She shakes her head vehemently, "No, no, no, no, no, no." she repeats, clearly in shock and unable to think through the vicious memories that are currently haunting her.

I lean in and wrap my arm around her back, the other sliding under her knees, and I lift us off of the elevator floor. She leans her head into me and continues to cry loud, heartbreaking sobs into my chest. I hit the button that will take us to the top floor, to my penthouse, where I plan to take care of her. Where I plan to stay with her, and hold her, like I should have done that night.

"Shhhh, Wendee, it's going to be ok," I try to calm her down as I take us through the penthouse and into my bedroom.

I lay her down on the bed and she curls up onto her side, holding herself as her sobs continue to wrack her body. I walk to the closet, grab an extra blanket, and kick off my shoes before I hurry back to her. I pull of her heels, tossing them onto the floor, and then I unfold the thick, soft blanket and drape it over her. She doesn't move, or protest, or give any indication she even realizes what's going on around her. She's lost in her own mind right now. She's lost in memories best left forgotten and there's absolutely nothing I can do to help her.

Except hold her. Be here for her.

I can't even think clearly myself. I have a moment of hesitation, a moment to ask myself, *what in the fuck am I doing?* But I push everything else aside and just act on impulse. On what feels right. And *Wendee* feels right. She always has.

So, I slide in under the blanket behind her. I push one arm underneath her pillow and snake the other around her waist, and then, I pull her in close. The position is foreign to me. I've never held anyone before in my life, but fuck! It feels like coming home. Like this is where I've always been meant to be. With Wendee. It feels like she was fucking MADE for me. Her body fits perfectly against mine and I wish I could feel her skin against my skin. And I don't even mean it sexually. I just want to be as close to her as I can be. No barriers. No clothes or frozen walls. And the thought of what all of this means, how I feel, fucking terrifies me for so many reasons. I force everything from my mind and focus on the woman crying and shaking in my arms.

"Shhhh, I'm here, Wendee," I whisper against her hair. Her head is tucked in under my chin. "I'm here with you and I'm not leaving you. I promise, I am *never* leaving you. You're safe. You're safe."

I keep whispering soothing words as I hold onto her with all of my strength, afraid she's somehow going to slip through my grip and disappear. After a while, I realize that my voice is the only sound in the room. Her sobs have stopped, replaced by a slow and steady breath. She's asleep. Wendee is asleep in my arms. I've fantasized about this moment more times than I care to admit, but it was never under these dreadful circumstances. I should have told her the truth. Now, I have no choice. She only knows one side of the story.

Well, she's here with me now, and I'll be right here when she wakes up. I refuse to fall asleep and potentially lose her. She's already made it clear that she'll leave me and head home the first chance she gets. No, I'm going to stay awake, stay vigilant, and hold her for every second that I can. I'm going to keep her safe, or as safe as I can, while she sleeps. There's nothing I can do for the nightmares that plague her dreams but I can be here when she wakes up. I will be here when she wakes up.

"I've got you," I whisper softly. "I've got you."

Dee – 1 Year Ago

TRAIN WRECK BY JAMES ARTHUR

I'm sitting across from a pair of dark, chocolate brown eyes. They're so rich and beautiful I could stare into them all day and never get tired of them. It's like getting sucked into an online rabbit hole of watching those aesthetically pleasing videos. Sometimes they're not even doing anything crazy, they're just cutting a damn foam square, but for some reason the simplistic beauty and perfection of it just pulls you in.

Those are the type of eyes I've been staring into over dinner. It also doesn't hurt that he's been smirking and smiling at me all night, showing off the sexiest dimples I've ever seen. I can't say that this man is the best-looking man I've ever seen, but something about him has me hooked. Maybe it's the dark hair and the almond skin? Maybe it's the muscles I can see straining against the sleeves of his dress shirt? Or maybe it's the bright, colorful tattoos I can see peeking out from underneath the rolled-up sleeves? Or maybe it is his eyes after all. And not just their beautiful color and shape but the way his eyes *look* at me.

HUNGRY.

He's looking at me like I'm dessert and he's got the biggest sweet tooth. It's such a powerful feeling when a man looks at you like this. You can't help but feel sexy and strong and in control. I hold the keys to unlocking the treasure he so desperately wants and it's all up to me if I want to give him a peek, throw the top open wide, or keep it locked up tight.

I Have. The. Power.

"You want to go grab a drink somewhere?" He asks, as he pays the bill for dinner.

Dinner was fantastic. We laughed and flirted all night. There's no doubt we have chemistry, and I'm not ready to have the night end so I'm grateful he offered a bar as a go-to and not one of our places. I'm not going to sleep with him on the first date and I was worried he'd think all the flirting meant I would. Then again, the nights not over yet and maybe he hopes some drinks will change the way this night ends. It won't.

"Yeah, that would be great," I say, with a big cheesy smile on my face.

"After you," he gestures for me to walk in front of him through the restaurant. A perfect gentleman, or a pervert that wants to ogle my ass. Maybe a bit of both, but it doesn't bother me.

Once we're out on the bustling sidewalk, he offers me his arm and I link mine with his, allowing him to escort me to wherever it is we're going.

"So, where are we headed?" I ask.

He shrugs. "Let's head over to The District and see what catches our eye."

"And here I was thinking that I already caught your eye." I look up at him, a sly smile playing on my lips.

He pulls to a stop in the middle of the sidewalk causing people to have to swerve around us. "Oh, Dee, you caught my eye the second I saw you in that coffee shop. I don't know what I would have done if you had declined my offer to take you out. I probably would have gotten on my knees and begged."

I throw my head back and laugh, he smiles broadly, showing his dimples. "Well, shit. Had I known that I would have said no just to see that play out."

He shakes his head. "That's nothing compared to seeing you in this dress." He lets his eyes travel slowly down my body and back up. The black and gold dress hugs my curves perfectly and leaves little to the imagination. My long legs peek through slits on each side, giving a glimpse of smooth skin with every step I take. It is probably the sexiest dress I own.

"My God, I may be on my knees by the end of the night anyway," he says with a devilish gleam in his eye.

I shake my head and laugh. "*That* is not going to happen."

"Begging to see you again," he clarifies.

"Oh," I feel the blush creeping up my cheeks at where my mind had gone. I was picturing him on his knees in a very different position.

He leans in and whispers in my ear, his voice low and husky, "Although, I'd be happy to be on my knees for an *entirely* different reason."

He pulls back so he can look at me. His eyes fall to my lips and my mouth waters and the thought of him kissing me... and of him on his knees kissing me elsewhere. I so want that to happen. I want him to kiss me and bring me back to life. I want to really be able to feel something deep as he pleasures me and not just pretend. The chemistry and tension between us are palpable. I haven't felt this type of chemistry in a long, long time. Maybe he's the one. I'm desperate to find out but I also don't want to move to fast and ruin whatever this could be by making it cheap and easy. But fuck, he's making it difficult to resist.

I clear my throat. "How bout we find that bar and get a drink? A very *strong* drink." I laugh nervously.

He smirks, as if he can sense my will caving. "A strong drink, coming right up."

Over the next few hours, we bar hop, experiencing a little of everything. The physical contact has slowly increased bar after bar and drink after drink. My body feels like it's on fire and I'm not sure of it's from his touch or from the alcohol. We're standing on the crowded sidewalk, the bars are emptying, and the streets are filling up even more.

"I've had a really great time," I beam up into his handsome face. "But I really need to get home and call it a night."

He nods, "I've had a really good time, too. Can I see you again?"

"You have my number. Use it."

"I will." He smiles arrogantly as his hand slide around my waist, pulling me in. "But maybe you can give me a little something to remember?"

"What did you have in mind?"

Without asking for permission, he leans his head down and places his lips on mine. They're soft and gentle at first but when I don't protest, he pulls me closer and probes at my lips with his tongue. I open my lips for him and he rushes in, impatient and starving. He tastes like alcohol, spearmint, and underneath that, cigarettes. He's only smoked two all night, a habit I am *not* a fan of, but it isn't something to completely turn me off.

Until now.

Until I can taste the smoke on his tongue, and now, in MY mouth. Even with the alcohol in my system, muting my senses, I can taste it as if I lit a fresh cigarette, put it to my lips, and inhaled. It makes my stomach flip and the alcohol churn, threatening to come back up.

I try to pull away from the kiss but I'm buzzed and unfocused, and he holds me tightly, devouring my mouth with a mixture of urgency and possession. Like he can't wait any longer to taste me and he has every right to claim my mouth for as long as he wants. It should be thrilling, to have this man utterly desperate for me, but all of the emotion is one-sided. He's ignored my attempt to pull away, taking what he wants in a selfish, greedy manner. All the chemistry I felt with him throughout the night is gone, replaced by a repulsion from the taste of cigarettes and the blatant disregard for how I feel.

I finally manage to push off his chest hard enough that he breaks the kiss and loosens his hold on me. "I really should get home." I try and smile through the disgust I feel. "I really did have a great time tonight, Luke, thank you."

"Me too," he smiles brilliantly. It does nothing for me now. "Can I call you a cab?"

"Oh, that's not necessary. I don't live too far from here, I'll walk."

"You'll walk?" He scoffs. "Not alone. Not at this time of night and not after you've had so much to drink. I'll walk you home."

"I appreciate the offer but that's really not necessary. I walk home all the time and really, it's not far."

"It's not up for debate. I'll make sure you get home safe and sound, come on." He tugs at my waist, still holding onto me from the kiss earlier.

I have little choice but to agree unless I want to be crazy and cause a scene. Besides, he's been the perfect gentleman all night long, I have nothing to worry about. I should be grateful that I actually have someone walking me home and caring about my safety.

I smile again, this one a little more genuine. "Alright, I'm a straight shot down to 43rd."

We walk for a while, walking slowly because apparently, I'm even more tipsy than I thought I was and my heels seem impossible to walk in. Luckily, we're back to talking and laughing, the earlier ease of the night is starting to come back as I forget about the aggressive kiss. The sidewalk traffic is thinning out as we get further away from The District but there are still several stragglers out this way. He starts to pull me towards an alley between two large buildings. My mind is slow to process things, my limbs feel like cooked noodles, and I let him pull me along. As we step into the alley, a spike of fear rocks through my body, sobering me slightly.

I stop walking. "What are you doing?"

"I need to take a leak real quick, come on, it won't take but a minute."

"I'll stay right here."

"I'm not leaving you alone on the sidewalk, Dee, just stand a little ways in here so I can keep my eyes on you and make sure you're safe."

I look over my shoulder, there are people walking along the sidewalks and I know I'm in no shape to be left alone. His reasoning makes a lot of sense and I can't argue. Maybe I should, but my mind can't think of why. Besides, he's the one keeping me safe.

He pulls on my hand and my feet continue to move as we walk a few feet into the darkened alley. He jerks on my hand and I stumble with the force of it. His arms are there, catching me, and then my back is being pressed up against the wall and his mouth is on mine again. It all happens so quickly I have a hard time keeping up.

I manage to turn my head. "Luke, what are you doing? Stop."

"Oh, c'mon, don't act like you don't want this. You were practically throwing yourself at me all night." His hand gropes my breast. "Isn't this what you want?"

"No!" I push against his chest, hard, and he takes a steadying step back. It gives me enough room to move out of his hold. I take one step before his hand is wrapped around my wrist and he yanks me back. Again, I stumble, and he uses my disoriented state to push my back into the wall. His left hand is holding me tightly on the waist and his body is pinning me against the wall. My heart is racing and the fear is now alive and rushing through my veins. The adrenaline has cleared my mind immensely and I know this is not a situation I want to be in. I need to get out of it, now.

"Stop being a fucking tease. You don't wear a dress like this unless you want to be fucked." His right hand finds one of the slits easily and rubs his fingers between my legs.

"Don't fucking touch me!" I lift my knee up, trying to hit him in the balls, but he blocks my attempt.

He laughs, maniacally. "Playing hard to get, I like it."

His fingers manage to find the edge of my panties and he pulls them aside. Panic shoots through me and I scream.

"Help! Someone hel—"

Pain shoots across my cheek as the back of his hand slams into me. I'm dizzy, seeing stars, and I taste blood filling up my mouth. I want to spit it out but there's pressure on my face. I blink rapidly, trying to clear the black and white spots swimming in my vision.

"I don't want to hurt you," he says, his voice is hot against the back of my neck. For some reason, the smell of the cigarettes on his breath is suffocating. "Just relax and be a good girl. I know you're going to enjoy it."

I feel the night air on the back of my legs as he pulls my dress up around my waist. His fingers find my underwear again and they're jerked roughly to the side. I get another dose of panic and fear.

"No! Please! Don't do this!" I beg. "Stop!" I taste the salt of my tears as it mixes with the metallic taste of my blood on my lips. I try to fight against him but he's too strong.

His large hand pushes my head harder into the wall. I can feel the porous, uneven texture of the brick scratching against my left cheek. He's pushing my face so hard into the brick that I feel like my head is going to explode. I cry out in pain but the cry is cut off as I feel him enter me. It feels like my entire world falls away from me and I'm left frozen in outer space. I'm not here. This isn't happening. This isn't real. This can't be real.

"Mmmm, do you feel that? Doesn't it feel good?" He moans, as he continues to hold my head painfully against the wall.

I squeeze my eyes shut, trying to shut out the truth of what's happening. I don't want to be here. I don't want to see this alley. I don't want to hear his voice as he moans and excuses this away with lies that I want it.

With every hard thrust into my body, my cheek rubs against the brick. I can feel my skin shredding against the force of it but I don't even register the pain. I can feel nothing except the violation happening between my legs. This isn't real. This can't be real. It's all I can repeat in my mind as my body is being abused.

I open my eyes and fix my gaze on the sidewalk that's only a few feet away from where we are, willing someone to walk by. Willing someone to see what's happening and stop it. People do walk by but if they hear my whimpers and quiet pleas, they don't acknowledge them. People walk by, literally feet from where I'm being raped, and no one notices.

No one sees me.

I swallow down the rest of my cries and let my pain run silently down my face. Then, I feel it. I feel electricity in the air. And then I see *him*.

And he sees me.

I lock eyes with a massive tidal wave of anger. A tidal wave so tall and powerful there's no doubt it's going to destroy every single fucking thing in its path. And that tidal wave comes down on the man, no, the demon, holding me against my will.

As soon as the weight of his body is off me, whatever strength I was holding onto vanishes and I crumple to the ground. I lose track of all time and place as I retreat within myself. I'm picked up off the ground in strong, comforting arms. I don't fight it. I don't think I have any fight left in my body. The worst has already happened. I tilt my head back and look into the most fiercely beautiful face I've ever seen.

He looks down at me, his cold blue eyes softening. "It's going to be ok, Wendee. You're going to be ok. I've got you."

And I don't know why, but I believe him. I'm going to be ok because he's here. He saved me. He saw me when no one else did. How does he know my name? I reach my hand up, my fingertips barely touching his cheek. His jaw clenches at the light touch and his eyes close for a long second before they're searing into mine again. Something like smoke is moving, wrapping all around us, but it feels more alive than smoke. And there's no scent of smoke suffocating me. No, they're dark and threatening. Dangerous. But not to me.

Shadows.

"Who are you?" I whisper.

My hand falls back into my lap. I have no strength to hold it up. I have no strength to keep my eyes open. I have no strength to even breathe. I fall into the darkness with the sensation of flying amongst the shadows.

With my dark, guardian angel.

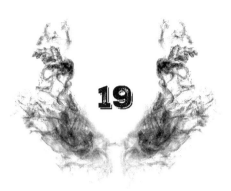

Dee ~ 1 Year Ago

CRAWLING BY LINKIN PARK

I wake up in a white sterile room that smells like antiseptic. I'm in a plain, scratchy hospital gown, and light coarse blankets cover my lower half. I push myself up into a more seated position and as the blood starts to flow, the throbbing in my face becomes more prominent. My entire head feels like one big heart beat. I can feel my head pound with each beat of my heart so fiercely I'd swear you could see it growing bigger with each pound, like a living, breathing cartoon head.

A nurse walks into the room, her bright red hair is plaited into a braid that hangs over her shoulder. Her warm grey eyes meet mine and they immediately put me at ease.

"Oh good, you're awake. My name is Sarah, how are you feeling, Wendee?" Her voice is soft and sweet, just like the rest of her energy, with a hint of an English accent. She smiles genuinely as she approaches and picks up my chart from where it hangs at the foot of the bed.

"Ummmm, I'm ok," I mutter. "What happened? How did I get here?"

"You don't remember what happened?" She asks, as she looks directly at me. Her question isn't accusatory though, she looks more concerned than suspicious.

I think back, trying to recall the last thing I remember. I reach for memories that just don't seem to be there. Maybe I'm just having a hard time remembering what happened because my head is throbbing so fiercely.

"My head," I cradle it in my hands. "Can you give me something for the headache?"

She moves to the table on the side of my bed. She hands me a little paper container with two pills in it and hands me a glass of water. "Here," she says softly, "it's just some Asprin but will help with the pain."

I take the pills and the water, downing them quickly. Sarah takes the empty glass of water and sets it back on the table, then she sits on the side of my bed holding my chart in her lap.

"Now tell me, what's the last thing you remember?"

I sigh and sink back into the pillows, thinking back on what happened and trying to figure out how I got here. "I remember... I was, ummmm, getting ready for a date. I remember dinner, and drinks." I lick my suddenly dry lips. The fact that I'm in a hospital is starting to sink in and I can feel my panic rising.

Sarah must see the fear and strain on my face because she grabs my hand. "It's ok, Wendee. You're safe. You're ok." Her words prompt a memory of vivid blue eyes and a deep voice.

It's going to be ok, Wendee. You're going to be ok. I've got you.

"How did I get here?" I ask again. "Who brought me here?"

Her eyebrows crease in confusion as she looks down at my chart again. "There's no documentation of anyone bringing you. It says that a nurse found you in the lobby, alone."

I close my eyes and I can see the deep blue eyes clearly. Cold and furious as the ocean itself. Did I imagine him? Did I dream him up?

"Do you remember how you ended up in the lobby?"

I shake my head.

"Well, how about I tell you what you told us when you got here, hmmmm? Maybe that will spark some memories for you?"

I nod but I'm terrified to find out the truth. "Ok."

Sarah clears her throat. "Well, like I said, it looks like a nurse found you in the lobby. You were sitting on a chair alone. No one saw you come in or how you got there. When she asked if you needed help, you said..." she stops and looks at me, sadness filling her eyes, "you said you had been raped."

I suck in a shaky breath. I was raped? Oh God, what the hell happened last night? I feel the tears building up and pouring over my cheeks before I can stop them.

Sarah continues, softly, "You gave us permission last night to do a rape kit. There was evidence of...penetration, but there was no trace of semen. Can you tell me anything at all about what happened before you got here? Even the smallest detail can be helpful."

I shake my head, the tears falling furiously and the emotion is so thick in my throat that I can't speak, even if I had something to tell her. Which I don't. All I remember is getting ready for a date, and then fear and panic so intense that I feel it now, all over again. It feels like my heart is going to beat out of my chest. It fucking hurts. Then I remember the taste of blood, the smell of cigarettes, and the feeling of the cold, hard brick tearing into my cheek. I lift my hand up to feel my cheek, but it's been bandaged.

"You had a pretty rough cut on your left cheek," Sarah explains, as she sees me reach for the wound. "Your lip was also busted and there's a small crack in your right cheek bone. All will heal in a few weeks." She grips my hand before she lets go and stands. "I'll let you rest and hopefully you can tell me more when I come back."

All I can do is nod my head. I want to be able to tell her something but I'm also so grateful that I *don't* remember what happened. It sounds so fucking terrifying. Just like so much of my past, this is going to be another piece of my life that gets locked away in an attempt to keep me safe. The only thing that's ever kept me safe is my own mind.

Sarah comes back a few hours later, I don't have anything new to tell her, and there's no reason for me to stay in the hospital any longer. There's nothing they can do for me. No one can help me. Nevertheless, she gives me a card to a psychiatrist that specializes in helping rape victims.

Rape victim.

How can I be a rape victim? The thought is almost impossible to believe. I don't want to believe it, and even though I can't remember the actual moment it happened, I know it's true. I get dressed in a pair of sweats, a t-shirt, and flip flops that Sarah bought for me herself. I took one look at the dress I came here wearing and had to run to the bathroom to throw up. Since the dress had already been processed for DNA, it promptly went into the trash, and I gladly accepted the clothes Sarah gave me. She also denied any mention of repayment. I think she might very well be an angel. I take the card with the promise to call, and I hug Sarah, thanking her for everything she's done for me.

"The type of genuine kindness you have isn't common," I say, as I hug her tightly. "Never lose it."

"I promise I won't as long as you promise to take care of yourself."

She pulls back, holding me at arms-length, staring at me expectantly, with a hint of demand. I manage to give her a small smile and nod my head but I can't bring myself to make a verbal promise. I know she doesn't miss that little fact but she doesn't press me. She just nods again and watches me as I walk out of the hospital and back into my life.

I stand in the outer entryway of the hospital taking in the world around me. Nothing has changed and yet everything has changed. The sun is shining and the heat immediately settles into my skin, but the warmth doesn't seem to penetrate deep enough. I shiver and I know it has nothing to do with the change in temperature from inside the hospital to outside.

How can life just go on spinning as if nothing happened? No one around me knows me. No one knows what happened. But as people pass by me, walking in and out of the hospital, I feel their eyes on me. It feels like they *can* see the shame radiating off me, the embarrassment, and the pain. I feel like they can see all of my deepest, darkest secrets as if I was wearing them proudly like a tiara and sash. I know it's absolutely ridiculous, I know they can't *actually* know what happened to me, but the feeling is real nonetheless and makes me want to curl in on myself.

I walk toward the line of waiting cabs. One man is leaning against the hood of his car. "Do you need a ride?"

He asks, gesturing to the cab. The idea of getting into a car, with an unknown man, alone, has my heart racing and my fear practically immobilizing me. I manage to push through the crippling fear and shake my head as I practically run away from him.

I see a woman sitting in a cab a few cars down and I hurry over to her. Her passenger window is cracked, and I lean down, looking at her through the window.

"Are you free?" My voice sounds foreign to me. It's hollow and weak. Scared. The voice of a victim.

"Hop in," she says blandly, barely even glancing at me before she starts the car.

I climb into the back seat, still stiff and tense with caution. And fear. Even though she's a woman, she's still a stranger, and I have no idea what she is and isn't capable of. I'm wary of everyone now and the ball of nerves and fear is tight and heavy inside of my chest. I feel it where my heart should be, but I think my heart was cut out of my chest last night, and all that's left are these emotions and a big fucking scar.

"Where ya headed?" She asks as she starts the meter and pulls off the curb.

"43rd and Marble."

As we get out of the hospital parking lot, I realize where we are. I'm clear across town, not at the hospital closest to where I live. The hospital close to where I live is known for being extremely busy and always understaffed.

This hospital though, is known to be the best in the city. I definitely didn't get here on my own. How the hell did I get here? Was it the blue-eyed stranger after all? Is he real? My gut is telling me that he's real but I have no way to find him. Hell, I don't even remember what he looks like other than his intense eyes. How will I ever find him?

You won't.

I sigh and slowly start to settle in the backseat as we make our way through the impossible traffic of New York City. Even though I obviously slept in the hospital, a sudden heavy exhaustion takes over my body and all I want to do is get inside the comfort and safety of my tiny apartment, climb into my bed, and sleep for weeks.

That's exactly what I do.

I shut the rest of the world out. I basically cocoon myself inside of my tiny apartment and survive, barely, off canned and junk food. And not even halfway decent canned food that requires heating, like corn or green beans. No, I eat fruit cocktail, applesauce, vienna sausages, tuna, peanut butter, chips, cereal out of the box, crackers and, of course, you can never have enough cookies.

So, basically, I'm just slowly poisoning my body with crap, but I just can't bring myself to care about a fucking thing. I feel like a zombie. Like my body is nothing more than a shell of the person I used to be. I don't know who I am anymore. My life was taken from me the night my choice was forcefully ripped from me. I still can't remember what happened that night. It's like something inside of my brain just snapped. Disconnected. Internet connection not found. And I don't know whether to be grateful that I can't remember or mad. Maybe, if I could remember, I would be able to connect with the woman I used to be. Maybe, if I could remember, I could face it head on and start to heal and then perhaps, there could be some semblance of moving on.

But I can't.

I can't remember.

I can't find myself.

I can't heal.

I can't move on.

I'm lost. I'm so fucking lost. And all that comes to me is darkness, fear, pain, blood, tears, the feeling of being invisible, and then...a riotous ocean storm. Blue eyes, so deep and fathomless, so cold and dangerous, and yet the memory of those eyes is the only sense of warmth and comfort I have. Day and night, awake or dreaming, I'm tormented by feelings, pieces of memories, sensations, and utter hopelessness.

Except when I remember those ocean eyes.

I've never been so drawn to anything, to anyone, before in my life. But those eyes have seared into my mind, into my skin, and into my soul. Every second of every day, they continue to save me from myself, from my past, from my pain, from the void trying to pull me in and devour me.

Every second of every day, I fall a little more in love with these mysterious eyes.

I cling to them as hard as I can, but the more I try to remember more about them, more about the man they belong to, the man who saved me and continues to save me, the further and further away they seem to get. And I'm determined to hang onto the ONE last good thing I have in my life.

What if he's looking for me, too? What if he can't find me because I've locked myself away from the world, and in doing so, I've also locked myself away from *him*.

If he's trying to find me, he'll go to the place where it all started. The place he saved me. It takes me five days to talk myself into leaving the apartment. I've gotten dressed, actually made it out of my apartment, down the elevator and into the lobby, before the fear stopped me dead in my tracks.

I'm paralyzed by it.

But not today. Today marks one month exactly since my life was destroyed. If I thought I had a shit life before, it's nothing to what I have now. Now I live in ruins of what used to be. I'm haunted at every turn. Ever pair of eyes that glance my way have my heart racing. Every smile directed my way has my skin crawling. And if anyone gets within a few feet of me, I start to hyperventilate, which only makes them want to get closer and make sure I'm alright. I leave them staring after me in bewilderment as I run away, back to the safety of my apartment.

Crazy.

I think I've gone completely crazy.

But not today.

I hang onto the vision of those eyes. My heart is racing and I focus all of my energy on steadying my breathing. I pull the hood of my hoodie up and around my face, blocking out as much of the world as I can, and then I grip the pepper spray hidden in the front pocket until I'm sure I'm going to crush the damn can in my hand.

I take one last deep breath and push out of the door onto the busy New York sidewalk.

Dee – 11 days ago

WORDS THAT DON'T EXIST BY CITIZEN SOLDIER

One year. It's been one entire year since that night. My life has stalled, come to a complete stop. I have nothing and no one in my life. Both of my sisters have their own lives, the day-to-day struggle of adulthood has us all consumed and focused on surviving, one day to the next. We keep in touch, but it's brief, and I sure as hell haven't mentioned anything about what's happened. As far as I know, no one knows what happened to me except, me, the piece of shit who did this to me, *him*, Sarah the nurse, and a handful of people from the hospital and police force, and I'm sure they've all forgotten about me by now.

But I haven't forgotten.

I stand in the spot where it happened. I've watched the stain of my blood on the brick fade just like everyone's memory of me and what happened has faded. How I found the spot where it happened, I have no clue. I just followed my gut, my instinct, but as soon as I saw the small pieces of my flesh still stuck to the brick, and the dark stain of blood, I knew I had found the right place.

I've been coming here every single day, for eleven months, right before the sun descends beyond the horizon. I stand here, in a trance-like state, staring at the place where it happened. I still don't remember more than the feelings of fear and utter brokenness. Coming here hasn't changed anything. I haven't had an epiphany, I haven't had closure, there's been no healing, and worst of all, *he* hasn't once shown up. I've come here every damn day, for almost a year, with the tiniest sliver of hope that he'd come and save me just one more time.

But he hasn't.

He's either not real at all or saw the truth of what I became. Nothing more than an empty husk with a broken soul. And if I was him, I would want nothing to do with me, too. Because even though he saved me that night, he was too late.

There was nothing left to save.

A year later, I'm completely empty. All of my hope for...*something*, is gone. I have nothing left inside of me. I have no words left to speak. At least nothing that would make sense to anyone else. I don't feel anything anymore. Not even the crippling fear that I thought I would go to the grave with.

I'm empty.

I'm numb.

I'm nothing.

This world has nothing left to offer me, but more importantly, I have nothing left to offer this world. I'm just a being taking up space that could belong to someone else. Someone with hope and a beautifully bright future in front of them. And so, I resign my life.

I sit down on the dirty ground of the alley, my back pressed up against the same wall that held me up while my attacker took everything from me. I do have one last thing to give to this world. And I'm going to give it up, right here, on this spot of Hell on earth. I remove the piece of broken glass from my pocket. I shattered the mirror in my apartment when I looked into it and couldn't recognize not *one single piece* of the face staring back at me.

I have no fear.

I don't fear the pain I'm about to feel because I know it will be fleeting. I don't fear what comes next because anything has to be better than nothing. I don't mourn the life I'm leaving behind because it wasn't a life at all. I don't mourn the people I'm leaving behind because they're all better off without me.

I don't hesitate as I push the jagged glass against the tender, paper-thin, skin of my wrist and cut...deep. I can feel the rough ends of the glass tear through my skin instead of smoothly cutting like a blade would have. It's fitting actually, that not even my suicide would be the easiest choice. There will be no stitching these wounds back together.

My blood is bright and vivid even in the dying light of day. It looks alive and flows from my veins rapidly and freely. It's a lie because no part of me is alive. I take the glass in my other hand, holding it seems more difficult, but I manage to cut, almost as deeply, into my right wrist.

I glance up at the sidewalk only a few feet away from where I sit, bleeding out. Much like that night, I have the same feeling of being invisible. People pass by but no one sees me. No one ever sees me, and just like my childhood, no one wants me.

I lay my hands gently at my sides and watch as my blood puddles on the ground, another blood stain that will just fade in time, until absolutely nothing and no memory of me remains. Not even in this spot.

Where I die.
Cold and alone.
Forgotten.

Dee

BROKEN BY SEETHER, AMY LEE

I slowly start to surface from a deep, dreamless sleep. It's the first time I've slept without some kind of nightmare or memory haunting me, and yet, I still feel exhausted. I feel like I could happily stay in this bed for another week. This bed. My mind starts to wake up as my surroundings start to take shape. This bed is way too comfortable to be mine, and these sheets are definitely way too soft and luxurious, but what has my mind jerking awake is the body surrounding mine.

My heart starts to race as I realize I'm enfolded in hard unforgiving muscle, warmth, and the smell of leather. The heavy arm that's draped around my waist is gripping me tightly, but not uncomfortably. I can feel the rise and fall of his chest as he breathes steadily behind me. My body is suddenly flushed with heat and I'm nervous and excited and fucking confused as all hell at this situation. But before I can ruin it, and before he changes his mind about what he's doing, I close my eyes and relish in the feel of him holding me. I feel protected and safe. I feel comfortable and, the way he's holding me so hard against him, with absolutely zero space between our bodies, I feel...*hopeful*.

Then I feel the twitch and stirring of his massive dick against my ass and I can't help the intake of breath that breaks the silence of the room.

"You're safe, Wendee." His deep voice comes out lazily and gravely, unlike I've ever heard it before. It feels real. Like he's not masking his voice to be a cold weapon, he's just allowing it to...be.

I'm not sure if he misunderstood the reason for my breath hitching but it certainly had nothing to do with fear and everything to do with his body pressed against mine. But as his choice of words sink in, *you're safe*, the damn is broken, and last night's memories come rushing in.

The Crocodile, the drink Tink gave me and that nasty gleam in her eye as I drank it down, Sinn finding me on the floor of the elevator, everything that happened to me a year ago, and the events that lead up to eleven days ago. This time, I DO remember everything. Every little detail of *that* night.

My breath hitches for an entirely different reason now. "I'm here, Wendee. You're safe and you're going to be ok. I've got you."

"Sinn," I whisper his name like a prayer as the tears flood down my eyes and I'm left sobbing in his arms. Again.

I don't know how it's possible, but he pulls me in tighter, all signs of his earlier excitement are gone as he comforts me with his unspoken promise of protection. And I don't know what makes me cry more, all of the new information and truth flying around my mind, or the fact that *he's* here, holding me and comforting me. The cold, dangerous, and untouchable man, is HOLDING me.

And I have so many questions.

I take a few minutes to let my tears run their course before I reel my emotions in. I've cried enough and I'm sure I'll cry even more, but right now I need to get my head straight. I need answers.

Especially the most important one. The one that's haunted me for a year. The one I never understood.

I turn in his hold and he loosens his arm from around my waist, pulling away from me. I grab his arm and feel the tension ripple through his muscles immediately.

"Please, stay," I say, as I come face to face with him.

His jaw clenches but he rests his arm over my waist again only this time he's not holding me like a vice grip. I move my upper body a bit further away from him, creating some space so I can see his face more clearly and cradle my arms against my chest. I know that being this close to me, in a way that has nothing to do with sex and everything to do with feelings, is hard for him. Even though I just spent the night in his arms, I don't want to push him, so I keep my hands to myself and allow him to hold me on his terms. I may not be able to touch him freely yet but I do need answers.

"Why didn't you come back?" I watch his clear blue eyes grow stormy. He's looking at me, but I imagine he's remembering that night just as much as I am right now.

"I couldn't." His voice is hard, clipped. The earlier softness is gone.

"Why?"

"I've been stuck here ever since that night."

"Here?" My thoughts get pulled to even more questions and look down to my wrists and the puffy pink scars running vertically down my wrists. "You knew. You saw my scars...and, you knew." I remember him laying a gentle kiss to my wrists when he washed me. He could always see the scars, unlike me. "You knew all along, didn't you?" I ask, as the tears well up in my eyes again.

"Yes," he says, softly.

"Where exactly is here? Is this...Hell?" I ask, hesitantly.

"No, Wendee, this isn't Hell and I'm not the devil."

"Please, Sinn, tell me everything because I feel like I'm going crazy. You saved me that night but I don't know how or why, and I don't understand how you're here now. And, I'm...," I can't bring myself to say it out loud. "I just...I don't understand." My voice cracks as the tears slide down my cheeks and I close my eyes, trying to gather my strength and bravery to face all the truths being thrown my way. "Please..."

Sinn moves, but not to get away from me. He sits up in the bed, his back against the headboard, and I realize, once again, he's fully dressed, but this time so am I. The memories of last night flood through my head. I was so consumed by remembering my past that I barely registered Sinn laying me down in bed and climbing in behind me. After my mind was literally blown, I pretty much just passed out from the onslaught of emotions and now, here we are.

I join Sinn by sitting up in bed as well. I cross my legs, facing him, and pull a pillow into my lap, hanging onto it for dear life.

Sinn lets out a heavy sigh. "I'm not even sure where to begin."

I sit quietly and patiently, waiting for him to find his voice and get his thoughts together. I don't know where to start either so I'll let Sinn narrate this story and shed more light on the truth, and just sit back and absorb it the best way I can. All I can hope for is that it doesn't break me further.

"You remember what happened eleven days ago? How you got those scars?" He gestures to my wrists.

"Yes," I swallow down my awful truth, "I took my own life."

He nods. "Yes. Ever since you woke up in this world and walked into Sinful Delights, you've been dead. Unlike the majority of souls who get transported to either Heaven or Hell, you have some kind of unfinished business, something inside of you that didn't allow you a direct route to the Afterlife. So, you ended up here, in Purgatory, also known as The Land of Never."

"Purgatory," I repeat the word in awe, still unbelieving that this is all real. "What happens here? Am I stuck here?"

"Let's circle back to that," Sinn says, and continues to explain everything that I don't know. "Normally, I would have been there when you died, to guide you and help you find your way to...well, to your next destination because I'm the Angel of Death."

I let out a whoosh of air as his truth punches me in the gut. "Holy..."

"But everything changed the night you called to me."

"The night you saved me."

"Yes. I've never been called by any soul still living. I only hear the cries of the dead or those close to death. You were neither and yet I heard you as clear as I hear you now sitting right in front of me. You begged for death with a fierceness that I've never felt so deeply. Your desperation, your pain, *gutted me*, Wendee. I've never felt so close to another soul than I have to yours."

I don't know what to say. I remember that night clearly now, and I don't recall begging for death but, apparently, I did. Because death's Angel came for me.

"When I saw what was happening," his jaw clenches and his eyes flash with anger, "I've never felt the cutting blades of death so fiercely." He closes his eyes and takes a couple of deep breaths. When he opens his eyes again, they've returned to their clear, cold blue. "Then I locked eyes with you and I saw everything that I've ever felt reflected back at me. It was like looking into a mirror. I saw a life of loneliness and heartache. A life of hardships and trauma. I saw you, Wendee, and in you, I saw me."

"Your scars," I say, softly. "You've suffered at the hands of someone who claims they love you, too."

A curt nod is all I get from him but it's all I need. I don't need him to cut open his chest and hand me his heart. Not yet. I have a feeling he's never talked about any of this with anyone else before and this is its own type of intimacy. I keep my mouth closed, waiting for him to continue and give me what he wants to give me. I know it will all come in time.

"Well, you obviously weren't dead, so I did the next logical thing I could. I took you to the hospital."

A small smile pulls at my lips at the thought of the Angel of Death taking me to the hospital. "I knew you were real. I knew it was you who took me to the hospital. How come no one saw you?"

"I'm an angel, Wendee, I can go unseen whenever I want to."

"Alright, Mr. All-Powerful, don't get all cocky on me now," I tease.

There's a slight twitch of his lips but he gets right back on task without skipping a beat. In fact, his face gets even more solemn, if that's possible.

"After that night, I was connected to you. I knew your soul, what it felt like, what it sounded like, and I heard you calling out to me every...damn...day. I heard the cry of your soul so intensely, it felt like it rattled my bones. Your agony gripped my heart and never once eased up on it's hold. For fifty years I've had to feel your sadness and your pain and have been utterly helpless to do anything about it."

"Wait...fifty years? What do you mean, fifty years? It's only been one year since that night."

He shakes his head. "Time moves differently here. Your one year has been fifty for me."

My mouth drops open in shock. Fifty years! He's been feeling everything I've felt for fifty years?! Fucking hell! No wonder why he's angry and as cold as ice. I would be, too.

"Sinn…," I grasp for words, trying to comprehend what he's telling me. "I'm so sorry. I didn't know you could feel me…I didn't mean to hurt you. I…" I don't even know what to say.

"There's nothing for you to apologize for, Wendee. It's no one's fault but my own."

"What do you mean?"

"After I took you to the hospital and made sure you were taken care of, I went back for him," he snarls, an angry growl rumbles in his throat and sends a shiver down my spine. "I found the motherfucker who violated you and I killed him. I pulled his evil soul right out of his body and took him straight to fucking Hell."

The image of Sinn ripping out the man's heart with his bare hands plays in my mind and I know he's telling the truth. Instead of feeling nauseous or disgusted at the thought of Sinn killing someone in cold blood, I only feel pride and a sense of peace. Maybe that makes me evil and maybe that's why I'm in Purgatory and not in Heaven.

"Good," I say with a tip of my chin.

I refuse to cower in my own truth. The truth that I'm glad he did what he did. I'm glad the motherfucker that hurt me, destroyed me, broke me…is dead. And not just dead but in Hell, burning forever.

"That truth doesn't bother you?" Sinn is looking at me curiously.

"No, Sinn, it doesn't bother me. I remember what you did to the man here in the hallway too, and it doesn't bother me. No one has ever saved me or put me first, until you. I've never felt safe like I do with you. I've never felt seen…until you looked at me that night," I whisper.

He leans forward and cups my face in both of his massive hands. His touch is gentle and comforting just like it was when he bathed me. It's a touch I've never experienced before him and it makes my heart ache with the need for more.

"I see you, Wendee." His voice is soft conviction.

His eyes sear into mine and I wonder if he can still feel my soul? Can he feel the amount of love that has built up over the past year for him? The love I have for my guardian angel...my Angel of Death.

He slowly pulls away from me, his touch lingers on my skin, and I want to crawl to him. I want to fall into his arms and feel his touch all over me. I want to kiss him and show him how much I appreciate all he's done for me regardless of how evil it might be.

He clears his throat and continues, "As an Angel of Death, I have one rule. Escort souls to their final resting place. I am never to interfere with divine destiny, with fate. I took a man's life before his time and that came with a grave consequence. My shadow wings, the very wings that allow me access to the earthly plain and the shadows that allow me to hide in plain sight, were taken from me. I was effectively trapped here with no way to get to the earthly plain again. With no way to get to *you*."

I don't know if I can feel him the way he can feel me but right now I feel his pain. I feel his loss. "I'm so sorry," I say through the thick emotions climbing up my throat and new tears threating to fall.

"I made the choice to kill him knowing what would happen. I don't regret killing him but I do regret not being able to come back to you, Wendee."

I close my eyes and I feel the tears slip through my lids and down my cheeks. I've been so desperate to feel something, anything, for so long and now I feel too much. I feel everything. I feel guilt for my role in Sinn's suffering. I feel relief knowing that he didn't abandon me. I feel happy, and sad, and angry, and cheated at the way everything happened, and uncertain about what the future holds, and just...*fuck*!

I feel his hands on my face again. His thumbs are wiping my tears away, but I can't bring myself to open my eyes. I don't want to see the emotion in Sinn's eyes mirroring my own. Because even though he says he doesn't regret it, how can he not hate me for all I've done to him? Whether I knew it or not.

"How can you not resent me?" I ask, my eyes still pinched shut. "I see the way you look at me, Sinn. You clench your hands at your sides and you look like you want to *murder* me." A sob escapes my throat. "And I don't blame you. I cost you your shadow wings!"

"Wendee, look at me." His voice is hard and demanding but it doesn't sound cold and angry.

I slowly open my eyes and meet his royal blue ones. They're storming with emotion, but I can't lock down anything that makes sense. His anger is easy to see, so is his desire. I don't know what this is I see in his eyes now.

"If I look at you with any type of... *hardness*, it's only because I'm mad at myself for not being able to be with you. And the only reason I clench my fists is to hold myself back from touching you because your skin calls to me as strongly as your soul does, because I want to hurt you, Wendee, but even more than I want to mark your skin and hear you cry out in pain, I want *everything* else even more. And I've never been soft or gentle. I've never loved anyone, Wendee. I don't know how to be that man."

"You do know how! I've seen it inside of you already. I know—"

"No, Wendee!" His sudden outburst causes me to jump. He curses and pulls away from me again. "It's not an option."

Now it's my turn to get angry. I can feel the frustration building up inside of me. He clearly has some kind of feelings for me, why is he being so fucking stubborn?

"Why won't you even try?" I yell back at him.

"Because we can't!" His deep voice rumbles with anger. "We can't!"

My brows furrow and I watch him closely. He said we can't, not that he doesn't want to. There's obviously still more to the story.

"What aren't you telling me?" I ask. "I remember something The Crocodile said. He said that I play a role in your past AND your future. He said something about time running out for you to be your full self. He was talking about your shadow wings, wasn't he?"

Sinn sighs in defeat and slumps back against the headboard. I don't think I've ever seen him this vulnerable and open before.

"You're the reason I lost my shadow wings so, your soul being taken to its rightful place, is the only thing that will give me my shadow wings back. A soul for a soul, to right the wrong."

"Oh. I see."

"My job now, since I've lost my shadow wings and can no longer escort souls to the Afterlife, has been to help the souls in Purgatory with their unfinished business. I'm basically their guide to finding their peace and then sending them to either Heaven or Hell where they will remain forever. A soul can only remain in Purgatory for thirty days before it has to move on. You've been here eleven now, so you only have nineteen days left here."

"That's why you said I would be the one leaving and not you," I scoff, and shake my head.

He's known all along what this was, how much time we had together, and I've been in the dark. God, I've been such a fucking fool. All the cards were on the table, I saw them, I saw how he kept his distance, but I chose to ignore all the signs. My fucked-up brain was still holing on to hope that I could finally find love. Fucking idiot. I think about everything he just shared, his role in Purgatory, and how I've seen him meeting with different people in his booth. It oddly makes sense now.

"So, if that's your job now, why haven't you tried to help me with my unfinished business? Why haven't you helped me move on, especially if it means getting your shadow wings back?"

He looks straight at me, his face completely unreadable. "For one, I've been selfish. I've wanted to keep you here for as long as possible."

He pauses. I wait for him to continue but he hesitates.

"And the other reason?" I prompt him.

He sighs heavily and runs a hand through his jet-black hair as he hammers the last nail into my coffin. "You're a suicide, Wendee. That's an unforgivable sin. When you move on, there's only one place your soul can go."

I try to swallow down the sudden fear that's threatening to choke me, but I can't. His words slice me open and it's like I'm watching the blood seep out of my veins all over again, but this time it's my soul I see seeping out. When I decided to take my own life, I never once thought of what that would mean beyond ending my empty and dark life. I didn't think of the consequences as I watched my blood seep into the dirty ground of that alley. I thought that anything would be better than the cold, bleak world I was living in. Now, faced with the reality of Hell...I was so wrong. And I'm fucking terrified but I can't say I'm surprised. Heaven has never felt real or close to me.

I scoff. "I think I've always known my fate. I've lived in Hell on earth so," I shrug, "I guess it was clear where I was headed all along."

A blood tainted soul.

Bound to an eternity in Hell.

Sinn

BAD HABITS BY NERV

After I pulled the curtain back and revealed the truth about everything, well *almost* everything, Wendee withdrew into herself, into her mind. I know she's not only struggling with the truth about who I am and where she is, but WHY she's here, and all the memories she now has to re-live from *that* night. If I could take the memories from her, if I could protect her from this, I would. But I can't.

I can't save her in the way she needs saving. And need is a strong word. Wendee has one of the most resilient souls I've ever felt. It's scarred and damaged, but it still manages to be pure somehow. It's beautiful. Just as beautiful as she is physically. Wendee doesn't need anyone to save her, she never has, but she fucking deserves it. And fuck if I don't want to be her savior.

But I'm no one's savior. Never have been and never will be. So, once again, I let her walk out of my penthouse when all I wanted to do was lay her down and hold her some more. But she said she needed time to process everything in her own way and in her own time. That was three fucking days ago. If she doesn't come to the bar tonight, it will be night four. And I'm on the verge of fucking insanity. If I can't even handle not seeing her for three nights, how am I going to survive when she moves on? She's been here for fifteen days, which means I only have fifteen days left before she'll no longer be in my world. Before she'll be gone...forever.

It doesn't make it any easier that I can *feel* her. I can feel all of her pain, her confusion, her need for comfort. And I can feel her soul calling out for me just like I've always been able to feel it, only now it's calling for so much more. Her soul wants connection. And not just sex, but intimacy.

Love.

And I can't give her everything she deserves. I just can't. So why the fuck am I power walking to her apartment? Why am I impatient to set my eyes on her, to make sure she's ok? Why am I desperate to touch her and feel her skin? Why am I strung out with the need to be inside of her? Fuck! She's worse than fucking heroine and I haven't even had a straight hit yet.

I still haven't tasted her.

I walk into her apartment building, and for the first time, I *really* see. I'm appalled at what I see. How can she live here? It's not the worst place I've ever seen but it's not the best either. It's old. Well taken care of, considering, but old. And the biggest issue I have with this place? It's not fucking safe. Anyone can walk in here, access the elevator, and all that's left between her and some fucking monster is a wooden door and a measly chain? Not to mention her apartment has access directly onto the fire escape. Anyone can break that window and be inside of her apartment without her even knowing.

"Fuck this," I growl, as I stalk down the dimly lit hallway towards her door.

My anger is rising and I'm using her safety as an excuse for it. I mean, I AM concerned about her safety, but I'm fucking pissed off at our entire situation. I'm fucking pissed off that I've wasted three nights without seeing her and I only have a short time left with her. I'm fucking pissed that she waited for me on earth and that I couldn't go to her. I'm fucking pissed off that she took her own life and damned her soul to Hell for eternity. How can such a beautiful soul be bound for such torment and destruction?

I knock on her door, harder than I intend too, and the door groans on its hinges under my strength. *Fuck, Sinn, get a damn hold of yourself.*

I hear shuffling inside of the apartment and a few seconds later the chain slides free, the lock clicks, and the door swings open, revealing my kryptonite. It doesn't matter how hard I try to stay steadfast in my feelings, or lack thereof, one look at her and all of my willpower is put to the test.

She's standing in the doorway, her hair is up in a messy bun, and there's not a trace of makeup on her face. I feel like I've been sucker punched in the gut. She's fucking perfect. And her lips, fuck, her lips are the perfect shade of pink, and they look so fucking edible. I manage to tear my gaze away from her lips and notice she's wearing nothing but an oversized t-shirt that hangs to the middle of her thighs, leaving her long, smooth legs on full display. I'm tempted to run my fingertips all the way up them, to slip underneath the shirt, and find out if she's wearing underwear or if she's bare.

Once again, my fists clench at my sides and I see her eyes take in my stance. Now she knows it means I'm trying not to touch her and not that I hate her, like she originally thought. The fact that she knows my secret makes me feel vulnerable and I fucking hate it. I don't know how to be vulnerable.

"Sinn." She looks surprised to see me. "What are you doing here?"

"It's not safe here," I snap, as I push past her to stand inside of her tiny apartment. "Get your things, I want you staying in the penthouse with me from now on."

She scoffs. "Excuse me?"

I did not plan this. Once again, I lose all of my fucking sense when I'm around Wendee. Do I really want her in my penthouse, *in my space*, twenty-four fucking seven?

YES.

Fuck, I hate that the answer is yes. It shouldn't be, *yes*. But ever since I held her in my arms, I've wanted to hold her every night since. Even though I stayed awake all night to make sure she was safe, it's the most relaxed I've ever felt. It felt right. Her body nestled into mine felt fucking perfect. I want to go to sleep knowing she's safe in my arms every night and I want to wake up to her body pressed against mine every morning. This just confuses me and pisses me off even more, and yet I'm committed to it.

"You heard me, Wendee. Get your things and let's go."

She crosses her arms and holds her ground. "No. I'm not going anywhere."

"Well, you can't stay here." I look around the room, because that's all it is, one room and a separate bathroom, and sneer. "This is unacceptable."

"What are you babbling on about?!" She throws her arms up in the air. "What's gotten into you?"

"You can't stay here," I repeat, clinging to my pathetic excuse to get her to stay with me. "Your room has direct access to the fire escape!"

"Ugh, yes, I know," she says, sarcastically.

"And what makes you think staying here is safe?" I argue.

"I've been here for years, Sinn, and nothing bad has ever happened."

"And that's ok to you? Just because something hasn't happened doesn't mean something won't. And I won't sit idly by while you're here, in this…. *this room*, alone. You're moving into the penthouse and that's the end of this discussion. Now," I say through clench teeth, "pack your things. Don't make me throw you over my shoulder and carry your ass kicking and screaming back to the penthouse because I fucking will, Wendee." My voice is cool and calm, a complete mask to the tornado of emotions clashing inside of me.

She stays rooted in place, but she tilts her head slightly, studying me. SEEING me, like only she can. It unnerves me and thrills me at the same time.

"Why are you really here, Sinn?"

I huff. "I—" I run my hands through my hair, clasp my hands behind my neck, and exhale heavily. I walk to the bed and throw myself down on it, hanging my head in my hands. I can't lie to her, I don't *want* to lie to her, but I don't even know what's straight in my own fucking head. "I don't know," I admit.

"That's fucking bullshit. You *do* know why you're here you're just still trying to fight it."

I sit up straight, gathering the confused and scattered pieces of myself, until I'm back in control... I think. But then I look at her, standing there, watching me knowingly and expectantly, and all of my so-called control and certainty about who, and what I am, is all fucking muddled again.

"You don't understand."

"You're right. I don't. I don't understand why you're trying so hard to fight what clearly *feels right*."

"This is who I've been for a millennia, Wendee. I can't just change because you think I should," I say coldly.

"I'm not asking you to change, Sinn, I've already told you, I want you just the way you are. All I'm saying is stop fighting what *you* WANT."

I run my hands through my hair again, letting out another heavy breath as I try to come to terms with what I want and how to act on it. "I've been the cold, untouchable, Sinn, for so long that I honestly don't know how to be anyone else."

"All I'm asking is for you to try," she says, her voice soft and warm...calm, as she approaches me slowly.

She stands between my legs, and I can feel the warmth of her body sinking into mine where her bare skin is pressed against my knees.

"Because I'm not going back to that penthouse with you until you can agree to try. I only have two weeks left of...whatever this life is, and I'm not going to spend it bending to your whims and getting nothing that I want in return. And I want *more*, Sinn. Two weeks. That's all we have. Please, say you'll try."

She takes the last step towards me, and I have to slightly look up into her face. I see determination in her eyes. She's not going to back down from this and that fucking turns me on. I love that she pushes me and challenges me because no one else ever has. Though, I don't think I'll ever admit that to *anyone*.

She moves her hands slowly, treating me as if I'm some wild animal and she's right to do so. Because I feel fucking feral. She gently lays her palms on my chest, sending my heart racing like a winning thoroughbred at the *Kentucky Derby*. My instinct is to grab her wrist and wrench her hands away from me but, somehow, I manage to control the urge. I *want* her to touch me.

My body is rigid and tense. It feels like the tiny tendons are the only thing holding my body together and they're bound snap from the tension any damn second. She's been closer to me than this but always on my terms. Always when I'm in control. And I'm not in fucking control.

Her sparkling green eyes are locked on mine, and they're filled with so much light. She shines so fucking brightly I don't know how anyone can't see it and I can't fathom why anyone would want to dim it.

"I know you feel the same pull I do," she says quietly, as her hands slide up my chest, behind my neck, and she sinks her fingers into my hair the same way she did the first night we slept together.

I close my eyes, reveling in the feeling of her hands on me and I can't help the growl that rumbles through my chest. I don't know if I'm angry that I'm allowing her to touch me or if I'm angry at how good it feels and how fucking stubborn I've been by trying to fight it.

When I open my eyes, her face is inches away from me. I see the need in her eyes. I see her desire and it burns so fiercely I swear I can feel it heating my skin. She's a beautiful, bright, hot flame burning for ME.

My eyes drop to her lips, so achingly close, and I'm so hungry for her. I want to close the distance between us, but I can't move. I'm fucking trembling with the effort not to move a single fucking muscle. Because I don't trust myself not to ruin this moment. I don't trust myself not to turn the tables around and fall back into my comfortable pattern. Which is to dominate her and deny her what she's asking for. I sit as still as a fucking statue, my heart pounding frantically inside of my chest, and my blood practically boiling in my veins.

She leans in further. Her next words are warm breath on my lips. "Let me in, Sinn."

Her command is barely more than a whisper, and her kiss is barely a brush of her lips against mine, but she may as well have shouted her demand and attacked my walls with a battering ram. And then her lips press more firmly on mine and I'm rocked to my core. I feel something inside of me snap, something deep inside of me awakening and flooding through my veins. It feels like I'm sinking and soaring at the same time, and I have no idea which way is up or down. I don't know whether I should be elated or fucking terrified.

I have no time to decide because she swipes her tongue along my bottom lip and I fucking break. I lose whatever feigned control I was attempting to cling to and I finally kiss her back. I do exactly what she asked for.

I let her in.

I open my mouth and her tongue dances inside, gliding against mine, and my entire body ignites. I groan at the sensation of her mouth on mine and my hands reach for her, bunching in her shirt as I bring her closer to me. She tastes exactly like I knew she would.

Like delicious, sweet...*sin*.

She's intoxicating and addicting and fucking devastating, because I know I'll never get enough of her, yet I have no choice but to let her go. She moans into my mouth and I'm pulled away from my depressing thoughts. Fuck me, it feels so damn good to kiss her. I pull her onto my lap as the kiss gets deeper, hungrier. Her hands are griping my hair tightly as she rocks her hips against the hard bulge in my pants.

My hands find her legs and slide up her thighs, under the shirt, and over her smooth, bare ass. She's not wearing any underwear. Fuck. I grip her ass hard, moving her hips even harder against my throbbing cock. The image of her walking into the bar in those fucking jeans flashes across my mind. I never did get to act on my impulses that night and the desire is even more intense now.

I break the kiss as I yank the t-shirt over her head revealing her beautiful naked body, and before she can protest, I slide my arms under her legs, gripping the backs of her thighs, and yank her forward as I fall onto my back. She lets out a yip of surprise followed by a beautiful laugh that strikes deep in my chest and sends another wave of pleasure to my dick. I want everything from her. Everything her body has to offer me, every sound, every look, every touch, I want it. I *need* it.

She finally realizes she's straddling my chest, dangerously close to my face, and I see the heat creep up her cheeks. "Sinn, what are doing?" She asks, already breathless and I haven't even gotten started yet.

Her naked body is displayed above me, and I swear to God, I've never seen anything more beautiful. "I'm deciding whether I'll be punishing you or rewarding you. Have you touched yourself since I told you not to?"

She shakes her head rapidly. I scoot down, putting my face directly under her sex. My hands are wrapped around her thighs, holding her tightly so she can't move.

"Don't lie to me, Wendee."

"I swear, I haven't."

"Have you not thought about me?" I kiss one thigh and then the other.

"You're all I think about, and I've been dying to be with you again," she breathes out, eyes glued to me and what I'm doing.

"You must be strung out. On edge. And desperate for a Release." I lick her thigh, dangerously close to her center. I'm having a hard time holding myself back and not diving into her, but I need some semblance of control.

Her body twitches in response. "Yes."

"Yes, what, Wendee?"

"Please let me come, Sinn. Please."

"Since you've been a good girl." I pull on her thighs, bringing her down lower, and swipe my tongue up the center of her beautiful pussy. Her mouth drops open and she moans loudly after just that one pass. "Fucking hell, Wendee." I close my eyes as I get the first taste of her and I know I'm fucked. "You're already soaking for me, and I haven't even made you come yet. Let's see just how wet you can get."

I stop holding back and I dive into her. My tongue slips between her lips easily, her juices already pooling out and coating my tongue. I eagerly lick it up and quickly move to her swollen ball of nerves. As soon as my tongue flicks over her sensitive clit, her body jerks and she gasps. I haven't done this in centuries and I'm suddenly terrified I won't be any good at it. And I want to be good at it, for her. I want to make her feel good in every way I can. I flatten my tongue against her clit and give her soft, gentle strokes. I move my tongue in a circular motion, slowly adding more and more pressure, listening to her as she tells me exactly when I get it right. Her head falls back and she lets out a deep guttural moan I've never heard from her before.

"Oh, that feels good," she pants. "So...fucking...good."

"Play with your breasts," I order quickly, before returning my mouth to her center.

She doesn't hesitate and runs her hands up her stomach until they're cupping her breasts. I watch her squeeze and pull on her nipples and a satisfied growl rumbles through my chest. I smack her ass with both of my hands, hard. Once, twice, making her cry out in pleasure before I return my bruising grip to her thighs. She starts rocking her hips, finding a rhythm with my tongue and I know she's close and chasing her release.

"Look at me, Wendee," I demand.

Her heavy lidded, green eyes land on mine, and I swear my heart skips a few beats. They're filled with pleasure but that's not what has my heart constricting in my chest. It's the trust that's so clear to see on her face as she looks down on me. She's putting all of her trust into me. Trust that I won't disappoint her. Trust that I won't hurt her. Trust that I can give her what she's asking for. And fuck, as she's staring down at me, rocking her hips against my face, her sweetness coating my tongue and her moans playing like music in my ears, I want to. I desperately want to. But I don't know if I can.

I focus all of my attention on her body and her cues. I add more pressure to her clit and increase my speed. Her hips move to match my pace. She groans and swears as she rocks above me.

"Take it from me, Wendee. Take what's yours."

Her knees fall further open and she sits harder on my face. My own moan of satisfaction adds a deep bass to the beautiful music we're making. Her hands sink into my hair as her hips start to thrash. She riding my face with abandon and her grip on my hair is close to painful, but I hold her gaze. Her eyes are so pure, her soul shining through, calling to me more than ever. I need her to come so I can take her completely.

I need her.

"Fuck, Sinn...," she pants, breaths coming hard and ragged as her orgasm starts to crest. Her legs are shaking, and her hips are losing their rhythm. "Oh, fuck. I'm going to come."

She gives me a quick warning before her thighs clench, squeezing my face tightly between them. I can't breathe, but I still manage to suck her clit into my mouth as the orgasm hits, causing her to cry out. Her body jerks violently above me and then her body is wracked with smaller shudders, one after another, after another. She's so fucking beautiful when she's completely consumed by her pleasure. She looks like a fucking goddess, and I want to spend the rest of my days and night worshiping her and making her come.

Her body finally sags in defeat as the pleasure subsides. She sits up higher, loosening her hold on my face, allowing me to breathe again.

"Holy fuck, that was intense." She's still looking down at me and her eyes are coming back into focus. Her cheeks immediately turn pink, and she starts to move off of me, muttering some kind of apology that's not necessary. "I made a mess on you. I can't believe I did that. I'm sorry, I don't know what—"

I get up quicky, using her own momentum to throw her down on the bed as I hold myself over her. I use one hand to unbutton and unzip my pants, pulling my rock-hard dick free.

"Does this look like I didn't enjoy every fucking second of that, Wendee?" I ask, my voice gritty with the need to sink so fucking deep inside of her. I wipe my face, her juices coating my mouth and chin, and use it to lube the head of my cock. "I fucking need to be inside of you, now. Right fucking now," I growl, as I use my knees to spread her legs wide.

"Wait." Her hands push against my chest, as if she could ever hope to stop me from taking what I want. "I want to see you, Sinn. I want to see all of you, please."

I gave in and let her kiss me. That's more intimate than anything else she could ever ask of me. Well, except her request to see me naked. I'm not ready to show her my scars. Not yet. No one else has seen them since I was a kid. Not even Hook.

I push all of that aside as I focus on Wendee lying naked and perfect beneath me. Her eyes are pleading, begging me to give her what I know she deserves, and I can't hold her demanding gaze. I don't want to see the hurt in them as I deny her request. My eyes drop to her lips and I'm suddenly filled with need to feel her lips on mine again. It's like I'm on the verge of madness if I don't sink inside of her while her mouth is glued to mine. I need to taste her as I take her.

"You can't ask or expect me to change overnight, Wendee. I've already given you more than I've given anyone in centuries."

I don't wait for her to protest and argue. I use my size and strength against her and lean down, claiming her sinful mouth. I push my tongue inside at the same time I push slow, and deep, inside of her. She hisses in pain as her body struggles to open up to me, but her hand is no longer pushing against my chest. She's accepted that this is what's going to happen and she has no fucking chance at stopping me.

Well, that's not true, if I knew she didn't want this, didn't want me, I would never take her like this. But she does want me. I can feel it just as deep in my soul as I am deep inside of her. I swallow down every whimper, moan, and breath she gives me as I start to pump my hips. I'm giving her long, hard strokes, her bed is screaming in protest at our weight and my relentless thrusts, and it's not long before I feel her body clenching around me.

I keep my mouth locked onto hers, our tongues dancing to the lyrical music our bodies are making. When we're joined together, we're literally one soul. It's like nothing I've ever experienced, and I want so badly to give her more. To give her all of me, everything that I am. The good, the bad, and the ugly. She consumes me and takes me over completely. All I want is her. All I see is her. All I feel is her. All I care about is her. Fuck this world. Fuck everyone else. And fuck whatever it is we're *supposed* to do. Fuck my wings and who I was before.

All that matters now is this.

All that matters is her.

All that matters is us.

Dee

NOTHING WORTH SAVING BY DANGERKIDS

I've been here at the penthouse with Sinn for a week. And what a glorious, sex and orgasm filled week it's been! I barely have any time to recover before Sinn is devouring me again, and again, and again. It's like he's the damn energizer bunny and literally has no off button. Not that I'm complaining. As far as my life is concerned, this has been the best fucking three weeks of my life, hands down.

Even though I ignore the fact that I'm settling for less than I deserve. Sinn is still holding himself back from me. He still refuses to let me see any part of him other than his dick. I have a feeling it has to do with the scars I saw on his arms the night he bathed me, and I'm trying my best to just be here for him, to show him in any way that I can, that I don't care about his scars. I don't care in the way that I think *he thinks* I will.

But I have seen his attempts at opening up to me. I've now experienced the tender and sweet side of him on several occasions. Not to mention the mind-blowing make out sessions. Holy fucking shit! The man can fucking kiss and he seems to want to kiss ME all the fucking time. And so, I pick and choose my battles. I settle. Like I always have. Like I always will. Because I'd rather have pieces of him than none of him. Because I want to be loved so damn badly, I'll focus on the effort I DO see. I'll hang on fiercely to the idea that he will eventually give me what I need. I'll continue being in a relationship with the *idea* I have of him in my mind. I'll continue being in a relationship with my hope.

It definitely doesn't hurt that I've never felt more beautiful, secure, and safe, than I do when I'm the center of Sinn's attention. I feel like he truly sees ME. All of me. And I never have to hide or pretend to be someone I'm not. Granted, having his full attention is not always pretty. He'll always like causing me pain, but I think the desire to cause me pleasure, to see me happy, is slowly taking the lead. And honestly, I don't mind the pain. It's physical and fleeting, and he never gives me more than I can handle. He may be causing me pain on the outside, but he's slowly healing all of the pain I've carried on the inside. Pain that is far deeper and way more excruciating than anything his hands have ever done or will ever do. Not that we have forever to test this theory because we don't.

I hate how quickly the time seems to be ticking by. I only have eight more days here, and as much as I try not to think about how all this ends, I can't control my thoughts from going there. I'm going to Hell. Like literally. I will be tortured in Hell for eternity. That really puts the pain Sinn puts me through into perspective. Obviously, I've never been to Hell, but I know there's no comparison. The hands of the Angel of Death are far more appealing than the Devil's will be. I'd gladly take an eternity with Sinn. I would choose an eternity with Sinn, if I had the choice, but I don't.

My thoughts are interrupted as the gorgeous Angel of Death walks into the living room and literally steals the air from my lungs. He dressed in his signature black, from head to toe, but it just accentuates his deep blue ocean eyes. Eyes that see me and see through me. He approaches me where I'm sitting on the couch, bundled up in a cozy blanket. He leans down over me, one hand bracing himself on the back of the couch, the other griping my chin and tilting my face up to his.

"What's wrong?" He asks, as his eyes search mine.

I try and give him a smile but I know it's weak. "Nothing. It's nothing. Just my treacherous mind doing what it does best."

"I'll stay with you tonight. I don't need to go down to the bar."

That does earn the devious angel a genuine smile. I love the fact that he'd stay with me if I asked him too and to hell, possibly literally, with the other souls waiting for guidance downstairs. *This* is the effort I see, and it warms me down to my bones to know that he does care about me on some level.

"No, Sinn, you have a job to do, and those people need you. Go. I'll be fine."

He stays staring into my eyes for a few beats longer. His stare is always so damn powerful. I can't help but get lost in them as everything else in the world fades away. Nothing else matters except him and I. And there's no hiding *anything* from him.

He must be satisfied with whatever he sees in my eyes because a small smile tugs at the corner of his lips and then those sexy full lips are descending on mine. My body automatically reaches for him. I stretch as far as I can in my seat to meet him for the kiss. I want to either climb up his massive body, feel his strong arms pick me up and hold me against him, or I want to pull him down and feel his weight on top of me. I've never craved someone as much as I crave him. He's the worst kind of drug and I'm past the smoking stage. I want to puncture my own damn vein and put him directly into my blood stream.

Is this what it feels like to be an addict? I've never been addicted to anything in my life before. I had to grow up watching a person I love become a slave to the high and I swore I'd never let myself become the same. I never understood the pull. I never understood how she couldn't control herself. I never understood how she couldn't just stop using what was clearly bad for her. How could she continue to use what was slowly killing her?

Now I think I'm beginning to understand because Sinn's kiss is clawing its way inside of me. He's going to wrap himself around my heart, sink his claws in, and absolutely ravage it to pieces when I'm forced to leave him in eight days.

Sinn pulls back from the kiss reluctantly. My body wants to protest and follow him, keeping our lips locked, and escalating this moment to something more. I fight the urge to reach out to him and slump back down against the cushion. I can't help but notice the bulge in his pants that's eye-level with me and it's my turn to fight a smile at what I see.

"Fucking hell, Wendee," he grunts, as he reaches into his pants to adjust himself. "Now I'm going to be hard all fucking night."

"Or I could just take care of it for you before you leave." I reach my hand out and rub him over his pants, reaching for the zipper.

Sinn clutches my wrist before I can pull it down and steps away from me. I look up into his face and I can see how hard he's fighting not to let me. His eyes are blazing with need and his jaw is clenched tightly. Just glancing at him, you would think he's pissed off, on the verge of unleashing his fury, and not on the verge of unleashing expertly crafted pain and pleasure. His face always looks so hard and mean, but his eyes have become so emotive, at least in private with me, reflecting what he's really feeling. His eyes are just like the ocean they remind me of, with so many different types of waves, depths, hidden dangers, and hidden treasures, and I'm slowly learning how to navigate them.

"No," he says curtly. "I want this need with me all night. I want the reminder of what I have waiting for me when I get back. And when I get back, I'm going to unleash it all *on you*."

Son of a bitch. Just the threat of his promise and the look in his eyes has me clenching. "I'll be waiting," I promise in return.

He rubs his thumb lightly over the scar on my wrist that's still gripped in his hand. He always caresses my scars, and kisses them, as if to show me that he doesn't mind, that it's all ok. I love the gesture because I know he does it from a place of deep understanding, but it always just reminds me of the clock ticking down and what those scars mean. They're my entry into the eternal afterlife of Hell.

He slowly releases my wrist and heads towards the elevator. I fall back into the fluffy couch with a sigh. We only have eight days left together and I want to spend every single second of those days with Sinn. But he has a job to do, a job he doesn't even want but has to do because of me. Because, as an angel, he also committed an unforgivable sin. He took a life, a soul, when he had no right to. But he did it for *me*. And I'm still trying to wrap my mind around how we're connected, how I called to him when no one else ever has. And why he made that sacrifice, knowing what would happen.

I hear the quiet whoosh of the elevator doors, followed by hushed footsteps against the marble floors, and I smile triumphantly.

"Did you change your mind about that blow jo—" My words get stuck in my throat and the smile falls form my face as The Crocodile comes into view.

He raises an eye brow, an amused smirk on his lips, as he takes me in with those eerie white-blue eyes. His hands are hidden in his pockets, and he exudes the same calm yet dangerous energy he did the first time I met him.

"I'm not exactly sure what Peter is thinking right now but *I* wouldn't have turned down *anything* if I was in his shoes." He smirks arrogantly.

I don't even want to THINK about him being in Sinn's shoes. He's attractive enough, sure, but he scares the bejesus out of me. There's just something about him that feels...*off*. So, I quickly change the subject.

I clear my throat and sit up straighter. "What are you doing here?"

He shrugs, the move looking graceful and elegant. "I came to talk to you, Dee. I can call you, Dee, can't I?"

"Ugh, sure."

"Let's take this little chat onto the balcony. I prefer the fresh air," he says, as he starts heading to the large sliding glass doors that lead to the balcony. I hesitate. I don't want to be alone with him much less on a balcony where he can throw me to my death. Well, then again, I'm already dead, aren't I? "Come now, don't be afraid of me. I'm not going to hurt you."

With no reason NOT to trust him, and no warning from Sinn about him, I throw the blanket off my legs and follow him onto the balcony. The warm night air immediately wraps around me, a huge contrast to the cold of Sinn's penthouse, sending shivers down my body. He passes by the large seating area and stands at the end of the balcony, overlooking the city. I may not have a reason not to trust him, but that doesn't mean that I do so I remain by the seating area and watch him as he takes in the view of the city and inhales deeply.

"It really is a great view," he says, more to himself than to me.

I look out over the lights of New York City and a new question comes to mind. "Why is Purgatory New York?"

The Crocodile looks over his shoulder at me and chuckles. "Other than Sinful Delights and Salvation Lights, everything else you see is unique to you. Every soul here sees something different when they leave the bars. Purgatory is only New York to you."

"Ohhhh. Wow." I try and wrap my mind around how that works and just can't picture it. Then again, how can a human mind conceive what angels do? Answer...we can't. I shake the thought from my mind and focus on why I'm here with Samuel.

"So, what exactly did you want to discuss?"

"Ah, right." He turns to face me. "I wanted to discuss your future with you. I'm assuming after my last visit that there's been some communication."

"Yes." I cross my arms over my stomach, partially defensively, partially to hide my scars, and partially to just hold myself. "I know that I'm in Purgatory and I only have eight days left before I move on to...," I hesitate and clear my throat again, "Hell."

He nods. "a suicide only has one place to go."

"You know?"

"Of course. I know every soul."

"Sinn called you, his uncle. You're an angel too?"

"Correct."

"So, what's your role here?"

"I think we're getting a bit off topic. We're talking about you now, Dee, and your future. Has Peter explained all of your options to you?"

I furrow my brown in confusion. "Options? No, he hasn't mentioned anything about options."

"I see. Well, I guess that doesn't surprise me, but you do have a right to know. I can't imagine an eternity in Hell would be your first choice."

I snort. "Not my first, second or millionth."

He sighs, as if he's disappointed with my answer. "That's what I figured and that's why I'm here, to make sure you know that you don't have to go to Hell. You can choose to stay here, with Peter."

I drop my hands from around my waist and take an involuntary step toward him. "What?!"

"You can choose to stay here, in Purgatory. If you don't move on by the thirty-day deadline, the portals to Heaven and Hell close forever. You'll be stuck here, to spend the rest of your eternity in Purgatory."

"That doesn't sound like a problem. If my choices are here, what I'm living now, or Hell," I scoff again, "there's no choice at all. Why wouldn't I stay?"

The Crocodile shrugs again.

My mind is racing with the possibilities. Living here with Sinn, for eternity sounds like Heaven to me. I don't have to live an eternity being tortured in Hell. I mean, c'mon, that's a win-win. Then it dawns on me.

"Why didn't Sinn tell me this?"

"Did he not tell you what happened the night he saved you?" Samuel asks, curiously. "What he lost?"

"His shadow wings," I whisper. "He wants his shadow wings back, and the only way for him to get them back, is if I move on. Like I'm supposed to."

"Bingo," he says, pointing his finger at me with a devious grin on his face.

I find the edge of the patio couch and sit on it before the disappointment of my situation can knock me down. I don't have to go to Hell. All I have to do is stay here passed the deadline and I'll be safe. Forever. But if I stay, Sinn will also be trapped here forever. Without his shadow wings. Without a huge part of him that makes him who he is. The Angel of Death.

As if what's left of my life wasn't already hard enough, now I have this new information to add to the weight of the world already on my shoulders.

Damn myself to Hell. Forever. Or...

Damn Sinn to purgatory, broken. Forever.

Neither are choices I want to make. But I have no choice. One of us is going to get what we want and the other is going to be left to suffer. I take back my earlier thought about this being a win-win situation. This is a fucking fucked up situation.

The Crocodile's voice is closer to me when he speaks. "I know it's not an easy choice, Dee, but...it's always better to have all the information, isn't it? I mean, at least now you know where Peter stands when it comes to what he truly desires. His shadow wings, not you."

I physically wince at his harsh words. I hate hearing them and I hate that they're the truth.

"If Peter was willing to let you go to Hell, for eternity, then you need to think long and hard about what you're willing to do for him and for *yourself*. Peter lost his shadow wings all on his own, Dee. No one, not even you, made him kill that man and take his soul, unbidden, to Hell."

We sit in silence for a few minutes. My mind is racing, right along with my heart, and I have no clue what the fuck to even think much less what to do with this new information. The feel of his hand on my shoulder makes me jump. He removes it quickly, now having gotten my attention.

"I'm sure I'll be seeing you again, Dee. Make the right choice," he says, solemnly. "Tick tock, tick tock," he adds, chuckling as he walks away.

I listen to his quiet footsteps as he walks back into the penthouse, leaving me to decide my fate on my own. I'm a mess of thoughts and emotions as I try and sift through all of this new information.

I don't have to spend eternity in Hell.

I can stay here, with Sinn.

But he clearly doesn't want me to. He doesn't want *me*.

I end up pacing the entryway in front of the elevator, waiting for Sinn to come back. I need to confront him with this new information. I need to hear him say the words out of his own mouth. I need to hear him say, *I don't want you here*, Wendee. I need to hear him say it, and make it real, because if he doesn't, I'll continue moving forward on hope. False hope. And lies.

And my entire life has been built on false hope and lies. If all I have left is eight days, then an eternity in the place I choose, I'll be damned for sure if I allow it to be based on false hope and lies. No, my eternity will be nothing but truth.

No matter how hard that truth may be to live with.

Dee

LOVELY BY BILLIE EILISH, KHALID

November 19th. A day that will forever live in my mind as one of the worst days of my life.

It's a Saturday. We just got back from another away volleyball game. The trip took longer than expected due to the first winter storm coming in with a vengeance, promising a harsh and cold winter ahead. We pull into the school parking lot and I'm not at all surprised to see that no one is here for me. Then again, I'm the only senior without my own vehicle. No one else has to depend on their parents. I sigh as the bus comes to a stop and we all get up and head toward the front.

Both of my sisters are gone now, leaving me here alone. My mom should be home but it's not surprising that she's not here, even though I told her I'd need a ride tonight.

My best friend sees what I see. "I'll take you home."

I give her a thankful, but sad smile. "Thanks, JoJo."

Even though I know this is my life, even though I know better than to expect anything different, it still hurts. At what point am I really and truly going to give up hope that one time, just one time, someone will be here for me? At what point will it stop hurting? At what point will I become completely numb?

I climb into JoJo's car, and she turns on the engine and we wait a few minutes for it to warm up before we head out. She knows everything about my life, just like everyone else in this damn town so, luckily, I don't have to explain anything or deal with fleeting looks of pity. She knows, it is what it is.

The drive to my house is quick since I only live a mile from school and JoJo lives right down the street from me. We can literally walk across a field to get to each other's houses. She turns off the highway and onto the dirt road that leads to my trailer. My mom's little ford pickup is sitting in front of the house and the lights are on in the kitchen, living room and her bedroom.

"Well, at least she's home." I sigh. "Thanks for the ride."

"It's all good. You know where to find me if you need me." I nod. "Kay, see you Monday."

"See you Monday," I say, as I shut her door behind me.

I heave my gym bag over my shoulder and march up the wooden steps to the small porch landing in front of the front door. I push inside, the immediate warmth from the wood burning stove welcomes me home. At least she got the fire going tonight. I shut the door and the cold out behind me.

"Mom?" I yell into the house.

I'm met with the sound of water hissing violently. I drop my bag and rush into the kitchen. A pot is on the stove and the water is boiling over, falling onto the hot stove top, the flame angrily surging against the onslaught of water being poured onto it.

"Shit!" I rush to lower the heat. "Mom? Where are you? You left the stove on!"

There's a bag of fideo noodles and the ingredients to make it sitting on the counter, but you don't boil water for fideo so, I'm not sure what she was doing. Still, Sopa de Fideo is one of my favorite things to eat when it gets cold and it makes me smile that she's making it for me, even if she got off on the wrong foot. I'm thankful that she hasn't started cooking yet and it's just water that boiled over. At least dinner isn't ruined. There's a win. I sigh again and head back out into the living room. I pick up my bag and walk down the hallway, the temperature getting cooler the further away I get from the living room but it's still not terrible. Last I knew our heat was still working, we just use the wood burning stove to add more heat without having to ramp up the furnace.

"Mom? Where are you?" I shout, as I open the door to my bedroom and toss my bag on the floor.

I continue down the hallway, passed the washer and dryer, the bathroom, and stop in front of the last door. The door to my mom's room.

I knock. "Mom, hey, I'm home. Do you want me to start the noodles?"

No response.

"Mom? Are you ok? Can I come in?"

No response.

I try the handle. It turns. I slowly open the door.

"Mom?"

I see her lying on the bed, on her side with her back to the door, and a tightness in my chest releases as I sigh. She's just asleep.

I close the door and head back into the kitchen to make dinner for us. Thirty minutes later, when dinner is ready, and she still hasn't come out of her room, I go back to wake her up.

I open her door. She's in the same spot she was in earlier. "Mom, wake up. Dinner is ready," I say, louder than before, trying to wake her.

She doesn't stir.

"Mom, hey! Wake up, dinner is ready." I walk into her room, pass the foot of her bed, and freeze.

She looks like she's sleeping. Her eyes are closed and she looks peaceful. But then my eyes take in her outstretched arm and the shoestring and needle on the floor beneath it.

I don't rush to her to check for a pulse. I don't run out of the house and across the arroyo to my aunt and uncle's house to use their phone to call an ambulance. I don't scream, or cry, or fall to my knees in horror. I don't react at all.

I freeze. I stand here, frozen as solid as a statue, not even breathing, and I stare at her lifeless body. I know it's too late to do anything else but stand here and accept it. I feel numb inside. Broken. Fuck, I've always felt so broken. I should feel something, anything would be better than the bleak emptiness inhabiting my chest. But it doesn't even matter how I react. No one is here to see me and judge me anyway. I have no one to turn to.

Once again, I'm alone.

And this feels....final. Like this is how the rest of my life is going to pan out. Dani left. Kizzy left. Mom left. There's literally nothing and no one left. Only me.

How fucked up of a person am I to be thinking of myself in this situation? My mom is dead, she took her own life, and I'll never know if it was an accident or on purpose. Maybe she was struggling with more than I could ever understand, but all I can think about right now is the fact that my own mother didn't want me enough to stay in this life with me. She continuously made her choice and now there's no coming back from it. No more chances of a regular, happy life. No more wasted breaths on empty apologies. No more wondering if she'll be there to pick me up from my game. She'll never watch me graduate, and date, and go through heartache, and get a job, and fuck up and make mistakes, and all the things that a mother should be here for.

Everyone is selfish.

Everyone lies.

Everyone leaves.

"Wendee, hey, wake up."

The sound of Sinn's deep voice pulls me from my nightmare. I jerk awake, sitting up quickly, my eyes frantically take in the penthouse. I feel disoriented and like I should be back in that memory, back in the trailer, back to being the broken young girl I've tried so hard to outrun.

I close my eyes and take a deep breath that shudders in my chest. The tears push against my closed eyelids, but I refuse to let them fall. I've cried enough for ten lifetimes. I don't need to spend the few days I have left crying and feeling sorry for myself.

Sinn's large hands are cupping my face with a gentleness that grips my chest. He may as well be squeezing my tear ducts, like you would ring out a wash cloth, urging the tears to flow. His quiet comfort and affection are too much for me. I'm seconds away from breaking apart in his arms. I grab his wrists and pull his hands away from my face, holding his hands in my lap instead.

"I'm ok." I blow out a steady breath and open my eyes.

Sinn is kneeling on the floor in front of me where I'm now sitting up on the couch. His face is inches away from mine and he's studying me like you would study an abstract piece of art in a gallery. With awe and confusion and intrigue but underlying all of that, I see his concern.

"I'm sorry, I must have passed out while I was waiting for you. I don't really remember sitting down, or falling as—"

"Wendee."

My name. Just my name on his lips is the sweetest sound I've ever heard. That's all he has to say to ensnare me. His tone is an order. One not to be disregarded. His eyes demand attention. MY attention. And who am I to deny this wicked king my attention?

"You know, I've always hated my name. I've gone by Dee for as long as I can remember. Everyone calls me Dee, too, everyone except you. And I've never loved the sound of my name more than when it comes from your lips."

My eyes drop to his lips. They're lush and beautiful. They're the only feature of his face that aren't hard and masculine. But right now, they're pressed into a flat line, no trace of a smile or anything to hint that what I just said meant anything to him.

He removes a hand from my hold and his fingers grip my chin, tilting my face up, forcing my eyes to meet his. His thick brows are pulled together but not in his normal scowl. No, the wicked king is definitely worried. About me.

"Your name is beautiful, Wendee, just like the rest of you. And you deserve to be called by a full, beautiful name, not just some half ass version that belongs to someone else. I don't want *Dee*. I want you, Wendee."

"You only want me temporarily. You don't want me forever. Just like everyone else in my life. You're no different. I thought you could be but I was wrong," I whisper, as the tears finally win the battle and run down my cheeks.

He grabs my face more solidly this time, his thumbs brushing my tears away as quickly as they fall. "Wendee, what are you talking about? What has you acting like this?"

His concern sounds so genuine but it's just another lie. Another beautiful façade to distract me until he lands the final killing blow. I close my eyes again, trying to center myself and gather whatever strength I have left. I feel like I've been fighting my whole life. Fighting an uphill battle that I was never destined to win. Why do I keep fighting when it's utterly hopeless? Why do I keep expecting people to be different, to be better, when they're not?

I inhale deeply and open my eyes to meet his again. "The Crocodile paid me another visit."

Sinn's entire demeanor turns rigid and cold. His scowl is back, and his jaw tightens with his anger. "And what did my uncle want?"

"What did he want?" I seethe. "Unlike you, he wanted me to know the truth. The WHOLE truth. I don't have to spend an eternity in Hell. I can choose to stay right here, with you, but that's not what YOU want. Is it, Sinn?

Before he can argue or come to his own defense with his perfectly distracting lies, I continue my outburst.

"You don't give a shit about me. You never did," I pull his hands off my face again. "You've always known who I am and what THIS is," I gesture between us, "you always knew that I'm nothing more than a means to an end!"

My anger and hurt are bubbling out of me, and I can't control it. I don't want to control it. I want him to know that I know how he feels. "You didn't tell me about the loophole because you don't want me. You want your shadow wings. And I don't blame you but…I can't help but hate you, too." My voice breaks on the last few words, my hurt outweighing my anger.

Sinn rocks back on his heels, a look of shock on his face as if I physically slapped him. Which I wouldn't mind doing.

"Is that what you truly believe?"

I scoff. "It's the truth, Sinn. Whatever you're doing with me, it might be fun for you, it might be a nice little distraction from the monotony of your life, until you get your shadow wings back, but it's not just FUN for me. And I'm done letting you use me." I move to stand but his strong fingers wrap around my wrist and tug me back down to the couch, hard.

"You're not fucking leaving until you hear the truth, the WHOLE truth, as you so indignantly stated. My uncle is the Prince of Lies, Wendee. Does that mean anything to you?"

I don't hear what he's trying to tell me. I'm too riled up to really listen to his words. "So, he lied to me about being able to stay here?" I yank out of his grip and cross my arms defensively as I battle with him.

"No."

I scoff again, ready to unleash more of my anger on him, but he continues before I can. "But he didn't tell you everything about making that choice."

A small sliver of doubt starts to creep in with his words. More half-truths and misdirection. Why do people keep trying to manipulate me? My head is spinning from trying to keep up and all I want is the goddamned truth! All of it!

"What do you mean?" I ask, giving him all of my attention now and not just my defensive anger.

"My uncle, The Crocodile, is the Prince of Lies. What does that name mean to you?" He repeats.

"The Prince of Lies," I echo, softly. It comes to me slowly at first and then crashes into me like a freight train with no breaks. I gasp, my mouth making a shocked O of surprise. "Oh, my, Go..." I cut myself off from saying the name. "He's...he's the devil," I look up into Sinn's eyes as yet another truth bomb hits its target.

"Yes, Wendee. He calls himself Samuel as a play on Samael. He thinks he's clever." Sinn rolls his eyes. "We call him The Crocodile because he camouflages himself in his surrounding and hunts, finding his unsuspecting and helpless victims, and then he attacks out of nowhere, dragging souls, down, down, down into the pits of Hell."

I sink into the couch cushions, once more completely knocked off guard and defeated. Another thought comes to mind, making a connection that I didn't understand before.

"The first night I was here, you told your bouncers...or, whatever they are, to take that man to H2, to meet The Crocodile. You were sending him to Hell."

It's not a question but he answers anyway. "Yes. H2 is the name of a dock. H1, as I'm sure you can guess, would be the port to Heaven. My brother, Hook, captains the ship that transports the souls from here, Purgatory, to either Heaven or Hell, when they're ready to move on."

"Fucking hell," I exhale on a weighted breath. "This is all..."

"A lot to take in," Sinn finishes for me, his voice growing softer as he watches my reaction.

"Yeah, you could say that." I laugh sarcastically. "So, back to what The Crocodile or, the Devil...Jesus, the fucking Devil." I shake my head. "What *didn't* he tell me about staying here, in Purgatory?"

Sinn's chest heaves and he lets out a weighted breath as well. "If you stay here, the portals to Heaven and Hell close, permanently. You'll never be able to get to your Afterlife.

I scrunch my brows in confusion. "Yeah, he told me that. I still don't see the problem."

"I told you this place is also called, The Land of Never. Do you remember?

"Yes."

"It's called that because if you choose to stay here, you'll never be able to leave. You'll be stuck here, and...," he hesitates, "if you die here, because you *can* still die here, Wendee, a *final* death. If you die in Purgatory, your soul will be lost, forever. Your body will not deteriorate so it would be sacrificed to the Mermaids in the ocean to feed on, and your soul will forever wander in darkness. Alone. With no light, no sound, no feeling other than emptiness." He pauses and finally brings his haunted eyes to mine. "If you die here, Wendee, your soul will be lost to *me*. And I would rather have your soul safe for eternity than lost to a place I cannot reach or feel. I don't care about my shadow wings. I'd give them up for you again and again if it meant I could save you."

His words pierce my heart like a poison tipped arrow. The pain starts in the center and then slowly flows outward, engulfing my chest until it feels like my lungs will collapse. The pain climbs up my throat and I can't breathe. No one has ever put me first. No one has ever sacrificed *anything* for me. Sinn still isn't able to open up to me completely, but he's given me more than anyone ever has, and yet his actions are still selfish.

"You've made me feel so special, in your way." I smile weakly. "You've done things for me that no one ever has. You've seen me, truly seen me, and put me first. But now you're being just like everyone else. You're making this decision for me and you're making it because it's the best option for YOU. You don't want to take the chance of losing me forever, but it's MY soul, Sinn. It's my choice to make and damn you for keeping this from me."

I stand up again and he lets me.

"I need some time alone to think about all of this."

"Wendee, I—"

I raise my hand up to stop him. "No, Sinn. I don't want to hear any more excuses. I don't want to hear *anything*. Just…give me some space."

He nods once and I turn away from the gorgeous man, no…*angel*, still on his knees, looking up at me with a deceptively blank face. But his eyes are a storm of emotion that I can't even begin to concern myself with. Right now, I need to figure out my own damn emotions. I feel elated that Sinn actually cares about me, but I also feel betrayed by his choices.

I need to figure all of this shit out and make a choice about my future. Once again, I'm left with impossible choices and I have no fucking clue what I'm going to do.

Sinn

CALL OUT MY NAME BY THE WEEKND

Once again, The Crocodile has shown up and stirred the pot. All he cares about is creating chaos and madness wherever he goes. He loves to misdirect people, whisper flat-out lies or partial truths in their ear, and then send them on their merry way while he sits back to enjoy the show.

And, once again, his machinations work. They work because I've kept information from Wendee. Fuck! And now she believes that I want her to go to Hell so I can get my shadow wings back when, in fact, it has shit to with my wings and everything to do with her soul. But am I making this conclusion because I'm being selfish?

Yes.

The answer is yes.

And if I was in Wendee's shoes, I'd be pissed at me, too. She's right. It's not my choice to make. I can't seem to do anything right when it comes to her. I just...I don't think clearly when it comes to anything that has to do with her. But I do know one thing. I need to make this right. We're down to seven days together, one fucking week, that's all the time I have left with her. Well, unless she chooses to stay, but that's not a guarantee so I need to make this right. I don't want time to run out on us and be left with regrets of wishing and wanting, and I should've, could've, would've. No, I need to know that I did everything in my power to show her how I truly feel. So, when she does make that final choice, at least I'll know she did it with all of the information and everything out in the open.

No secrets.

No lies.

No more hiding.

"Fuck," I swear to myself as I leave my bedroom in search of her. I honestly don't know if I can do this.

I find her on the balcony, standing at the edge, looking out over the night lights of New York City. She's been out here for two hours. I know she asked for space, but I can't stay away any longer. My mind can't stop thinking about her, worrying about her, and wanting to make everything right. The only problem is I don't have the power to make everything right, and that's another thing crawling underneath my skin, adding to my anxiety.

I'm not in control.

I slide the glass door open and lean against the door jam, silently watching her. Her long hair is cascading down her back, blowing in the gentle breeze. She's wearing a black tank top and a pair of black pajama shorts that hug her ass way too fucking tight, barely covering her ass cheeks. And I fucking love them on her. I take in her long, smooth legs, and every beautiful curve of her body on display. Just looking at her turns me on and the devious thoughts running rampant through my mind send blood rushing to my dick. I've never had this happen before. Getting hard at just the thought or presence of someone. It's heady and new and makes my chest tighten and my stomach start somersaulting like a damn Olympic gymnast.

Feelings I've never experienced.

Feelings I don't know how the fuck to handle.

My fingers are itching to touch her skin and I can't fight the temptation any longer. I don't want to. I walk toward her in controlled, steady strides instead of like the raging bull it feels like I'm containing inside of me. I don't stop until my entire front is pressed against her entire back. I lean in and place my hands on the ledge outside of hers, caging her in. Her body is tense and stiff against me, letting me know that she's still upset about everything that's happened. I don't say anything, content to stand here with her looking out over the city.

After several minutes, her body slowly starts to relax against mine and she presses slightly harder into me. I close my eyes, relishing in the feel of her body against me, and let out a small sigh, letting go of some of the anxiety that's been gripping me. I won't be able to relax completely until I know she's okay though. That *we're* ok.

I remove my right hand from the ledge and find the smooth skin of her thigh. I gently but firmly grip her thigh with my fingertips, massaging her and working my way higher and higher until I reach the edge of the shorts. I trace them, feeling the curve of her ass barely being contained before I move my fingertips forward. I slide them under the hem of the shorts just like I did the night she was on the dance floor in that short dress. Only this time, I don't plan on stopping.

I can feel the change in her breathing at my roaming touch, but she still hasn't said a word. I continue moving around her leg until my fingertips come to her center. I glide my thumb over her clit, on top of the shorts, my dick jumping with the knowledge that he'll be touching her here next. But then her hand clamps down on my wrist, stilling my movement.

"You can't keep doing this, Sinn." Her voice sounds tired and sad. "You can't keep using my attraction and feelings for you against me. It's not fair."

I lean down and whisper into her ear, "I'm sorry."

Words I've never said to a single soul before. Not even as a kid when I was doing devious and hurtful things to others. I wouldn't have meant the words, so why say them? But now, with Wendee, I truly mean them.

She turns in my hold to face me. Her eyebrows are raised, eyes wide in shock. "What?"

"I'm sorry, Wendee. For everything. For not being able to go to you when you needed me the most. For not being honest with you about everything. For not being able to change our circumstances. I can't change a lot of things, but I can promise to tell you everything you need to know going forward."

I slide one arm behind her back, pulling her into me, while my other hand slides into her hair, gripping a handful and pulling her head back exactly where I want it. Her lips part as she inhales sharply with the force of my grip.

"But I will never apologize for needing to touch you. For needing to feel you, and kiss you, and fuck you." I lean down and run my tongue across her slightly parted lips. My teeth clenching as I hold myself back from voraciously claiming her mouth. "I don't think you understand what you do to me, Wendee."

"Sinn." My name on her lips is heavy and breathless. It calls to the predator in me. The one that wants to unleash every ounce of muscle and ferocity onto its prey.

A growl rumbles in my chest, the predator dying to be let loose. "Don't say my name like that unless you want me to fuck you right here, right now." I pull her head back further and move my hand to palm her ass, sliding down until I feel the heat between her legs. "And you do want me to fuck you, don't you, Wendee?"

"We can't just keep having sex and acting like everything else is ok."

"Now who's the one fighting against what they want?" I taunt. "If I pull these shorts aside, I know I'll find you drenched and ready for me. Don't deny us what we both want. Especially when we only have a few days left together."

"You know what I want." She stares at me with blazing defiance in her eyes.

"I give you more than I've ever given anyone else, Wendee." I'm trying to contain my aggravation and my need to take her. "What more do you want?"

"Everything, Sinn. I want everything." She stares up at me with heated and hopeful green eyes.

Fucking motherfucking fuck! This woman fucking challenges me and pushes me at every goddamn turn. And when she's in my arms, looking at me like this, I don't know why I can't give her what she's asking for. A part of me wants to tear off that final mask, that veil that's separating us from being completely whole together. That gut-wrenching, soul crushing part of me that she makes me feel wants to give in to her demands and be *free*.

I'm at war with myself and I don't see an end in sight. All I can do is lean down and claim her sweet, beautiful mouth with mine. My tongue sweeps into her open mouth and clashes violently with hers. She kisses me back just as fiercely; all of her frustration and anger being expressed with lips and tongue and teeth. Her hands bunch in my shirt, pulling me harder against her, even though we can't get any closer.

She breaks the kiss, gasping for air. "I want to see you, Sinn. Please, give me something." She's looking up at me, pleading with her words and her eyes.

We stare at each other, her eyes searching mine for something. What, I don't know. But I want to give it to her. Whatever it is she's trying to find, I want to be the one to deliver it. And in true Wendee fashion, she continues to challenge me as her hands let go of my shirt and slide up my chest, slowly and calmly undoing the first button.

I clench my jaw, holding her determined gaze as her hands slide to the next button, setting it free. My heart starts to pound in my chest and my hold on her tightens even more in my panic. I haven't been exposed to anyone…*ever*. Not as an adult with the choice to do so. She doesn't know what she's asking of me. She doesn't know this is an impossible request. She doesn't know I'm fucking terrified.

"Wendee." My voice is low, and slightly shakes, betraying my fear.

"Trust me, Sinn. Trust me the way I trust you."

She sets the last button free and then I feel her soft hands gently settling on my stomach, but her eyes remain locked on mine. My muscles clench at the touch and my eyes close for several frantic beats of my heart. The feel of her hands on my skin is beyond compare. I've never felt anything more peaceful or electrifying in my entire life. It's perfect. She's fucking perfect. Her hands slowly start to glide up my stomach and I can't help the shiver that shakes my entire body or the groan of pleasure that escapes my lips. My body somehow relaxes underneath her attention and touch. Both of my hands move to rest gently on her hips.

"Fuck, Wendee." I open my eyes to find her eyes traveling along with her hands. Seeing me for the first time.

Her hands reach my chest, and she slides them to the sides, opening my shirt up further. "Fucking hell, Sinn, your beautiful," she says in awe, as she continues to explore my body with her eyes and hands.

Her fingertips find a thin scar above my collar bone, and she traces it gently before she tiptoes and lays a gentle kiss against it. I can feel the genuine love and care in her touch, and it sinks my heart like an anchor in my chest. No one has ever seen my scars much less touched them or kissed them...except Wendee. And the ones she has seen are the smaller, less noticeable ones. The thought of her seeing the devastation on my back rockets my anxiety back up full force. What will she think of them? There's no way she'll think I'm beautiful once she sees them. She'll gape in disgust and flinch away from me. She'll finally look at me like the monster I am. No, I can't risk it. I can never have Wendee look at me that way. It would destroy something inside of me. The only good thing I have left. I need to regain control of this situation before it goes too far. Before we can't turn back from the edge of cliff and tumble over into death.

Death of us.

I grab her wrists, stopping her exploration, and I kiss her again. I kiss her hard and deep. Showing her with my mouth how much she means to me. I kiss her with the desperation and fear I feel inside of me. I desperately want her to see me, all of me, and get to know every piece of who I am, but I'm scared she'll never be able to fully accept me. So, I kiss her, telling her all of my wants and all of my fears the only way I can.

She moans into my mouth. I swallow it down, and it's the spark that ignites my flames. The fire rages inside of me, starting in the pit of my stomach, climbing and climbing, until I'm consumed by flames. Her flames.

"Fuck." I break the kiss and twist her around, pushing her body down and over the ledge. "I need to feel you, Wendee. I need to be inside of you."

I unleash my aching cock and angle her hips where I need them. I yank her shorts to the side and run my fingers up the middle of her center, soliciting another breathy moan as she pushes her hips back against my fingers, needing me just as much as I need her.

"You're so fucking hungry for me, Wendee." I push two fingers inside of her, sliding them in and out slowly. I lean over her body and whisper into her ear. "Do you hear how sweetly your body is begging for mine?" I ask, as I pump my fingers into her wet pussy, adding a third, preparing her for my dick, although there's no real way to prep her for me.

"Yes," she pants, as I continue to stretch her open. "I always want you, Sinn. Always."

Her words twist up my stomach. I want her to always want me. That's why I can't show her everything that I am. I can't risk it. I can't risk losing her this way. I remove my fingers from her pussy and wipe off her wetness on my dick, pumping myself hard a few times before I bring my head to her opening. I rub her slit up and down, up and down, and then I slap her sensitive clit with my slick and heavy cock before I tease her opening again. She squirms and pushes her hips back, trying to capture my dick.

"Sinn, please!"

"Please what, Wendee. Tell me what you want."

"I want you, Sinn. I want your dick inside of me, please."

My balls clench at her words. "Fuck," I groan deeply, as I push inside of her.

I have to pull out and push in again, and again, and again, slowly pushing my way further inside of her. She's always so fucking tight that I have to fight for it every damn time. Once I've pushed all the way inside of her, I pull all the way back out, and slide in again. Tip to base in one fluid motion. Again and again, until she's taking all of me with no resistance.

"Oh, fuck, Sinn, you're so deep. You feel so fucking good," she moans.

I wrap her hair around my left wrist, my other hand gripping her waist, holding her in place as I pull her head toward me. Her back arches in the sexiest fucking way, and I pull on her hair until her eyes are able to meet mine as I lean over her body. I pump my hips faster, driving into her harder.

"Don't ever fucking deny me what's mine again, Wendee. This pussy is mine and I get to fuck it whenever I fucking say I get to fuck it. Do you understand?"

I think she tries to answer me but all I get is a guttural sound coming from her throat as she moans. I let go of her hip and tug the top of her tank top down over her breasts, setting them free. I grip one in my hand then gently squeeze her nipple, her groans and pants for breath intensifying. Then I slap her tender breast; once, twice, three times. She whimpers, her skin turning red under the power of my heavy hand, and I continue to drill into her from behind. I can feel the walls of her pussy starting to clench around my dick. She's close to coming, her eyes are closed, she's getting lost in the pleasure, but I need her to fucking answer me.

I slap her cheek.

She lets out a surprised cry and her eyes jerk open. They finally focus on mine and I know I have her attention. "You're mine, Wendee. Every fucking inch of your skin and every fucking piece of your soul. You belong to me. Do. You. Understand?"

"Yes," she manages to get out.

"Good. Now come on my dick and don't you dare fucking close those eyes," I demand, as I reach down and rub her clit, sending her over the edge.

She tries to scream but I still have her neck pulled at a hard angle, restricting her voice. Her pussy drenches my cock and I finally let go of her hair. She hangs her head and leans over the ledge for support. Her legs go limp, and I pick them up, holding them on the sides of my hips, as I continue to pump into her.

I look down to where my dick is punishing her. The sight of her creamy orgasm coating my dick makes my heart soar, released from its heavy anchor. I love making her feel good. I love watching her beautiful face as she comes. I love seeing the proof of her pleasure on my dick.

She regains the use of her voice, we're both moaning and panting as we add another haunting melody to our playlist. A playlist that will forever torment me in the years, weeks, days, hours, minutes, and every fucking second, that she's absent from my life. A playlist that will cut and scar me far worse than anything that's been done to my flesh.

My orgasm rips through me as I sheath myself all the way inside of her. I lean down and rest my forehead on her back as my dick spasms and throbs inside of her. And for this split second, I release all of my fears along with my orgasm. I let go of everything except for the feeling of Wendee in my arms and how good it feels to be wrapped around her and inside of her.

For a split second, life is perfect.

For a split second, I think that maybe I can keep this feeling, keep Wendee, forever.

For a split second.

Dee

CAN YOU HOLD ME BY NF, BRITT NICOLE

I'm such a weak piece of shit. I was actually making progress on the balcony, I thought that I'd finally broken through Sinn's barriers and that he was going to allow me to see him. WRONG! I got as far as he wanted me to get and then he turned the tables on me. I swear, all that man has to do is kiss me and I melt faster than butter in a hot frying pan. I melt and bubble and boil and eventually burn under his touch. Damn, I AM butter and Sinn is the fucking scorching hot, unyielding frying pan.

I know I should hold my ground better. I know I should speak up and demand what I want. But I don't really *want* to demand anything from him. I want him to give it to me freely. And, as much as Sinn IS a demanding and arrogant control freak, I know he wants the same from me. I know that no matter how hard he tries to be cold and dictating, he'd never take something I wasn't giving him freely. It's a silent understanding we have with each other. The only problem is, I'm the fucking butter! I have no chance in hell against him.

Still, I can't help but be satisfied with the progress we made on the balcony. It's the furthest he's ever let me get to seeing him and I'm soooo not complaining. I knew he was all hard muscle under the shirt but seeing it…fucking hell… his skin is golden and beautiful, soft and smooth over chiseled abs and strong pecs. I got a nice glimpse of his devastating V-cut, and the trail of dark hair disappearing into his pants before my eyes caught sight of the scar.

It was nothing more than a thin white line on his skin but it's almost like my eyes knew where to look to find it. Like I was drawn to it. It was the same type of scar that he has on his forearms, and I have a feeling there are more of them. I think that's why he's refused to let me see him. And to be honest, I've given up hope that I'll get to see him in all of his beautiful, Greek God-like body. We're making progress but progress that's too slow for the time we have left.

I'll still continue to push his boundaries, I can't NOT push him and see how far I can get, but I'm not holding my breath either. I don't want to push too hard and ruin all the progress I *have* made. I still haven't decided what I'm going to do when my time is up so we may only have a few days left together and I don't want them to be wasted. I don't want to spend them arguing and fighting. So, when he carried me inside and insisted on bathing me again, instead of showering with me like I asked, I let him.

I let him wash my hair. I let him wash my body. I let him dry me off and rub lotion into every inch of my skin. And when he laid me down on his bed, spread my legs wide and devoured me with his skilled mouth and tongue, I let him do that too. Then, I put on one of his large t-shirts that I like to sleep in, climbed under the covers, and that's where I'm waited patiently for Sinn to shower. Alone.

It doesn't take him long to shower though, and my eyes greedily take him in as he walks back into the bedroom wearing a long-sleeve black t-shirt and, the kryptonite to any hot-blooded, breathing female…grey sweatpants. The only thing that would make this view better is if he was shirtless and I got to see the sweatpants sitting low on his hips, revealing that sexy as fuck V-cut I got to see earlier leading down to that impressive bulge. Sweet baby Jesus, and just like that, I'm fucking wet again. The motherfucking Angel of Death. Who would have thought?

"Wendee." His voice is low and husky as he walks toward the bed and pierces me with his deep blue gaze. "You better stop looking at me like that and get those thoughts of yours under control or there will be no sleep."

I lick my suddenly dry lips. His eyes drop to them, the muscle in his jaw twitches and his nostrils flare as his fists clench at his sides. Fuck. I didn't mean to rattle the cage and get the beasts attention.

"Sorry," I murmur, closing my eyes to try and settle my racing heart and liquid fucking insides.

I feel the bed dip under his weight as he climbs in and slides to the middle of the bed where I'm waiting for him. He lays on his back and then pulls me into his side tightly. I tuck myself into him, throwing my leg over his and hugging his waist. This position is a new development for us. He's always been the big spoon, not allowing me to be in a position to touch him, but we woke up in this position the other day and he must have been ok with it because this is the second night, or day rather, that he's initiated this position. I continue to behave and not push him too hard, keeping my hands still, content to relax in his safe embrace and let him hold me.

I let his body heat sink into my skin, relaxing me further. I inhale his heady scent of soap and leather. Everything about him has always meant safety to me. A feeling I've never been fortunate enough to feel in my waking life. Not even as a child.

"Wendee." His deep voice pulls me out of my tranquil thoughts.

"Hmmmm?" I hum against his chest, not wanting to speak and break this peaceful moment.

"When I found you earlier, asleep on the couch...," he hesitates for a second, "you were whimpering and calling out for your mom. What were you reliving?"

The mention of it brings my nightmare crashing back into my thoughts. So much for not wanting to disrupt my peacefulness. I feel my body stiffen and my breathing getting heavier at the image of finding my mother. Dead.

"Tell me." It's not a demand but a request, and he tightens his hold on me, reminding me that I'm safe.

I've never really talked about that moment with anyone other than the police. I mean, I told my sisters obviously, but not in detail, and I never expressed the thoughts that have haunted me the most since that night. If there is ever going to be someone who I want to tell, who I know is asking me because they genuinely want to know every part of me, it's Sinn.

I sigh. "When I was seventeen, a senior in high school, I played on the volleyball team. Hell, I played every sport and joined every group and activity that I could to keep me busy and away from home."

"Why?" He asks, softly.

"My mom wasn't always the...most present mom. She was an addict and the drugs took her away from everything and everyone. I'm the youngest of three and my older sisters had already graduated and left. I was always alone so I kept myself as busy as I could." I shrug my shoulders. "Anyway, there was a Saturday afternoon game at the other team's school. We were supposed to be back home by seven o'clock, but the game ran long and then the weather was terrible on our way back. A storm came out of nowhere, delaying us further. We didn't get home until almost nine. Of course, my mother wasn't there to pick me up so I had to get a ride from a friend, but when I got home my mom was there and all the lights were on in the house. I just assumed she forgot that I needed a ride. Or maybe, because we were so late, she got tired of waiting at the school. I guess I don't blame her for not wanting to wait two hours."

I hesitate as I remember everything that comes next in the memory. It's one thing to relive the memory in a nightmare, it's another to voice it out loud but somehow, I manage to keep going.

"When I walked in, my mom had started a fire in the wood burning stove and had started boiling a pot of water for one of my favorite meals, but she wasn't in the kitchen or the living room. I went to her bedroom, opened the door, and saw that she was asleep on her bed. I decided to let her sleep until I finished making dinner for us. When she still hadn't come out of her room, I went back to wake her up, only..."

The weight of what I have to say next seems to sit on my chest, threatening to crush my ribs and suffocate me. The emotion is thick and heavy, clawing its way up my throat, making it impossible for me to speak.

Sinn's hand starts to rub up and down my arm in a slow, steady, comforting motion, letting me know that he's here with me in this moment. He's here for me. That small gesture gives me more strength to keep going.

"Only, she wasn't just sleeping. She was dead," I manage to whisper against his chest.

Sinn is silent but his hand is still steadily rubbing my arm, never hesitating or skipping a beat. I suppose discussing death with the Angel of Death is just another day in his life. He's experienced in this, and he's patient, giving me time to continue without interrupting or pressuring me.

"I didn't really...*react*, when I found her. I always knew it was a possibility that I'd find her that way one day. I know I should have been sad or shocked or hysterical, but all I felt was emptiness. I know I should have done something but...I just stood there. Staring at her. And all I could think about was the fact that she left me, too. That everyone who was supposed to love me, left me. They all made other choices, selfish choices, and didn't give a fuck about me. No one has ever put me first. No one has ever saved me, Sinn."

I push up on my hand so I'm sitting up and looking down at him. I need to look into his eyes. "But you have. You've saved me over and over and over again. You may not give me everything I want, but you've given me more than anyone else ever has, and for that, I'll always be grateful."

His hand comes up to cup my face, his thumb wiping away a single tear that slides slowly down my cheek.

"There's more bothering you. Tell me," he repeats, urging me to reveal the deepest, darkest parts of me.

I swallow down the rest of my emotion and meet his tender gaze. "She died that night because of me. She clearly didn't *plan* on killing herself. The fire was going and dinner had been started, but I was late. Had I been on time, had I been there, I know that night would have ended differently. And maybe she would have overdosed in the future but maybe she wouldn't have. If I had just been home, if I had just been there with her instead of always being gone, then maybe..." my chin wobbles as I try to rein in my emotions.

"Wendee." His voice is firm and he grabs my chin in his hand. "Look at me."

I do, trying to blink away the tears blurring my vision of his handsome face and failing. The tears unleash like a flood and a sob echoes my internal pain. Sinn is moving, he twists his body so I'm on my back and he's leaning over me.

His lips fall onto my cheek. "Your mom made a decision that night." He kisses my other cheek. "Nothing you could have done would have changed that." He kisses my forehead. "I'm the Angel of Death, Wendee. I know things about death and the souls that fall into its grasp." His lips gently brush against mine. I can taste the salt of my tears on his lips. "It was not your fault or anything you could have prevented." He pulls back and looks at me, his eyes holding mine, demanding that I see him. He's like gravity and I have no choice but to concede to him. To those stormy eyes that have saved me again and again. "I need you to trust me on this. Do you trust me?"

His words, no, not just his words, but the *conviction* in his words, releases something inside of me. Something I didn't even realize was rooted so deeply in my core being.

Guilt.

I swear I feel a gust of air blow through the room as the guilt leaves my body. It wasn't my fault. IT WASN'T MY FAULT. I feel lighter than I've ever felt and a realization rushes through me.

"That was my unfinished business," I whisper.

Sinn nods. His hand is still on my face, caressing my cheek, and I see the sadness in his eyes. This is it. This was the last piece keeping me here, in Purgatory. I'm ready to move on now, officially. And even though I've released the guilt that has controlled my entire life, there's no way to go back and change the past. I'm still a suicide. There's still only a one-way ticket to Hell with my name on it. There's nothing Sinn or I can do to change my fate.

"I would never leave you, Wendee. Just know, if I had the choice, I would never choose to leave you. Not for anything."

I'm flooded with so much emotion, the emotion from finally understanding myself better and everything I'm feeling and seeing from Sinn. Even though he hasn't given me every single piece of himself, he loves me. I can see it in his eyes. I can feel it in his touch. I can hear it in his words. He loves me and I love him. I've loved him since the night he saved me in the real world. And I've fallen more and more in love with him every single day, when just the thought of him saved me again and again.

Another choked sob escapes me as Sinn continues to wipe my tears away and tells me everything I need to hear with his actions and his beautiful blue eyes that see me like I've never been seen before. And now, I know what my decision is going to be.

"Sinn?"

"Yes, Wendee?"

"Can you hold me?"

I see his throat bob on a hard swallow, and I wonder if he knows what I'm thinking? I wonder if he knows how much I'm in fucking love with him? I wonder if he knows I've made my decision?

He nods and lays down behind me, pulling me into his chest, his strong arms enveloping me and holding on tightly.

"I'll hold you until I can't hold you anymore."

Dee

Everything between Sinn and I has been perfect since the night The Crocodile paid me a visit. That night was a huge moment of healing for me and it wouldn't have happened without Sinn. Granted, the person I've become because of the guilt I carried is still me. I'm not going to radically change overnight. No one is capable of change like that but I do feel...different. It's something inside of me. It's a new way of seeing things. I don't know, it's hard to put into words, but I feel it.

Sinn is leaning against the doorway of his bathroom, arms and ankles crossed, looking like an angelic fucking snack in his signature all-black outfit. My eyes keep roaming over his impressive body and keep get caught in his ocean eyes. I imagine him stalking towards me until his body is pressed against mine. Then he'll reach down and slowly pull up the material of my dress until he reveals my bare ass. I imagine him sliding his hard cock inside of me, all while keeping eye contact in the mirror, and then fucking me into oblivion. Just the image has my stomach clenching and my arousal firing.

"You're distracting me," I scowl at him in the mirror as I continue to apply mascara.

The bastard smirks, no doubt reading the thoughts that were clearly displayed on my face. "Are you sure you want to go down to the bar? I can think of several things I'd rather do if we stay here."

Sometimes I swear he can see exactly what's in my head because he pushes of the wall and stalks toward me, exactly like I imaged him doing. He stands behind me, pushing his hips forward, letting me know he's thinking the same things I am.

"Yes." The word comes out breathy, I clear my throat and try again. "Yes, I'm sure. It's my last night and I want some semblance of normalcy. I want one last normal…ish night before…" I swallow the rest of my words down.

"If you're sure that's what you want." His fingertips graze up my bare arms, sending goosebumps racing across my skin.

"It is," I confirm my decision, as I put the mascara down and reach for my scarlet lipstick.

Sinn's hand gently grabs my wrist, and he spins me around to face him. His fingertips gently trace my lips. The simple touch causes butterflies to flying frantically in my stomach and up into my chest. The swell of my cleavage is noticeably heaving as my heart races and breathing becomes harder. Fucking butter.

"No lipstick." His tone tells me there will be no debating this, but I don't understand what his issue is against lipstick.

"Why," I whisper.

I watch as his eyes change from a lukewarm interest into a full-blown wild fire. And I'm standing entirely too close. I can feel the temperature change as my body begins to burn from the inside out.

"Because I like the taste of *you*, Wendee. And I plan on feasting to my heart's content tonight."

He holds my gaze with his wild eyes and my chin with his strong hands as he lowers his head. His lips land on mine and begin to move in our familiar dance. Once his tongue finds mine, I can't help but close my eyes and get lost in the feelings consuming me. If he wasn't holding onto me, I'm sure I'd fall. Id fall, and I'd fall, and I'd fall, forever. His other hand slides behind my neck and settles against the back of my head. He doesn't grip the usual fistful of hair but holds me tenderly instead and moves my head to the side, kissing me deeper, longer. I moan and lean into his body, so fucking desperate for him.

He slows the kiss down and then slowly pulls away from me. I open my eyes to find him still staring at me. His lips are still so close that they brush against mine as he says, "I love watching you get lost in your pleasure. *In me.*" He pulls further away, caressing my kiss-swollen lips with his thumb once more, then lowers his hand to take a hold of mine. "Let's go."

He keeps a firm grip on my hand as he leads me to the elevator and then out into the bar. I don't know why such a simple gesture means so much to me, but it does. He's showing everyone that he's with ME. That he chose me. I know he's done other things to make this clear too, but it feels like it means more now. Now that we've spent so much time together, and I'm happy he's not pretending to be someone else with me in private and then someone entirely different in public.

We slow down as we pass the bar, a few people already sitting at it and drinking. "Tink, our drinks to the booth."

She acknowledges him first, but her eyes quickly slide to our joined hands, a sneer of disgust and anger pulling at her lips, and then her eyes meet mine and there's no mistaking the look of murder in them. Sinn must see exactly what I see because he's suddenly pulling me toward the bar.

When we reach it, his huge six-foot five frame leans over it easily. His free hand moves so fast I barely register that it's wrapped around her neck. He did this to her once before, when she brought me water and ibuprofen. Granted, she was trying to tell Sinn what to do and he didn't like that very much. Pissing this man off is not something that is conducive to a person's bodily safety.

"I'm getting real fucking tired of your blatant disrespect, Tink. If you ever look at Wendee like that again, or do anything to hurt her, I fucker swear you will fucking cease to exist," he threatens her through clench teeth. Meanwhile, his hold on my hand has remained the same.

Jesus. This man.

I know I shouldn't like his violence, but I do. Especially when it's at my defense. It makes my insides all gooey and I want to fuck his brains out even more than normal.

"Well, looks like I got here just in time to stop whatever *this* is. Brother, let her go. C'mon, whatever she did or said can't be that bad. Let's have a drink!" Hook's cheerful voice booms across the room and I can't help but smile when I'm met with his contagious one.

"Awwww, Dee, don't you look lovely this evening." He steps around his brother to take my free hand in his, bringing it to his lips.

Sinn is turned around now, facing us, having let go of Tink at some point. A growl escapes his lips as he watches his brother kiss my knuckles.

"Oh, Sinn, calm down," I laugh and lean into his body.

He lets go of my hand and pulls me in tighter, one arm around my back and the other coming across his body to hold my waist. Fucking possessive. And I fucking love it. Not that he has anything to worry about. His brother is good looking but I don't want to be anywhere else in the world except right here, with my Angel of Death.

The three of us make our way to the booth and slide in. Sinn doesn't waste any time questioning Hook. "What are you doing here, AGAIN?"

Hook laughs easily. "Instead of just being happy to see me and spend more time with me, *your brother*, you're angry and suspicious because this visit doesn't fit into your controlled routine."

"Our *routine*," Sinn throws the word back at Hook angrily, "has been the way it is for as long as I can remember. And you, *brother*, have followed that routine to a T, never once deviating. Now you are, and The Crocodile is being summoned behind my back, and who knows what else is fucking happening around here. I think my suspicion is fucking warranted, don't you?"

"No one is out to get you, Peter. Everyone here, including me, wants nothing but the best for you."

"No one knows what's fucking best for me except for me."

"Alright guys," I chime in. "Do you mind if we maybe put the family drama aside for now? It's literally my last night here and I don't want to spend it watching you guys fight."

Sinn's eyes stay locked on his brother, the suspicion clearly not going anywhere, and I can't say I blame him. When your gut is telling you something is off, you really should listen to it, but I don't want him listening to it right now.

Our drinks come and Sinn immediately downs his glass of bourbon and requests another one. He's definitely not going to let this go but, luckily for me, Hook is the most easy-going person I've ever met. He doesn't let anything or anyone phase him, and before I know it, we're laughing and talking as if we've known each other forever.

"Ok, ok, last one. I promise," Hook says, as he's catching his breath. "Why don't whales wear underwear?"

"Oh my gosh," I giggle. "Why?"

"Because they prefer a *Free Willy*."

I throw my head back and laugh, thankful that I've seen the movie and can make the connection to the joke. It doesn't hurt that the whiskey I've been drinking is running through my veins in a smooth relaxing way, allowing my laughter to come more freely. My stomach and cheeks hurt from laughing and smiling so much over the last hour with Hook entertaining me. Sinn hasn't really joined in on our conversation much, but he's kept his hand on my thigh, or around my shoulder, holding me close the whole time. And I've felt his eyes on me, like I'm feeling them right now.

My laughter is still dying in my chest and the smile is still plastered on my face when I turn to look at him. His stunning blue eyes capture mine and everything around us fades away. I don't even remember what I was just laughing about.

All I can see is Sinn.

All I can feel is Sinn.

All I can think about is Sinn.

He reaches out and brushes my hair behind my ear and then traces my jaw with his fingertips until his thumb is brushing my lips again. The touch, combined with the fire in his eyes, penetrates my senses and I'm lost. I'm so utterly lost in Sinn's universe and I never, EVER, want to be found.

"You're so fucking beautiful when you laugh," he says in awe, as he continues to hold my face in his large hand. I lean into his touch, closing my eyes for a second, before I meet his fierce gaze again. "I've never wanted to make anyone laugh. I've always only wanted to cause pain, to control and manipulate, but you...I want so badly to be the one who makes you look this beautiful, but I don't know how. It's not who I am," he says sadly.

I'm still completely lost in Sinn's world but I hear Hook clear his throat and make some comment about his que to leave. I don't care if he goes, and I don't care if he stays. All I care about is this gorgeous man sitting next to me, sharing with me his inner most thoughts and insecurities. I don't want him to be insecure because he's *exactly* who I've always needed.

"Sinn, how many times do I have to tell you that I want you exactly the way you are. I don't want you to change for anyone, especially me. You're the one person I waited my entire life to find. You're everything I've ever wanted and needed. You keep me safe and put me first, above everything else, you don't need to make me laugh."

"But I want to," he confesses. "I want to be the one to give you everything you deserve, Wendee. And you deserve to be chosen, to be safe, to be put first, and you deserve a lifetime filled with laughter."

I push down the immense emotions his words stir up inside of me. They're threatening to claw me open from the inside and break me apart into a million pieces. I don't know what kind of good karma I have that has allowed me time with this man, but the bad karma must heavily outweigh it since I can't actually have him in my life forever. Karma is a nasty fucking bitch. But I do have him right now. I have him for another night and I'm not going to waste it.

Before I can suggest it, he's sliding out of the booth and reaching his hand out for me. "Let's go upstairs." I'm more than willing and beyond eager to comply with his request.

One last night.

One last time.

Sinn

STAY BY RIHANNA

My heart was breaking as I watched her laugh with Hook. Not because I was jealous, although, admittedly, it didn't feel great to watch her laugh so easily with my brother, but it was more than that. My heart was breaking because I know the kind of life she's lived. She didn't have a joyous childhood or life. She's deeply wounded and scarred, like I am, but she hasn't let that kill the part inside of her that can laugh.

I envy her for it.

She deserves so much. She's been an open book, has given me everything I've asked from her, and wants to give me more. Meanwhile, all I've done is take. What have I given her? The basic fucking things every soul deserves, like being cared for, being protected. That's all I've given her. Things that have come easy to me and cost me nothing.

She deserves better.

She deserves more.

I hang on tightly to her hand as we take the elevator up to the penthouse, but it's no longer just desire fueling my need to claim her.

It's panic, too. I don't know why, but I feel like if I let go of her, she's going to disappear. It's fucking ridiculous but I don't want to take the chance of it happening when I need her tonight. I need her more than ever.

I can feel her mood shift to match mine. She's no longer relaxed and carefree or full of desire. She's concerned. I can feel it in the way she's holding my hand, the stiffness to her body, and the way her eyes keep examining me, no doubt trying to read me and understand what's wrong. What she doesn't even realize is that she already reads me better than anyone ever has.

She's not interrogating me and demanding answers to my drastic mood swing. She's not blaming herself, assuming she did something wrong to cause this change. She's giving me time I need to deal with my thoughts, to try and fucking figure out these foreign emotions, until I'm ready to speak.

I lead her into the bedroom, finally releasing her hand, and shut and lock the door behind us. No one would dare interrupt me on purpose, but everyone has access to the elevator and I'm not going to chance anyone walking in and witnessing what's going to happen tonight.

Wendee still hasn't said a word. She quietly walks into the bathroom, giving me space and not expecting one fucking thing from me. And that's why I want to give her everything. Because she hasn't demanded it and she doesn't expect it.

I pace the bedroom for a few minutes, needing an outlet for my pent-up emotions and energy. Needing time to find the strength and courage that Wendee deserves from me. I end up back where we started the night, standing in the doorway to the bathroom, watching her. No, not just watching her, admiring her. I'm in constant awe of her. I'm in constant *need* of her. I know what decision she's made for tomorrow, and even though I told her I didn't want her to stay here, in Purgatory, because of the risk to her soul, now...now that I'm faced with the reality of her decision, knowing this will be our last night together, the last time I ever get to see her, touch her, feel her next to me, and under me, and on top of me...fuck! I don't want to let her go.

"You know I only see you, right?.I've only ever seen *you*, Sinn."

Her voice pulls me out of my chaotic thoughts. She's watching me in the mirror as she uses a wipe to remove her makeup. I don't know why she bothers with makeup when she's the most beautiful thing I've ever seen without it. I tilt me head, refocusing on her and what she just said. She thinks I'm upset because of Hook. I guess my past reactions give her every right to think that but that's the last thing on my mind.

"I know."

It's her turn to tilt her head and examine me. I can see the confusion clear on her face. "Then I'm not sure I understand what caused you to become so...*unsettled*."

"I don't want to be just another selfish person who's come and gone in your life but neither decision I have leaves me free of that burden."

Her brows furrow and she frowns. "I don't understand."

"You told me something last night that, once it registered, it really fucking pissed me off. You said that I've given you more than anyone else ever has, and to be honest, Wendee, I haven't given you shit. And the fact that what little I have given you is the most you've ever received is fucking bullshit."

She turns to face me directly. "That's not true," she huffs incredulously. "You've put me first soooo many times, Sinn. You saved me during the lowest and worst point in my life. You've opened up to me and—"

"No, Wendee, I haven't. I've still kept myself closed off from you while you've been eager and willing to give me everything, including going to Hell for an eternity so I can get my wings back."

"I—"

I shake my head. "Don't try to deny it, Wendee, I know you've made your decision to leave tomorrow. No doubt that's why Hook is here once again, which brings us to my current frustration. My choice to keep the information about staying in Purgatory was selfish. I want your soul safe, so that I can always feel you, always have you with me. For eternity. And if I ask you to stay…" I slowly walk toward her, still trying to gather my courage, until I'm standing right in front of her.

She tilts her head back, her green eyes remaining locked on mine. I swear I'm going to lose myself in their depths. Or maybe, just maybe, I'm going to find myself.

I hold her face in my hand and continue, "If I ask you to stay, I'm still being selfish because it's truly what I want. I want to be able to touch you, and kiss you, and—"

"Fuck me," she interrupts with a smirk.

I chuckle. "Yes, Wendee, and fuck you. Because having you here makes this miserable life bearable. *You're* my Heaven. You're the missing piece of my soul and I want you here more than anything else in this fucking universe and to fucking Hell with the risks."

"Sinn…"

"Hush," I silence her with a finger to her lips, "let me finish." She nods. "I'm asking you to stay, Wendee. I'm asking you to choose me, like I've chosen you." I watch as her eyes tear up and I don't know if they're tears of happiness or sadness. Maybe both.

"But I also know that if I'm asking you to stay, if I want you to *choose* me and share this life and the risks with me, I need to prove to you that I'm worthy. I need to give you everything that you deserve and not just the basic fucking things I've given you so far. You deserve to be *loved*, Wendee, wholly and fully. And I've loved you since I laid eyes on you."

"I love you, too, Sinn. Ever since that night," she whispers, voice tight, as a tear finally falls down her cheek.

I close my eyes for a brief second as her declaration sinks in. She loves me too. Thank fuck. Because I don't know that I would have been able to handle it if she didn't. If she left me. But she's not going to leave because she loves me, too. Her feelings for me solidify what I need to do.

"I didn't want to acknowledge it because I'm fucking terrified. I've never been in love, Wendee. So, you'll have to be patient with me, but I'm done fighting. I'm done hiding...from *you*."

I take a step away from her as I begin to unbutton my shirt. My hands shake slightly and my heart feels like it's about to explode inside of my chest. Fear and uncertainty are coursing through my veins stronger than ever before, but I hold onto Wendee's gaze, taking all the reassurance I need from her steadfast resolve.

She's looking at me like I'm her entire world. The way she looks at me penetrates through my skin and caresses my fucking soul. No one has ever seen me past my carefully constructed masks. No one has ever even tried to truly see me before. Only Wendee. And still, I hesitate once I've unbuttoned and untucked my shirt. My hands freeze as I'm about to pull the shirt off.

Wendee reaches out, her small, soft hands lay gently on top of mine. "You don't have to do this, Sinn."

"I want to."

I can barely hear myself speak over the frantic pounding of my heart as I fight the overwhelming fear that's threatening to ruin this moment. Threatening to rear its ugly head and leave me running from Wendee, like a coward, with my tail between my legs.

She deserves all of me.

She deserves everything.

I finally remove my shirt and toss it to the side. I quickly kick off my shoes as my fingers fumble with my belt buckle. I move quickly, before I lose my nerve, and run from this room. I don't want to run away from her but I'd rather be the one running away from her versus the alternative. Her running away from what she's about to see.

My pants and underwear are tossed to the side, somewhere along with my shirt, and I'm finally standing in front of her, completely naked. I've never been naked with another person in my entire life. I feel utterly terrified and so incredibly free. Her eyes are roaming over my body in a slow and heated perusal. I can't help but grow hard at the look I see in her eyes and the arousal I smell coming off of her.

But I need her to see ALL of me. The worst of me.

I turn around, and for a brief moment, I squeeze my eyes shut and the world around me disappears.

I can't see anything.

I can't hear anything.

I can't feel anything.

I'm suddenly transported back to my past. When I was no more than eight years old, being whipped by my father, the infamous and divinely perfect Archangel Michael. I was never good enough in his eyes. I was too rowdy, too distracted, too cruel and evil for an angel, much less the son of an archangel. Everyone kept comparing me to Lucifer and would talk about me in hushed tones behind my back. This only coaxed my father's need to *fix* me. He attempted to RIGHT me by whipping me when I was too young and small to fight back. I suffered at his cruel hands for years, and the only one who ever came to my aid and tempered my father's hand, if only by a little, was Hook. He's the only one here, in Purgatory, who knows what I went through.

My grandfather never stopped my father either. There was no GRACE in my childhood, no divine hand to intervene, no God. There was only ever Hook, and he was never able to stop the abuse on his own. Once I turned eleven, I refused to let him, or anyone else, aid or see me. Therefore, even Hook has never seen the destruction and devastation that covers the entire backside of my body, from shoulders to ankles.

My ever-loyal brother has seen me suffer enough. I know he feels guilt for not being able to stop our father. I think a huge part of his loyalty to me, him being here when he doesn't have to be, is because of that guilt. And now he thinks the loss of my wings was the final blow that harden me into an impenetrable iceberg completely, but he's never really known me. He's wounded more by the loss of my wings than I am. And he longs for home but refuses to leave me here, alone, despite my best efforts to assure him I'm fine. And I'll only be better with *her* by my side.

Wendee.

She awoke something in me the night her soul called out for me. The night I found her at the worst moment of her life. The night I swore to myself that I would never let any more harm come to her. The night I gave up what little I had left to avenge her because I knew from that first moment I saw her, that she was going to be the one to save me. As soon as I locked eyes with her, my frozen barrier started to crack, and for the first time in my life I felt something other than coldness and anger. Her being here now has made me realize that it was never the loss of my wings that caused me to be crueler all these years.

It was losing *her*.

And I don't think I can handle losing her again. Not now. Not after everything that's happened in these past thirty days. Even though I've tried to fight it, knowing the ending can't possibly be happy, it's inevitable. WE are inevitable. She's here in Purgatory for a reason. She didn't go straight to Hell. She was always meant to be here, with me, and I'll be damned if I lose her again without a fight.

A rush of determination floods through my senses and I open my eyes. I stand up straighter, my attention now solely focused on Wendee. I'm watching her in the floor to ceiling mirror next to us as she takes in my naked appearance for the first time.

I can feel the heat of her hand as it hovers just above my skin but not touching me. Not touching the scars. There are fresh tears running down her cheeks but she doesn't look sad. It's not pity making her cry. What I see in her eyes is something I know all too well. Anger. I see the flame of anger in her eyes before she takes the last step between us, wraps her arms around me, and lays her cheek against my back.

I can feel the warm wetness of her tears on my back as she squeezes me tightly and holds me. I expected her to cringe at the mere sight of me, to go running and screaming from the room in a hurry to get away from me. I never expected her to *hold* me. Every last lingering piece of my defenses crash to the floor underneath her touch. I feel lighter than I've ever felt, and even without my wings, it feels like I could fucking fly.

"Wendee." My voice is clogged up with all of the immense emotions flooding through me. I turn to face her and I'm met with more of her fiery rage.

"If I could kill the son of a bitch that did this to you and take his soul to Hell with me I would."

Her protectiveness over me makes my heart soar inside of my chest. I swear, it feels like a damn helium balloon and I'm certain I'm seconds away from floating off the damn floor.

I smile down at her, a smile full of all the warmth and love I feel inside of body and soul for this woman. A smile and a feeling I never even knew existed until this moment. I take her beautiful face in my hands and wipe away her angry tears.

"But you're NOT going to Hell, Wendee. You're going to stay right here, with me, for eternity. I will never let any harm come to you while you're here. You're mine, Wendee, and I will damn all the souls that come to this realm if it means keeping you safe."

"Sinn—"

I smother whatever argument she was about to make with my lips claiming hers. I gently lick her lips, coaxing her to open them for me. All the urgency and anxiety I felt minutes ago are gone. I take my time exploring her mouth as if it's the first time I'm kissing her. And as this new man, with these new feelings running through me, it is.

She moans into my mouth and it sends a shock of pleasure straight to my cock. Fuck she tastes so good. The feeling of her lips on mine, her tongue dancing with mine, I've never felt anything better. What is it going to feel like sliding inside of her? Fuck.

My fingers find the zipper at the back of her dress and slide it down, then they slip underneath the straps pulling them off of her shoulders and the dress falls to the floor. I pick her up and carry her back into the bedroom and never once break our kiss.

Once I have her on her back, in the middle of the bed, I finally pull away from her. We're both breathing hard, trying to catch our breath as our chests are heaving against each other. Skin on skin. The entire length of my body is pressed into hers. Skin on fucking skin. It feels better than I've ever imagined. She's warm and so fucking soft. So alive. Her eyes are literally shining like two north stars, guiding me to her.

Guiding me home.

"Fucking hell, Sinn, you've *never* kissed me like THAT before." She laughs softly and the sound sinks inside of my chest, tightening it, and making me feel things I can't even put into words.

"That's the way you deserve to be kissed, Wendee. Every fucking time. And that's the only way I'm ever going to kiss you again because I'm not holding anything back from you anymore. There are no more barriers and rules to hide behind."

"You are so fucking gorgeous, Sinn. Every. Single. Inch of you. And I'll spend whatever time I have left with you showing you just how fucking sexy you are. I never want you to hide form me ever again."

I prop myself up on my left arm and trail my right hand down her stomach. I don't waste anytime sinking two fingers inside of her.

"Fuck, Wendee," I growl. "How are you always so goddamn tight and wet?"

I don't wait for a response as I claim her mouth again. I hungrily drink down all of her gasps and moans. I could fucking live on her breath, on her taste, on her body, on her LOVE. She's writhing under my touch, her fingers are tangled in my hair, and her hips are rocking against my hand, chasing her release. I force myself to break away from her lips long enough for me to watch her fucking fall over the edge of pleasure.

"That feels so good. Fuck," she groans. "You're going to make me come."

"Look at me, Wendee," I demand. Her eyes flash to mine and hold steady even as the rest of her body loses all control. "You've never been more beautiful than you are right now."

I remove my fingers from inside of her and climb on top of her. I spread her wide, giving myself room to settle between her legs. I'm pushing inside of her before she's even had a chance to recover from her orgasm. She feels the same and entirely fucking different. I've never had sex with someone so openly and freely before.

I'm almost completely lost in the euphoria of it all but I can feel Wendee's hesitation. Her legs are wide open, but not wrapping around me, and her hands are clutching the comforter...instead of me.

I stop pushing inside of her. "Wendee?"

"Yes, Sinn," she asks, breathless.

"Touch me."

My permission is all she needs. Her legs wrap tightly around my waist, and her hands start at my forearms and work their way slowly up my arms. I close my eyes and hang my head at the intense and overwhelming feeling of her hands on my skin. Her hands move over my chest and then down my sides, and around to my back. Her fingertips gently trace over my scars and my entire body fucking shudders.

I lift my head and meet her eyes once again, blown away by the sheer amount of love pouring out of them. I start to push into her again as we keep our eyes locked on each other and her hands continue to explore and roam over my body. My mind and body are over loaded with sensations I've never felt before, both on my body and in my fucking soul.

Heaven.

This is everything I've ever been told Heaven is.

Wendee is my savior.

Wendee is my grace.

29

Sinn

WHAT IF I WAS NOTHING BY ALL THAT REMAINS

For the first time in my life, I slept like the dead. For the first time in my life, I made love to the person who claimed my body, heart, and soul completely. I made love to Wendee three times and fell asleep with her wrapped in my arms. Her naked body pressed against my naked body. For the first time in my life, I was content. I AM content.

A lazy smile pulls at my lips as I stir from the peaceful depths of sleep, but my peace is quickly interrupted, and I jerk awake. I feel it immediately and I sit up as if I've been electrocuted. I glance to the side where Wendee was asleep by me, but the bed is now empty. *No, no, no, this can't be fucking happening.* Panic is racing through my body and adrenaline has me out of bed and on my feet in two seconds. Once I'm on my feet, I release and stretch out my shadow wings.

Anger like I've never felt before erupts out of me. I scream. I scream a deep, guttural and soul piercing scream that shakes the entire building. It feels like a damn earthquake is about to tear the earth wide open. Me. I'm the fucking earthquake and I will fucking destroy this entire goddamn realm if Wendee is gone.

My wings are proof that she is but I refuse to believe it. I can still feel her soul but I know she's no longer close. I can feel her slipping further and further away by the second.

I pull my wings in and dress in record time, not giving a fuck about my appearance as I storm from the penthouse and into the bar. "Tinkerbell!" I yell for her.

She pops up from behind the bar, her eyes are wide as saucers and filled with fear at the sight of me. I'm in front of her in the blink of an eye, grabbing her throat and lifting her up before slamming her back on top of the bar.

I can barely contain my rage as I squeeze her throat. I want to fucking rip it out. I want to pry her chest open and watch her heart beat before I crush it in my hand. I want to damn her soul to the realm of nothing. I want to damn everyone until I get answers. Until I get Wendee back.

"Where is she?!" I yell in her face. "You're going to tell me everything, Tink, or I swear to God, I will fucking destroy you."

"She left," she wheezes out.

"Did you have anything to do with this? Do not fucking lie to me!"

"I…can't…breathe…" She taps on my hand that's clutching her neck. I somehow manage to loosen my grip enough to let her speak, but I don't remove my hold entirely. She's one fucking second away from dying if she doesn't tell me what I want to fucking hear.

"Tell me," I say through clenched teeth as I stare daggers at her.

"I summoned The Crocodile," she admits. "I needed gold dust to make her remember. I just wanted her to move on, Sinn. She's not good for you."

My hand clamps down on her throat again. She's clawing at my hand, trying to remove it, her mouth is opening and closing like a fish out of water, gasping for air. I can feel my fingertips sinking into her flesh, needing to rip out her throat right this second for what she did to Wendee. The only thing that stops me is the need to find out where Wendee is right now.

I release her and step away from her. My hands are balled into fists at my side and my entire body is thrumming with barely contained rage. I feel like I'm about to fucking detonate and no one is safe.

"Where is she, Tink? What did you do?"

"I didn't do anything, I swear," she explains, as she sits up on the bar. "*She came to me. She* asked me to get a message to Hook, to have him come so he could ferry her to the Afterlife. She said she was doing it for you, Sinn, so you could get your wings back and be whole again. I've only ever wanted what's best for you! Don't you see that?"

I pick up a bottle of alcohol and throw it across the bar, glass and liquid exploding everywhere. "Don't fucking lie to me!"

"Sinn..." Her voice is full of tears. "I love you," she whispers.

"You don't think I fucking know that? What you've done to Wendee has been because of your fucking jealousy. You want what's best for you, Tink, not me! Because what's best for me is the woman you just sent to fucking Hell, and I will never forgive you. You had my friendship but that wasn't enough for you, was it?"

"Sinn," she pleads as the tears fall down her cheeks, "please."

"You're banished, Tink. You will spend the rest of your time in Purgatory on Hook's ship ferrying souls to the Afterlife. You will leave the next time he ports, which will be as soon as I find him, and if you ever so much as set one motherfucking toe on my land again I will rip your soul out of your body and send you into the darkness."

I jump over the bar and head toward the front doors.

"She's already gone, Sinn. You'll never reach her in time." There's a hint of satisfaction in her voice as she yells after me.

I set my wings free and I hear Tink's gasp at the sight of them. "I'll get her back or I'll die trying."

As soon as I step outside, I'm airborne. It's been fifty years since I've felt the wind on my face and in my hair. It should feel like coming home, where I belong, but all I feel is dread. I'm terrified that I'm not going to find her. That I'm going to be too late and she'll be behind the gates of Hell where even I can't go.

I focus on the connection I have to her soul. I follow the pull and fly harder, faster, across the choppy waters of the Mermaid Lagoon and out into open water. It's as if the realm can sense my mood and is matching my chaotic thoughts and feelings. Dark clouds are moving in above me and the ocean below me is raging with dangerous waves and even more danger lurking below its depths.

Thunder rumbles the sky with a battle cry seconds before lightning crackles and sizzles close by. The storm wind is behind me, pushing me forward, urging me faster toward my destiny. I hear Hook's booming voice on the wind as he yells directions to his crew. I can barely make out his ship in the distance, fighting against the merciless waves threatening to take it under.

I pull my wings in tight to my body and shoot like a torpedo toward his ship. I don't slow down as I approach it. I land with the force of a damn nuclear bomb, and if the ship wasn't literally a divine vessel it would have blasted into pieces at my assault.

I lift my head up and push off of my knee. "Wendee!" I yell for her as my eyes quickly scan the deck of the ship, desperate to lay eyes on her, desperate to make sure she's ok and that she is still here and my senses aren't tricking me.

"Sinn." I hear her voice and turn toward the sound.

She's emerging from below deck, the wind whipping her hair all around her face. The ship is still being rocked by tempestuous waves caused by my reckless emotions, and she's struggling to remain on her feet. The sight of her, here, unharmed, eases the rioting storm inside of me. The winds die down and the sea calms as if it was all an illusion or daydream.

I flap my wings once and I'm launched toward her. I land softly in front of her and take her into my arms. "Wendee," I swallow down the emotion threatening to explode once again. "I thought I lost you. What in the fuck were you thinking? How could you leave me like that?"

When she doesn't answer, I realize her body is shaking in my arms. I pull away from her but remain holding her arms as I look down on her tear-stained face.

"I'm so scared, Sinn," her chin wobbles as she tries to fight the urge to break down.

I cup her face in my hands, wiping her tears away as quickly as they fall. "Wendee, it's ok. I'm here and I'm not letting you go to Hell. I'm not going to let you go, period. I refuse to let you go and you can't change my mind or fight me on this. I'm nothing without you, Wendee. This life is nothing if you're not in it with me."

I lean in and kiss her. She sobs and tries to pull away from me, but I hold on to her tightly. I'm not letting her out of my grip or out of my damn sight ever again.

"Look at me, Wendee." She slowly brings her tear-filled eyes up to mine. "You're ok. We're ok. And we're going to live a long and wonderful life together. You and I. Do you hear me?"

She swallows again and nods, then her eyes go wide as she seems to take in my wings for the first time. "Sinn," her voice barely more than a whisper, "you're wings…but, how?"

I shake my head. "I'm not sure. When I woke up and felt them, I thought for sure I had already lost you. I thought you had crossed through the gates and I'd be lost forever. It would be worse than the realm of darkness if I had to live even one day without you. But you're here, you're safe," I pull her back into my chest, holding her tighter than is probably comfortable for her.

"But if I don't go, won't you lose your wings again?"

"I don't give a fuck about these wings, Wendee. All I care about is you. Being with you. I love you, Wendee. I mean it when I say I'm nothing without you."

"Love." Hook's voice interrupts us.

I loosen my hold on Wendee so we can both turn and face my brother. "What about love, Brother?"

"That's what made you whole again. That's why you have your wings even though Wendee's soul didn't go to Hell. Love, Brother," Hook laughs heartily, a huge smile splitting across his face. "Love is the strongest thing in any realm, and the love you both have for each other trumps all else. You are both willing to sacrifice everything for the other person therefore, you don't have to sacrifice anything at all."

"What are you saying?" Wendee asks. Her cute, confused face stares at him with eyes full of hope.

He laughs again as he approaches us and grabs my shoulder, giving me shake. "I'm saying that I never thought I'd ever see the day where this little shit loves anyone. It's truly a damn miracle and you both deserve this happiness." He turns to face the bow of the ship. "Smee! Change course! Sail straight back to The Land of Never! We have some stowaway souls on board that need a ride home!" Hook pats me on the back and then chucks Wendee under the chin. "Welcome to the dysfunctional family, Dee. I'll leave this outcast in your capable hands." He whistles as he strides across his deck toward the wheel.

Wendee and I stand at the front of the ship. Her back is pressed against my chest and my arms are wrapped around her as we watch the waves pass us by on our way back to land. To The Land of Never, where I never have to live without Wendee ever again.

Once we dock, I take some time to fill Hook in on Tink's situation. "She's forever banished from these shores. If she steps even one foot on this sand, I will rip her soul from her body and feed her to Serene."

"Serene is already going to be after her. She made quite the hefty deal with her when she was scheming."

"That's her burden to bear," I say, not one ounce of sympathy in me. "There's always a price to pay for your actions."

"Indeed," Hook agrees.

"She'll spend the rest of eternity ferrying souls to the Afterlife and fighting Serene's call. You know, she could take your place, Brother. You could go back home."

I watch his reaction closely. I see the spark of hope in his eyes at the thought of going home but he's still hesitating. "There's no reason for you stay and keep an eye on me anymore. For the first time in my lie, I'm good. I'm *more* than good," I say, as a huge smile spreads across my face.

Hook throws his head back and laughs joyously. "You love sick fool. I feel sorrier for you now than ever before." He winks.

I laugh and then I'm suddenly yanked, once again, into his bear hold. As he pulls away, he grabs my face in his hands. "You deserve this life, Sinn. Don't fuck it up."

I nod, words seeming to allude me in this emotionally charged moment that I've never had with my brother. He nods in response, no doubt feeling the same way, and then I watch him walk down the deck and onto his ship. His voice carriers on the wind as he yells orders to his crew. I have no doubt that he's going to teach Tink everything she needs to know about the job and, once he's comfortable that his ship and crew are in good hands, he'll finally return home. Where he belongs.

I stand on the shore, watching them depart, until I can no longer see the ship on the horizon. I turn and head back to land. Wendee is sitting on a bench where she's been patiently waiting for me to handle my business. She stands when she sees me and my feet move faster. I'm eager to have her in my arms again.

"Everything taken care of?"

"Yes."

I wrap one hand around her waist, pulling her body into mine as my other hand sinks into her hair and grips it tightly, pulling her head back. Here eyes fill with heat and her lips part on a gasp. Fuck, I love how responsive she is to me, how much she trusts me implicitly, and I can't wait to spend an eternity learning and exploring every single thing about her.

"What's that look?" She asks, with a voice low and raspy with seduction.

"I'm just contemplating whether I'm going to be punishing you for fucking leaving me while I slept, again," I growl, "or rewarding you for loving me so fiercely you were willing to accept an eternity in Hell for me."

"Hmmm," she contemplates, as her devious little hand slides over my already aching cock. "How about both?"

A satisfied hum rumbles through my chest as I scoop her in my arms and stretch out my wings behind me. "Let's go home."

EPILOGUE

Wendee

There's really not much left to say except that I've still never found a good man, but I have found a man that's only good to me and, well, that's all I've ever really wanted.

AUTHORS NOTE AND ACKNOWLEDGMENTS

Where do I even begin?! These things are so hard to write because I'm overwhelmed with so many feelings every time I'm here, at the end of another book that I put my time, blood, sweat, heart, soul, and tears into. This is my fifth book and, honestly, it never gets easier. Writing a book is extremely challenging and equal parts rewarding and terrifying. Even more so when the book is personal, which this one is for me. So, here's your reminder to always be honest in your reviews and opinions BUT always be kind. If you don't have anything nice to say... you know how it goes.

First, I would like to thank my husband. Writing a book requires a HUGE amount of your time and that means something always has to be sacrificed. Often times, it's the husband and fur babies who get the short end of this stick due to the fact that I also work full-time. Luckily, my husband is so incredibly understanding and supportive. On the hard days, he's the one reminding me that all of my hard work is going to eventually retire him! Haha That's the goal babe, that's the goal.

Second, I would be nothing without my readers! I adore every single one of you! It means the world to me when you choose to pick up my book and spend YOUR time reading it. Thank you for making that choice and that sacrifice of your time. All I can hope for is that it was worth it.

Third, I want to thank my bookstagram family! I have been so incredibly blessed with the most amazing support group! To my Alpha reader, Jenny, who took on this role on a whim and gave me the BEST feedback. I adore you and appreciate you so much. To my Beta reader, Kara, who made me realize how comma heavy I write (cringe) thank you for also taking on this role and being so kind and gracious with your INCREDIBLE feedback. I appreciate you so much! To my ARC/Street Team, you're the BEST group of ladies I've ever had the pleasure of knowing, truly. Your excitement, your efforts, and your feedback are so appreciated and valued! I would not be where I am without each and every one of you by my side and I am forever grateful!

Last, but definitely not least, I want to thank my beautiful artist Çağla or @fire_foxdesign on Instagram. You are one of the sweetest souls I have ever met (online haha) and I cannot wait to work with you on the next adventure! It's hard to put your characters in the hands of an artist and hope that they capture them and do them justice and you absolutely did not disappoint! You're beautiful, you're talented, and I'm so grateful we connected.

As always, please don't forget to write your review on Amazon, Goodreads, and share on any social media platform you have! Reviews and referrals are seriously the BEST ways you can support us. Don't be afraid to TAG ME or DM me!

XOXO,
Harmony

MORE FROM THE AUTHOR

If you enjoyed this read, stay tuned for my next book, a Beauty and The Beast Reimagining...coming soon!

Also, check out my complete urban/paranormal fantasy series, The Amarah Rey, Fey Warrior Series.

Awaken

Fey Blood

Dark Temptations

Divine Destiny

You can find them on Amazon here: Amazon Author page or the kindle version here: Amazon Ebooks/Kindle

Stay up to date on news and exclusive content and follow me on social media!

Instagram

TikTok

Newsletter

Thank you for being here and all of your support! Again, I could not do this without You. Leave those reviews ▯

Made in the USA
Middletown, DE
30 May 2023

31502019R00182